D1417739

A TASTE FOR RABBIT

LINDA ZUCKERMAN

ARTHUR A. LEVINE BOOKS ◻ An Imprint of Scholastic Inc.

For Phyllis, my sister and dearest friend

Text © 2007 by Linda Z. Knab

Library of Congress Cataloging-in-Publication Data

Zuckerman, Linda.
  A taste for rabbit / by Linda Zuckerman. —1st ed.
    p. cm.
  Summary: Quentin, a rabbit who lives in a walled compound run by a militaristic government, must join forces with Harry, a fox, to stop the sinister disappearances of outspoken and rebellious rabbit citizens.
  ISBN 0-439-86977-3 [1. Government, Resistance to —Fiction. 2. Rabbits—Fiction. 3. Foxes—Fiction. 4. Animals—Fiction.]   I. Title.
  PZ7.Z78Tas 2007
  [Fic]—dc22   2007007787

ISBN-13: 978-0-439-86977-5; ISBN-10: 0-439-86977-3

10 9 8 7 6 5 4 3 2 1   07 08 09 10 11

Book design by Elizabeth Parisi

First edition, October 2007

Printed in the U.S.A.

CONTENTS

I think I could turn and live with animals, they are so placid and self-contain'd;

I stand and look at them long and long.

– Walt Whitman, *Song of Myself*

1

Harry:
Can't a Brother Be Brotherly?

Harry the Fox, standing at the end of the line that coiled like a snake through the snowy streets, peered up at the sky — gray, leaden, low to the horizon. It had been snowing for weeks, with no end in sight. He pulled up the collar on his jacket and dug his bare paws into his pockets, feeling once again his last few icy coins. *This will be pointless,* he thought. *By the time I reach the market, there will be nothing left.*

As the line shuffled slowly forward, the volunteer members of the Foxboro Cleanstreets Department, bundled in their brown uniforms, approached and began to work; but after a short time, the snow, falling with a silent ferocity, buried the newly cleared paths under a blanket of white. Harry watched as the volunteers shrugged and gave up in disgust, dropping their brooms and shovels, which quickly began to melt into the white streets and soon vanished.

The snow kept coming.

In front of him stood an older fox in a threadbare brown coat. "It's moving, but slowly," he said, turning to Harry. "I'm sure there will be enough for all of us."

Ahead of him, a fox with gaunt face and hollow eyes, turned and snarled. "Are you crazy? There's no food anywhere!"

"Get off the line, then," Harry said calmly. "We'll be happy to move up."

The fox thrust his face close to Harry's. "Make me."

Just then, the line turned a corner; the front door of the market was now in view, its windows spattered with driven snow. The fox scrambled to return to his place. "We can take care of this later," he muttered, but the threat was gone.

The line inched forward. Every so often, there was a scuffle as someone tried to push ahead and was challenged, but mostly foxes of all ages stood close together for warmth, jamming their paws deep into their pockets. Even from this distance, Harry could see the bare shelves with only a few wrapped items remaining. *No wonder everyone is on edge. Probably nothing left but mouse tails and squirrel paws,* he thought. *Not much nourishment there.* But saliva filled his mouth and his stomach growled just the same.

The fox in the brown coat turned again. "My name's John."

"Harry."

"I keep wishing I'd been able to get here sooner, but my children were sick," John said. "It's the rich who benefited from this storm," he added bitterly, and lowered his voice. "The price-gouging at the other markets didn't bother *them.*

They got all the food and *still* have their money." He stopped to cough. "I had to borrow. . . ."

Harry just nodded absently. *Not long ago I was one of those rich foxes,* he thought. *Not anymore.*

"What do you do?" John asked.

"Recently I've been a hunter."

"Not much work for you these days," John said sympathetically. "Not in this weather."

It was true. Still, just yesterday, Harry had ventured into Wildwood Forest, floundering through the drifts that blanketed the paths, watching, listening for a sign of life — but there was nothing. He'd returned to his apartment, cold and filled with frustration.

The line reached the front door of the market. The thin, gaunt fox hurried in and emerged in a few moments, tearing at the wrapping of a small package and chewing hungrily at the contents, which Harry could see was the shriveled, frozen carcass of a squirrel. The fox hurried away, avoiding Harry's eyes.

John shuffled inside. The owner, an old-timer everyone called Popsy, who was never seen without his white apron and a striped scarf about his neck, opened the door quickly and then shut it firmly. Harry watched as John took the last package from a low shelf and dug into his pockets for change. Popsy pushed his paw away. John tried again to pay, but the older fox was insistent. John tucked the package into his pocket and opened the door. Popsy followed, shook his head at Harry, and turned the OPEN sign over.

"This was the last," John said to Harry. "Mouse tails." He started to walk away, then turned back. "Listen," he said. "I wish I could share . . . but my children . . . I'm sorry."

I wish you could share too, Harry thought. *Children couldn't eat* that *much.* But he just nodded and left.

Harry trudged home through the icy streets of Foxboro. No income, no food, no resources. It was definitely a low point. Of course, there was always Isaac, his younger brother. *He never seemed to run out of money. Maybe I could visit him and ask for a loan.* Harry stopped in his tracks, imagining Isaac's insufferable arrogance, his condescension. *No! I'd rather die of starvation.*

As night fell and the sky darkened, the snow began to fall in thick, heavy flakes, muffling his footsteps. Children who had been sledding down the slick hills in the park near downtown made their way slowly home, pulling their sleds behind them. The streets grew quiet.

Harry stomped the snow off his boots at the front door of his apartment and turned the key. Inside, he reached for a match on the nearby table and struck it; the flickering light illuminated the cramped space, but left the outer corners in darkness. The apartment had a close, familiar smell — Harry's nose detected the odors of unwashed clothes, faulty plumbing, and days-old garbage — in stark contrast to the fresh cold air of the outdoors. But in a few moments it was gone. Home.

He lit the stub of a candle and prowled around his little space, looking for a relatively clear spot where he could rest. Unwinding the scarf from around his neck, he flung himself down on the used couch that stood against the wall near a grimy window. He dug around in the rubble behind it, found a moldy sandwich, and gnawed on it gratefully.

What about the rabbit warren? he thought. Everyone had heard the rumors that several years ago a huge colony had established itself within the abandoned fortress far to the south. No one knew who built it or when, but the high, crumbling wall, perched on a steep hill, was difficult to reach and impossible to climb. The rabbits who were said to inhabit it had been simply too much trouble to bother with, especially with other food so readily available. No one had eaten rabbit for a long time, although Harry had a faint recollection of some superb dinners from the distant past, and had often heard old-timers like Popsy reminiscing and trading recipes as if it were yesterday. *If I can find a way to get inside the fortress,* Harry thought, *the rabbits will be an easy kill. Even squirrels and chipmunks are more intelligent than rabbits, who, when faced with a predator, freeze stupidly in their tracks, their hearts pounding beneath their fur, their eyes staring. Yum.*

5

He swallowed hard. *The only trouble is that after struggling through this miserable weather and the snowbanks, icy winds, and blinding, howling storms, I'll be back here, exactly where I started: hungry again.*

I don't need food — I need money.

The front door opened. "Anybody home?" asked a familiar voice. Isaac. Harry reburied the remains of the sandwich under a rag he found in a dark corner.

"Close the door, will you!" Harry said. "It's freezing." He watched his brother limp into the apartment. "What do you want?"

In the dim light, Isaac looked even shorter than usual. For a moment, his broad shoulders and thick neck, backlit by the candlelight, made him appear menacing, even to Harry. Not long ago, Harry had read in the local paper that Isaac had been elected to the position of Managing Director, the highest administrative post in Foxboro. *It must have been Isaac's wealth — how had he acquired it, anyway? — that had given him entrée into the complex and notoriously corrupt political system,* Harry thought. The tabloids had proclaimed Isaac "a champion of the common fox." Harry knew better.

Now he observed, with surprise — considering the scarcity of food — that in addition to being well dressed and protected against the cold with a heavy, fur-lined coat and fine wool scarf, Isaac was looking extremely well fed.

Something's up.

"Gods, this place stinks," said Isaac, looking around for a comfortable spot and finding none.

Harry sat back on the couch. He knew Isaac wouldn't join him; since childhood, Isaac had always needed his *own* chair. He would wince when he sat down and that would inevitably bring someone running to get a pillow for his weak leg.

Harry didn't move.

Isaac brushed the snow off his shoulders and unwrapped the scarf. The snow puddled around him, but he took no notice. Finally he settled on a stool near the cluttered kitchenette and rested his cane against the table. He winced and looked around for a pillow. "Don't you ever clean it?"

"Is that why you lowered yourself to come here? So you could criticize my living quarters? Don't you have something better to do, some sweet, young potential voters to impress, some bribes to take?"

Isaac shifted on the stool, trying to get comfortable. "Don't be ridiculous. You know bribery greases the wheels. You should try it. Or hire someone to fix the plumbing, for the gods' sake. Surely you have *something* left from our inheritance!"

Harry was silent.

"No?" Isaac shook his head. "Harry, Harry! All right, then. Give one of those sandwiches you've been hoarding to some young fox to clean this place. Stop living like this."

"Let's get back to bribery," Harry said. "Speaking of which, I haven't congratulated you on your recent election."

Isaac didn't respond. He shifted again, gave up, and stood with difficulty, leaning on the cane. It was a new one, Harry noticed — carved mahogany with the head of a rabbit, its ears flattened into an easily gripped handle, at the top.

"Listen," Isaac said. "I need to talk to you about something important."

Harry tried not to show any interest. Clearly his brother was about to ask for a favor and was feeling uncomfortable about it. Harry was not going to make it easy.

Isaac took a deep breath. "We have never been close," he began and then stopped at the sound of a barely suppressed snort from Harry. "All right, that's an understatement. I know you don't like me and I must say, I don't . . . understand why, but I accept it. Still, we are brothers and we are family."

The stubby candle flickered and sputtered.

"Harry," he went on. "I need a favor."

"I figured as much," Harry replied coldly. "You have never come by this place on a social visit. Your brotherly love speech notwithstanding."

"There is something strange going on at the fortress, the one that protects that rabbit warren," Isaac continued, ignoring Harry's comment. "You've heard the rumors, haven't you? Well, I've sent several scouts to the area. They . . . have not returned. There could be a food supply behind those walls that would get us through the rest of the winter. Hundreds, maybe thousands of rabbits . . ." He stopped.

Harry waited for Isaac to spit it out.

"I need you to find out what's going on over there, what happened to the scouts, everything," Isaac said. "We need that food! It's our only hope. I don't have to tell you what this terrible storm has done. The roads have been completely impassable for weeks. Even the ermine traders — and you know how resourceful *they* are — cannot penetrate this storm. No one can get in or out, not even to hunt — as if any of us, other than you, knows how anymore. If this weather continues, we will starve to death. We must have those rabbits!"

"I don't get it," Harry said. "Why send scouts at all? Why not the traditional hunting party? The fortress can't be that much of an obstacle if rabbits could find their way in."

"As I understand it, the rabbits arrived years ago, and you know perfectly well there's no road to the southeast that goes that far. Besides, it's . . . complicated," Isaac said. "Trust me. Scouts were a good idea. Until they didn't return."

Trust you? Harry thought. *I'd sooner trust a bloodhound.*

There was silence in the cold, dark space. Harry finally sat up and poked around the sofa pillow cushions until he found a box of matches he'd dropped there several days ago. He struck one and held it up — very close — to his brother's face for a long moment. The flame danced in Isaac's eyes. He blinked. Harry blew out the match.

"Why me?"

"Because you're the best. Maybe the others didn't come back because they weren't up to the job — I don't know. I just know you're smarter than they were. You're the best we've got," he repeated. "And . . . I'm offering a reward."

"A reward? For what?"

"Information."

A reward for making a trip to the fortress, which I had been thinking about doing anyway? I like the sound of this, Harry thought. *Maybe my luck has turned. On the other hand, why do something for Isaac?* "Suppose I say no?"

"You can't do that," Isaac blurted out. "Think of the children!" he added, in what Harry recognized as the phony voice of an elected official. "Already some have collapsed, the poor little things. . . . Damn it, Harry," he went on in a different tone. "Don't you have any other light in here? It's like a tomb. I can't carry on a serious conversation this way!"

"*Why* can't I do that?"

Isaac was silent for a moment. "Because I've given my word that I, meaning *you*, obviously, since with my leg . . ."

Gods, do I have to hear about his leg again? "Oh, yes, your poor leg. You've been using that excuse ever since we were children. I would think even you would be sick of it by now."

"Really, Harry." He sounded hurt. "It *is* a disability. You should know that. You were there, after all." Isaac cleared his throat. "Anyway, as I was saying. We — *you* — are the only one who can find out what's going on at the fortress. It's incredible to me that four of our best scouts have . . . disappeared without a trace. Incredible and . . . frightening, if you must know the truth. If I don't find out what's going on — if *you* don't — I'll be thrown out. Or worse. There have been some . . . irregularities. I had to make promises."

There was a long silence. *Make him wait*, Harry thought gleefully. *Make him wait*. "How much time would I have?"

Isaac's faint sigh of relief hissed into the darkness. "I knew I could count on you!"

"Hold on. I haven't said I'd do it. I just asked how much time I'd have. I have a life, you know — obligations, commitments. I can't just drop everything to do you a favor. Especially if it's as fraught with apparent danger and mystery as this." Then he paused. "Is there something you're not telling me, my dear brother?"

"Of course not." A little too quickly.

More silence.

"What's the reward?"

"One thousand. Cash."

"One thousand?" Harry laughed. "Are you serious? I am not going out in this filthy weather to help get you off the hook for one thousand anything. Try again."

"One thousand now and another five when you return with the information," Isaac said. "But I can't wait forever. You have two weeks to get there and back. Otherwise the deal is off. What do you say?"

"I'll think about it," Harry said, but a smile of deep satisfaction lit up his face in the dark.

The next day, after Harry and Isaac had visited the bank, tromping with difficulty through the snow-covered streets, Harry returned to his apartment with the down payment.

"Bills or gold?" Isaac had asked, and when Harry said, "Bills," Isaac had simply withdrawn the cash by signing a note. The teller had put away the little burlap sacks of coins and instead counted out the cash impassively, tucking it into a paper envelope stamped with the bank's logo: an elaborately calligraphic *FB* for FoxBank.

"I can't imagine how you could have accumulated enough wealth to part with a thousand so easily," Harry had said, impressed in spite of himself as they left the building and faced the icy streets. "Our inheritance was relatively small and real estate values have been dropping. What did you do — rob a bank?"

Isaac looked him in the eye. "None of your damn business. All you need to know is that if you come back with the information I need, the rest is yours."

"Are these" — Harry indicated the fat packet of bills — "the 'irregularities' you referred to? Am I now the recipient of stolen goods? Delightful," he said, rubbing his paws together. "I had no idea extortion, embezzlement, and blackmail could be so lucrative."

Isaac ignored him. "Well?"

Harry carefully stuffed the envelope into his coat pocket. "Brother," he said, holding out his paw, "it's a deal." They shook on it.

Harry and Isaac walked slowly and silently through the icy streets. It was a while before Harry became aware of footsteps behind them.

Isaac turned, and Harry saw the fox who had stood in line ahead of him the day before. "John? What do *you* want?" Isaac said with obvious irritation.

"Forgive me for troubling you, sir," said John. "I need to have a word with you, if you wouldn't mind." He looked at Harry. "Oh, hello," he said. "It's Harry, isn't it? I didn't know you were . . ." He glanced at Isaac. Then he seemed to remember his conversation. "I . . . I didn't mean . . . I wasn't referring to . . ."

"Don't talk to *him*," Isaac said. "Talk to *me*. What do you want?" he repeated.

"It's about the loan," John said, turning back to Isaac, his voice trembling. "I need more time. My children have not been well and . . ."

"Are you telling me you can't pay?" said Isaac. His bulky frame loomed over John and his voice was suddenly filled with rage. "You pathetic . . . !" He stopped and cast a furtive look at Harry. "Let's not discuss this here," he said, taking John's arm and roughly walking him across the snowy street. "Wait for me," he called to Harry, as they disappeared behind a building.

It seemed a very long time that Harry waited, the swirling snow blowing against his back. He walked up and down and stuck his paws under his armpits for warmth. This was cold even for a fox. *What was Isaac doing? How long could it take to negotiate a new arrangement? Why not meet indoors later to discuss it?*

When Isaac returned, he was alone. He approached Harry with a smile of satisfaction. "Sorry for the intrusion," he said. "These things happen."

"What things happen?" asked Harry. "Where is John? What took so long? It's freezing out here."

"I know, and I'm sorry. Let's walk — we'll stay warmer that way."

He picked up the pace and they continued toward the town square. Harry turned to look across the street. Three ragged fox children were running toward the building where Harry had seen Isaac and John disappear. As Harry watched, they emerged a few moments later, crying, and carrying something limp and bloody. Harry caught a glimpse of a faded brown coat.

"What did you do to that poor fellow?" Harry cried. He glanced down, saw blood on Isaac's cane, and turned to run back.

Isaac put a firm paw on Harry's arm. "Go there and our deal is off. I'll find another way to get the information I need. I mean it." His eyes were cold.

Harry argued briefly with his conscience: There was nothing he could do to help; John's children would care for him; no one would believe Harry if he accused Isaac; and besides, he hadn't actually witnessed anything. And there was money in his coat pocket.

He turned back, and they continued walking.

Harry and Isaac parted company at the town square.

"When will you leave?" asked Isaac. His face, almost hidden behind the fur collar of his coat, showed no trace of the icy anger Harry had seen moments ago.

"You said I had two weeks," Harry replied. "If I start tomorrow that should give me enough time to get there and back, even in this weather."

"If the weather improves, you may be able to return sooner, although the forecasters are not optimistic." Isaac coughed and reached into a deep pocket. "I thought you could use this." He removed what looked like a thick wooden ruler, the kind that folded on itself.

"What is it?"

"A collapsible walking stick," Isaac said. "Look. I had it made for me, but I don't use it anymore." With a few quick movements he unfolded the stick and locked the segments into position. He tapped it on the snowy street. "See? Very steady. It's not going to be easy getting to the fortress if the snow continues," he said. "You know what those trails are like even in good weather." He offered the stick to Harry. "This could help."

"You're giving this to me?" Harry said, surprised.

"Not giving, lending. I want it back. Take it."

Harry tried it. The stick was straight and sturdy, the segments jointed with brass fittings. Isaac's initials were carved into the top. "I'll see. It might be useful. Thanks." He collapsed it and put it into his other pocket.

"By the way," Isaac said, "I wouldn't stop at Inn the Forest if I were you." He rubbed his gloved paws together for warmth. "I've been hearing those badgers who run it cannot be trusted. And I have never understood how you could tolerate the awful food."

"I've always enjoyed the food. Besides, it's not like you to express concern for my creature comforts," Harry said suspiciously. "First the walking stick, now this. What's going on?"

Isaac shook his head. "For the gods' sake!" he said with irritation. "Can't a brother be brotherly? Are we that far apart? Stay where you want, then. It's not my concern."

"No, it's not."

"Well. I'll be looking for you in two weeks. The mothers and children of our community thank you," he said, switching into his political voice. "The weak and the starving will praise your name."

"Save it for the newspapers," Harry said. "We both know who is going to benefit from this little arrangement."

"Yes," said Isaac, and he glanced at Harry's coat pocket, which bulged slightly from the presence of the envelope. "We do."

Now, back home, Harry stomped the snow off his boots and walked into his bedroom. He opened the narrow closet, pulled out a large, heavy wooden box with an old-fashioned latch, released it, and surveyed the neatly arranged contents with satisfaction.

"Preparation, Planning, and Perseverance — the three Ps — the keys to successful hunting, as Dad always said," Harry murmured. He removed a carefully folded map, a small penknife, a miniature box of matches in a waterproof container, a canteen, and a large, clean leather pouch with several compartments. At the bottom of the box was a compass in a worn leather case.

Harry held the compass in his paws for a moment, staring into space, then he carefully put the compass and everything except the map into the leather pouch. He locked the box and put it back in the closet.

He packed a change of clothes and some extra socks. In the kitchenette, he brushed crumbs and dirty dishes off the table and spread out the map.

2

Quentin:
A Chance to Get Even

Quentin the Rabbit stood on the library steps, looking out at the white world and the snow that flurried around him. "I hate this weather," he said to Zack. "It's been snowing for weeks and the streets are still piled with snow. Why doesn't the government do anything about *that*?" He shifted his backpack to his other shoulder and pulled on his mittens. The snow stung his face.

"I know," Zack said. "We could try to bring it up at the next community meeting, but I read this morning that they've been postponed until further notice. You know what that means." He started down the stairs.

"Yes. Forever," Quentin said, following him. "I always thought the long walk from home was worth it — it's the library, after all — but these days I keep wishing there were an easier way."

"You *always* wish there were an easier way." Zack wrapped his fuzzy black scarf securely around his neck, tucked the ends into his black jacket, and breathed deeply. "But you wouldn't be my friend Quentin if you loved the outdoors."

Quentin noticed the streets were emptying quickly; rabbits, bundled up in coats and jackets in the traditional blue, walked purposefully toward home without looking up. *It used to be different,* he thought. *I wasn't always afraid — but it's been so long since I felt safe in Stonehaven that I can hardly remember what that was like.*

At the corner, a tall rabbit, mufflered up to his nose, approached them with outstretched paw. "Pamphlet?" he said in a friendly voice through layers of scarves. "There's a prayer service in a few minutes over at the meeting hall. It will end before curfew," he added, reassuringly. "Please come."

Zack shook his head, but Quentin took the paper as they continued to walk.

"What does it say?" Zack asked.

"What they always say. Oh, no — wait. This one's a little different. A prayer ritual to soothe the angry gods — *and* they're offering free samples of a new potion to increase body strength for 'all your defensive needs.'" He crumpled up the paper and stuffed it into his pocket. Anti-littering laws were now severely enforced.

"And cure gout too? Prayer ritual!" Zack said scornfully. "What about our belief that we could control our own lives without needing the gods?"

Quentin laughed. "No one thinks *that's* going to work anymore."

They trudged through the snow in silence. At the next corner, another rabbit approached, this one wearing a sandwich board. Zack read, "'Rabbits! Beware the Gray Forces of Night! Change your ways or we will all die!'" The rabbit wore neither jacket nor scarf, and his eyes burned with zealous fire.

"Poor fellow. He's obviously lost his mind. . . . 'The Gray Forces of Night!'" Quentin repeated. "How does *he* know what color the Forces are? Maybe they're pink!"

"I like pink," Zack said, "but it doesn't scare me in quite the same way."

"I guess that's the point."

"How much time until curfew?"

Quentin reached into his pocket and looked at his watch. "Not much. I really have to get home and try to finish my farming-methods paper before guard duty tomorrow night," he went on. "I'm not looking forward to it — guard duty, I mean."

"Don't you hate the idea? The phoniness?" Zack said, turning to him.

"Yes," Quentin said. "It's a joke. Rabbits are still disappearing, no matter what they do."

Zack didn't answer.

"I can't decide which is worse — the waste of time or the horrible uniform," Quentin went on. "Besides, I feel ridiculous marching around like some military type. I'm not a soldier — I'm a *student*, for the gods' sake!"

"I know," Zack said grimly. "And they're getting closer to the end of the alphabet. My turn will be coming."

It's more than all that, Quentin was thinking. *It's being up at the top of the high perimwall, walking for hours on that narrow pathway looking out over the tops of the trees in Wildwood Forest. With nothing to hold on to except a torch. One slip on the icy path and . . .* He shuddered.

"It's cold, huh?"

"Yes. Very. I don't want to talk about it anymore," he said. He'd never told Zack he was afraid of heights. It seemed too silly. "Maybe we can pick up a hot drink in the park. It's on the way."

They headed toward one of several carefully planned open spaces that appeared at regular intervals in Stonehaven, but the park, dotted with benches and paths for runners — Quentin had a favorite bench, near a fountain — was now obliterated by snow. The little shop that sold cool drinks in the summer and hot tea in the winter was closed and looked desolate and abandoned.

"I heard another speech from the Leader yesterday — did I tell you?" Zack said as they turned away from the shop and continued on the path.

"No. Anything new?"

Zack shook his head. "There was a big crowd, though. He explained why the new laws were for our own good, and how we have to trust him because they are working — a lie, of course, because another family disappeared the night before. I guess the news hadn't reached him yet."

"Anyone we know?" Quentin asked with a sinking heart.

"No."

"Remember — we didn't vote for him," Quentin said. "It's not our fault. Anyway, I hear his advisors keep him in the dark about everything. I wonder if that's true."

"It wouldn't surprise me," Zack said. "He also talked about the new draft, and that it was necessary for our protection. I was amazed that most of the crowd seemed to support the idea."

The faint tracks of sleds across the snow were fast vanishing in the oncoming gloom of an early dusk. Quentin turned to see their footprints filling quickly behind them as they walked the diagonal path to the other side of the park. The streets had become very quiet.

"It's awful, isn't it."

Zack nodded glumly.

"I don't know," Quentin said. "We used to be so peaceful. What happened?"

"Everyone's afraid. I guess that's what rabbits do when they're scared. They try to be strong. Or pretend they are."

"Do you think it will work?"

"Nope. Listen, I've been thinking," Zack said. "Remember we used to talk about the rebels? What would you think about joining them?"

Quentin stopped and turned to look at his friend. "Joining them?" he said with a disbelieving laugh. "Do you really think we could live a feral life?"

"I'm pretty sure *I* could do it. I'm not so sure about you! But who knows how the rebels live? Maybe they *like* a cozy fire!"

"Somehow I doubt it."

They started to walk again. Zack sighed. "You're hoping this repressive nonsense will just go away."

"Yes, I am."

"I hope you're right."

Quentin checked his watch. "Curfew." He looked around. Night had fallen; the streets were deserted. Houses all down the block were tightly shuttered; the light that filtered through the wooden slats made yellow stripes on the small mountains of snow that filled yard after yard. "At least there's no one around to notice." He stopped under a streetlight. "Oh no. I think I left my identity card home." He patted his pockets and dropped his backpack to the ground, rummaging through it, feeling panic. "Maybe it's here," he said. "Gods, I hope so."

"I left mine at home on purpose," Zack said quietly, and

Quentin looked up at him, shocked. "You did? Why, for the gods' sake?"

"Because it's all a fake — guard duty, identity cards, curfews!" Zack leaned over and whispered angrily, "The only point is to try to impress us with what a great job the Leader is doing. I refuse to play along."

"You're asking for trouble," Quentin whispered back, and then thought, *Why are we whispering?* He looked around again, but saw only the lantern posts flickering with yellow light at regular intervals, creating bright circles on the snow beneath them and vanishing into the distance. What about the guards who supposedly looked for strangers and loiterers?

Quentin stood and picked up his backpack. "This curfew thing really worries me," he said. "Can we walk faster?"

"I never thought I'd hear you say those words, Q," Zack said with a smile. "Sure."

But it was not possible to walk faster, Quentin realized. The snowdrifts made the streets difficult to negotiate, and his socks were beginning to feel wet and icy through his boots. *Gods, I hate this weather.*

As they stepped from one illuminated circle into the dark and back into the light again, Quentin could see the falling snow — large, wet flakes now — that melted at first on the arms and shoulders of his jacket, then gradually layered into fluffy mounds, only to be blown away by the wind and rebuilt again. He stood under the light and looked closely at the elegant, fragile snowflakes that landed softly on his blue sleeve and then vanished.

"Hey, Q — remember this?" Zack said. He walked over to the next lantern post, dropped his backpack, and stuck out his tongue.

"Yes," Quentin said. "The best part of a snowstorm. That . . . and *this* — !" Impulsively, he reached down, made a snowball, and threw it hard at Zack, hitting him on the chest.

"Hey! Cut that out!" Zack said with a surprised laugh, then scooped up some snow and threw back.

In a few minutes they were scrambling through the dark, gasping with the exertion. Quentin could see Zack moving in and out of the light, sometimes illuminated, sometimes not. Each time he saw him, Quentin threw, but Zack dodged and aimed and scampered away. Once, Quentin heard a satisfying yelp of surprise from Zack and then quickly felt a thump on his own back. They were both laughing.

"Got you!" Zack cried.

"Did not! You couldn't hit the perimwall if you were standing in front of it!"

"Well, how about this?"

Smack. Quentin felt a soft, wet hit on his cheek. "Missed me again!" he called, wiping the snow from his face. He leaned down to scoop up more snow and was aiming for where he'd last seen Zack running, when he heard someone call out.

"What's going on?" a high-pitched voice said from the darkened street. "Loiterers? After curfew?" A thin rabbit wearing military gray stepped into the circle of lamplight. "You'd better have a good reason. And, incidentally, there *is* no good reason."

Quentin was so surprised at the contrast between the rabbit's high-pitched voice and his straight-backed, military demeanor that he struggled not to laugh.

"Just coming home from the library," he said, breathing hard and trying to keep a straight face. "Nothing nefarious." With his paws behind his back, he dropped the snowball he held and then brushed off his mittens.

"I'll be the judge of that. Let me see your identity cards, both of you. You know loitering after curfew is against the law." The rabbit pulled a short, thick club from his belt and slapped it rhythmically into his paw.

Quentin looked at Zack and said, "Oh. All right." He knelt over his backpack and pretended to search. "I know it's here somewhere."

"What about you?" the rabbit said to Zack.

"We weren't loitering," Zack said, with a slight quaver in his voice. "We were . . . having a . . . snowball fight. Just some innocent fun. Or has that been outlawed too?"

I can't believe he said that, Quentin thought. *Sarcasm? To a rabbit in a uniform holding a club? Has Zack gone crazy?*

"Not here," Quentin said, standing up. "I must have left it home. Sorry. Officer," he added as an afterthought.

There was a moment of silence while the rabbit looked them up and down. "So," he said. His voice was so high-pitched he sounded like a female, or a child. Yet he was obviously neither. "Two rabbits without identity cards, alone on the street at night after curfew. One, oddly dressed and with an attitude problem," he said, looking at Zack. "Hmmm. What shall we do about this? I know!" He raised the club and brought it down, hard. Zack cried out and fell to his knees, grabbing his arm. The rabbit kicked him in the ribs, and Zack fell over into the snow. Quentin knelt down to help and felt harsh blows on his back that pushed him to the ground. Throwing his arms over his head, he tried to protect himself from the blows that rained down from above.

When the rabbit finally stopped, Quentin looked up. Standing under the streetlight, pounding the club into his paw, the rabbit seemed to tower over them; his eyes, deeply shadowed by the overhead light, were hidden. The snow fell like a curtain around him and settled on his military hat and shoulders. "Next time it will be worse," he said, and turned and disappeared into the darkness.

Quentin lay on the ground, stunned, his back throbbing. "Zack — are you all right?"

Zack groaned. "My arm," he said. "Gods, that hurt!" He struggled to a sitting position. "What about you?"

A door opened and two rabbits holding lanterns walked slowly toward them, their boots crunching in the snow.

"We heard," the older one said. "Here — let me help." He held out a paw, and Quentin pulled himself up. Zack grabbed onto the arm of the younger rabbit and stood with difficulty.

"Thanks," Quentin said. "I think we'll be all right now. Can you walk?" he asked, turning to Zack.

"Yes. I can't believe what just happened, though. We weren't doing anything wrong!" he said to the two rabbits. "It was a snowball fight! It's just one more law that has nothing to do with the real problem," he said, brushing off the snow with his good arm. "Nothing!"

The older rabbit held up his lantern and Quentin could see his faded brown fur and gray-white face. "Are you sure you're all right? You're welcome to come in for a moment and sit by the fire if you need to."

Quentin shook his head. "I think we should get home."

The two rabbits started back to the house, then the older one turned. "I'm sorry for what happened to you," he said, "but I don't believe this one officer's action represents the entire system. And you *were* breaking the law. . . . Listen," he went on, his brown eyes sad. "I have grandchildren. We can't protect them alone. And if there's even a *chance* that these methods might work . . ."

The younger rabbit walked back to stand beside him. He had the same brown fur and eyes. He nodded in agreement. "I hate the restrictions too," he said. "Especially the curfew. But rabbits continue to disappear and no one knows who's responsible. What else can we do? I agree with my dad. At least it's something!"

"But don't you ever ask yourself if this is really helping?" Zack said, rubbing his arm. "Guard duty? Identity cards? The draft?"

"Yes," said the older rabbit. "I think it is. The surveillance will allow us to notice anyone who acts peculiarly, who stands out — like you, for instance," he added, gesturing to Zack's black jacket and scarf.

"Me?" Zack said. "I'm a student! I've lived in Stonehaven my whole life!"

"So you say," the younger rabbit said, and seeing Zack's expression, added, "and I believe you. But these days, it's risky to look different from everyone else. You know that."

Quentin took an instant dislike to him. "You could be next," he said.

"I don't think so."

"We believe this is the right direction — and so do many of our friends," the older rabbit said. "You have a right to your opinion, but I think you should know you are in the minority."

They stood in awkward silence for a moment. "Well, good night," said the younger rabbit, and the two walked back to the house, closing the door firmly. In a moment, the lights inside were turned down and Zack and Quentin stood alone under the street lamp, the snow falling around them.

The next evening, Quentin climbed the tower staircase with difficulty. The stairs were steep, and his bruised back ached with every step. He opened the door at the top and stood looking out at the length of the narrow path stretching before him to the distant tower. There was the low guard rail, the only thing separating him from the fall that would surely kill him.

A voice from high overhead shouted, "Is that the guard reporting?" The supervisor was supposed to have met Quentin on the ground when he arrived, but there had been no one there when he lit the torch. Now, looking up at the guard tower through the snow, he could barely glimpse the rabbit's face looking out and quickly withdrawing. No wonder — it was cold up here.

"Guard reporting, sir," Quentin shouted back, as required by the training manual. There was no further word from the supervisor, so he started down the path, holding the torch low to get the best possible light.

After a while, he stopped and peered over the edge. *Maybe I can do this,* he thought. *Maybe I'm over it.* He stood as close to the low guard rail as he could and leaned over cautiously, holding the torch at arm's length. The ground was so far away, the light didn't reach it; the tops of the distant trees that surrounded the old fortress were below eye level; the snow fell in a funnel-like descent to the distant forest floor. His vision blurred and his heart beat faster. He stepped back.

Quentin took several deep breaths of cold air and felt his balance return. *I'll never try that again.* He stomped along, trying not to notice the ache in his back and the shooting pain in his knees. His boots crunched on the path, which, he realized, would soon be smooth and slick from his footsteps and even more treacherous.

He reached the far tower, turned — in what he hoped was an appropriately guard-like manner — and began to walk back. There are many worse things than walking on the perimwall in the freezing cold, he told himself. Cauliflower juice? Premature baldness? Fleas? Unpleasant, inconvenient, and socially unacceptable, in that order, but not as bad as this.

What would I do if I actually saw something suspicious? The training guidelines said: *Alert supervisor by sounding the alarm bell at the base of the tower* — he could just imagine the panic — *and draw weapon,* which happened to be a standard-issue knife. The supervisor would bang the gong, made of brass and suspended from the top of the tower. The sound alone could cause temporary hearing loss — Quentin had noted the guidelines provided no further details about *that* — but the volunteer militia (or would it be the newly drafted army?) would be at the wall in a few moments, with torches, clubs, and arrows at the ready. And then what?

Maybe Zack's right — maybe we should join the rebels. But how would that work, exactly? And what about my friends, and my classes? I'll be graduating in a few years — could I simply leave, after all my hard work, and just throw everything way? No. Things will change for the better, sooner or later. They have to.

Now, as he came to the end of the walkway, Quentin noticed the snow had stopped and the stars were suddenly bright. His face was numb from the cold, and he could hardly feel his feet. Stomping the snow off his boots, he looked up and called loudly, "All clear, sir!"

The supervisor's face appeared again, leaning forward, and this time Quentin could see it clearly. "Password?"

The face was familiar.

It was Wally.

Wally, his nemesis from childhood.

Quentin's first real encounter with Wally had taken place almost nine years ago, on a midsummer afternoon when the heat had been intense, the sun high in the sky, and there was little shade.

He had walked, reluctantly, to the swimming hole at the encouragement of his mother.

"It will do you good," she'd said, handing him a towel and a neatly wrapped sandwich of lettuce and squash — his favorite — in a faded blue cloth sack. "They're going to cover up that swimming hole someday," she called out to him, "and then you'll regret you didn't spend more time there!" She ran after him and handed him a straw hat with a visor. "Wear this."

"I won't regret it," Quentin had responded, "and I don't need a hat." But his mother paid no attention. Since his father had died of lung congestion three years earlier, Quentin's mother had been even more protective than usual. There was no point in reminding her how old he was. It would not have made the slightest difference. All his other siblings from previous litters were grown and had started their own families. Quentin had been the rare only child. His mother hovered over him.

"You are my youngest," she'd say. "My last. My baby. I can't lose you."

Quentin would much rather have spent his time reading under the huge elm that shaded his backyard. But when Mother made up her mind, she was like a badger. There was nothing to do but go along. Maybe it would be fun — at least he'd cool off. *Maybe,* he thought hopefully, *the threatening clouds on the horizon will bring a thunderstorm and I'll have to come home.*

He'd walked the dusty road, holding the hat, his bare feet

kicking up brown clouds. It was hot. Flies circled slowly over a drying mud puddle. Dead weeds and wildflowers baked in the sun alongside the road. As he approached the swimming hole, he saw a small group of females clustered ahead.

"Hi, Quentin!" It was Beth, from his class in school. She had large gray eyes; her fur was completely white. She wore a pink straw hat that shaded her face, and a long pink shirt that covered almost all of her. Quentin thought she was the most beautiful creature he'd ever seen.

"Hi."

Beth left her friends and joined him. They fell into step. "It's hot."

"Sure is."

"I have to stay covered. I've got albino blood. Sun isn't good for me."

"Oh." He'd wanted to talk to her for weeks. Now he had an opportunity and he couldn't think of a thing to say.

"Want to walk home together later?" Beth said.

"Sure."

"I'll wait for you, then. Bye." She left him to rejoin her friends, who had been watching. They whispered and laughed, and one of them nudged Beth and glanced back at Quentin.

Females were strange, but very, very interesting.

At the swimming hole, the others had already been

splashing and fooling around. Just ahead of him, a big brown rabbit named Clovis had jumped from the rocky ledge above the pond, pinching his nose and yelling the traditional cry when jumping from a high place: *"Rackjabbit!"* Except it always came out like *"Ra-a-ackja-a-a-a-!"* with the last syllable lost as the falling body hit the water.

Quentin left his stuff near a tree already crowded with towels and shoes, and climbed up the hill behind the pond to the stony ledge. Below him, rabbits splashed and swam in the dark water, forcing the green algae that had covered much of the surface to the grassy edges of the pond.

"C'mon, Quentin!" a voice called. "The water's perfect!" It was Beth. She and her friends had walked into the pond, shrieking with delight over the cold and the antics of rabbits who were jumping up and down and doing headstands in the water nearby.

"Yeah," someone else called. "It's freezing. Jump! You'll love it!"

Quentin stood near the edge of the rock, looking down. From up here, the water seemed far below; the hill on which he stood was covered with small boulders and scrubby weeds. A hummingbird whirred near his head and he turned to look.

"You're not scared, are you, Quentin?" Wally asked. A

minute earlier, he'd been splashing noisily in the pond. Now he stood behind Quentin, his brown paws planted at his hips. Quentin smelled the cold water that dripped from his shoulders. Wally's icy blue eyes were lined with red. "Are you?"

Quentin was not afraid, but Wally had been teasing him in a nasty way at school. How far would he go? *If only I'd seen him first*, he remembered thinking, *I could have jumped and avoided this*. "What's the matter?" he said, stalling for time. "Is the water too cold for you?"

"No," Wally said with a sneer. "Maybe it's too cold for *you*!" He smirked at his own wit. He moved toward Quentin, and Quentin backed away, closer to the edge.

Desperate, Quentin said, "You know, they say that really cold water on a hot day does permanent damage to your . . ." He looked up at Wally's ears. ". . . you know."

Wally grabbed his ears. "What do you mean? What damage?" He pulled at one ear and tried to look at it, but it was too short to reach his eye level.

"See what I mean?" said Quentin. "They've shrunk already. Cold water does that to blue-eyed rabbits. They'll never grow now. Didn't your dad ever mention it?"

"What? What are you talking about?" Wally had said, looking alarmed. He twisted around, trying to see first one ear, then the other.

Quentin tried not to laugh. Everyone knew it was impossible for a rabbit to see his own ears, unless it was in a mirror. It was like trying to lick your elbow.

Wally recovered. His face got red. "You're not a rabbit," he said in a loud voice. He walked to the edge of the rock and shouted down to the pond. "Hey, look, everybody! Quentin's afraid to jump. He's a vole! A little baby vole!"

The swimmers stopped splashing. Quentin could see Beth's white face beneath her hat, looking up at him. Wally began to sing, "*Vole, vole, jump in the hole,*" and in a few moments some of his friends took up the chant.

"Well, little baby?" Wally moved closer again and poked Quentin on the shoulder hard.

I am not going to let him get to me, Quentin thought. *He's stupid.* "Maybe the cold water won't be a problem for you, after all," he'd said loudly, his voice wobbling in spite of himself. "Maybe you never had much to worry about to begin with."

"You . . . *weasel!*"

Quentin felt a hard shove on his shoulder and was suddenly falling backward. Taken by surprise, he'd had no time to hold his breath. In seconds he slammed into the pond on his back. He gasped for air, a second too late, inhaling the icy water.

Quentin was an adequate swimmer — good enough to enjoy splashing around — but the shock of having breathed the water into his lungs was terrifying. He panicked. His feet touched the slimy bottom of the pond as he flailed and struggled to reach the surface, trying not to breathe at all but needing desperately to expel the fluid from his lungs. *I'm going to drown,* he thought. For a moment he was aware of the silent, murky green water, the distant legs and arms of the others, the floating debris — the algae, the twigs and branches — the layers of dark brown leaves that covered the bottom. Then there was a roaring in his ears and a pounding as he gave a sharp kick with his legs, struggling upward. His effort finally brought him to the surface, where he gasped for air.

Quentin swam weakly to the edge of the pond and stumbled onto the grass. He stood next to a tree and bent over, trying to breathe without coughing and wheezing. Finally, he looked up.

The sun was shining, hot. Rabbits shouted and splashed. Wally was back in the pond, surrounded by a noisy circle along with a few of his buddies, trying to prevent themselves from being ducked below the surface.

Beth stood still in water up to her waist, the sleeves of her shirt rolled up to her elbows. She looked at him briefly, and turned away. Quentin found his towel and dried himself off. He sat down under the tree, breathing shallowly at first, then more deeply as he saw he could. It felt wonderful to breathe, wonderful.

He began to imagine what he must have looked like: pushed

off the ledge, unprepared, splashing into the water on his back (he felt it now), sinking to the bottom and rising to the top, coughing and choking and gasping for breath like a beginner who'd never swum before. Looking like a fool with Beth watching.

"Hey, Quentin. Are you all right?" It was Zack, standing next to him, his pale brown legs dripping.

"I didn't know you were here," Quentin said. He stood up. "I guess you saw?" He wiped his face again with the towel to cover his embarrassment.

"You landed on your back," Zack said, "and I noticed Wally up there, so I figured he had something to do with it. What happened?"

Quentin told him. "I hate him."

"I know. I do too. But you got him to try to see his ears," Zack said. "That was great." He patted Quentin on the shoulder.

"Yeah. But now my back is killing me, and Beth . . ." He gestured. "I'm sure she saw me looking like an idiot."

Zack looked surprised. "Why does that matter?"

Quentin shook his head. It was too hard to explain. "Never mind. She wanted me to wait, but I'm going home."

"Going to say good-bye to . . . Small Ears?" Zack nodded toward Wally.

Quentin smiled weakly. "No, not today. See you." He picked up his stuff and left.

But that was not the end of it. Wally hadn't left him alone. All year he called him Vole-hole and the name stuck. On the court he mocked him when he dropped the ball or threw badly, which happened a lot. Quentin saw Wally's buddies nudge one another and laugh, happy that Wally had found a target other than themselves.

Quentin and Zack privately referred to Wally as Small Ears, then just S.E. It helped a little. Some time later, Wally had abruptly moved away.

Since then, Quentin had sometimes found himself at a high place — a ViewPoint, perhaps, with the lake and valley far below, or looking out over the vast Black Mountain Range and forest to the North. While his friends ran to the edge, or stood against a low retaining wall, or climbed a tall tree on a dare, Quentin would find a shady spot and pull out a book, trying not to think about the swimming hole, and Beth, and falling like an idiot. He'd been able to hide his fear from everyone.

Now on the perimwall, Quentin thought, *Of course it would be Wally up here, stuffed into a military uniform.* He could see that the older Wally had put on weight: The military gray jacket fit snugly. His fur had turned prematurely white, his paws were encased in heavy mittens, and his familiar expression of mean stupidity was now mixed with something else — a sense of his own great importance.

41

"I know you," Wally said slowly, looking down. His voice was a deep growl. "I know you. . . . It's Quentin, isn't it! It's old Vole-hole! Well, well, well." He began to laugh. "What a pleasant surprise!"

Quentin felt a surge of anger as all the old memories flooded back. *I won't let you scare me now,* he thought. "Do I know you?" he said.

"It's Wally! Remember? The swimming hole? The ball court? I sat behind you in rabbit history class." For a moment, he sounded genuinely disappointed at Quentin's response.

"I remember an ugly, stupid rabbit named Wally," Quentin said. "I remember the ugly, stupid rabbit had some embarrassing problems with cold water at the swimming hole." He squinted up at the tower. "Oh, yes. Now I see. It's *that* Wally, isn't it?"

Wally's voice turned icy. He suddenly seemed to remember his duty. "Shut up," he said coldly. "What's the password, Vole-hole? I'm waiting."

Quentin didn't answer.

"Password, Vole-hole — did you hear me? I'm giving you another chance, since this is your first time. Say the password, or else!" Wally's deep voice had become a menacing growl.

"I'm thinking," Quentin said. "Wait, I've got it, I've got it!" he cried, pretending to be excited. "*Bloody foxes!* That's it, isn't it?"

"No, it's not," Wally said, his voice expressionless. "Now

who's the stupid one? The manual says I have to shoot you."
He raised the bow he'd held at his side and positioned an arrow.
"I don't think I'll mind that a bit."

Uh-oh. "All right, I remember now, " Quentin said. "It's
Foxblood, right?"

"Right," Wally said, and put the bow down. "Don't forget
it, Vole-hole. Or you'll be sorry." He pulled his head in and
disappeared into the tower.

Quentin turned and walked back along the wall, smiling to
himself. *This could be my chance to get even,* he thought. *I can
hardly wait.*

3

Harry:
Some Things Are Not Fair or Logical

The next morning, just after dawn, Harry was outside of town, trotting along a road on the edge of Wildwood, which was blanketed in snow. The sky was barely light, with no glimmer of sun, but for the moment it had stopped snowing; the air was cold, and his breath clouded in front of him. His heavy brown boots crunched softly on the path, and he was grateful for the squirrel hide that lined his coat and his gloves.

Briefly Harry wondered what promises Isaac had made to his friends. Clearly his brother's interest in learning about the rabbit warren at the fortress had to be more than simple concern about food for the community. Harry had witnessed for himself how much Isaac cared about his fellow fox. The image of John's limp body filled his mind, but he pushed it away. *Let that be on Isaac's conscience,* he thought. *It's no concern of mine.*

The sky lightened as the hours passed, but not by much. Snow fell in feathery flakes at first, then with a blinding fury. The cold gray clouds, low in the sky, and the bare, brown-black trees, their branches covered in snow, made the landscape seem rinsed of color, like an old engraving from a schoolbook. By the afternoon, Harry, having decided to take a short cut, was traveling through an area of dense wood where the snow was deep on the trail and the terrain hilly. Rocks and buried logs occasionally blocked the path completely, forcing him to struggle through the snow and uncertain footing in the woods before finding his way back. It was slow going.

Once or twice he glimpsed a retreating shape in the deep forest on one side or the other of the rudimentary path. Once or twice he heard a muffled, thumping footstep in the near distance that quickly faded. *I knew I wouldn't be the only living creature in these woods!* he thought. *And if there are creatures, there is food.*

He was hungry. Using some of Isaac's money, he'd treated himself to an early — and very expensive — breakfast at a local restaurant that was still serving small portions of the last bits of pre-frozen, spicy mouse-and-squirrel sausage. Now, after the cold struggle through the drifted woods, Harry was suddenly aware of a familiar gnawing in his belly.

He stopped, mindful of his failure a few days ago, and stood motionless, waiting until his breath slowed. Then his keen ears picked up the sound of an animal scurrying beneath the snow. He listened intently. In a moment, the sound was repeated, and it was close by. Harry detected the scent of vole, and his ears told him there was more than one.

In the stillness of the snow-covered forest, the scurrying

sound was like a clap of thunder to Harry's ears. In another moment, he located the source: a mounded shape, perhaps a fallen log, a short distance away. The faint movement of the powdery white surface told him he was correct.

Harry carefully removed his coat and placed it gently on the ground. Then, in a flash, he was digging at the snow, and in less than a minute his effort was rewarded. Two adult voles and three out-of-season young, buried beneath the snow in a pile of decaying leaves and pine needles, were exposed to the cold air. The babies squealed in fear and the voles scrambled to escape. Harry barely noticed the terror in their eyes; he snapped the spines of the adults one at time, then, holding the babies by their tails, he bit off their heads. The hot blood and tender bones seemed to melt in his mouth, and his saliva dripped into the snow. In another moment, he had devoured the voles, skin and all.

The first time he'd tasted vole he'd been a child on an excursion into Wildwood Forest with Isaac and Dad. They had left early in the morning, and following Dad's instructions and his "Preparation, Planning, and Perseverance" motto, had decided in advance exactly where they'd be hunting. Each of them carried a small knapsack and an informally drawn map. Dad had a compass, folded into a leather pouch.

"Just because we live in a civilized society," he'd said as they started out at dawn, "doesn't mean you don't need to know the basics. Our ancestors found all their food this way. I want my sons to know how to fend for themselves. You never know."

They were walking through the early light. The air was cool, and on the horizon, the Black Mountains were hidden by a pale gray fog. Following first a long, wide trail out of town at the eastern end of the forest not far from their house, they gradually turned onto narrower paths until they were in the middle of the pleasant woods. Dad checked the map frequently, his gray-brown felt hat pulled down over his brow for shade, his sharp blue eyes alert and vigilant. His father was big — or at least that's how Harry remembered him — and he strode through the woods with a relaxed confidence. Isaac and Harry trotted behind him.

"You never know what, Dad?" said Isaac.

"Just you never know. Your mother thinks fresh-killed prey is more easily digested and nutritious. She may be right. Anyway," he went on, "I want you to experience this. It's part of growing up."

Harry had felt himself to be in an exalted state almost from the moment they entered the woods. There had always been a serious injunction against going to the forest alone, and Harry had never violated it. Isaac claimed to have heard — and seen — monsters lurking in the trees at night. Harry didn't think he believed him.

Now Harry found every tree and shrub to be an object of intense beauty and interest; every sound — the crackle of leaves and pebbles underfoot, the snapping of twigs, the wind sighing through the firs, the calls of birds — a song of the gods. The smells alone made him dizzy with delight and excitement. He had found his true home.

Dad had forged ahead, talking, explaining, warning. He pointed out dangers and opportunities. He told them how to trot silently (they couldn't do it), how to distinguish the scent of different creatures, and which ones were most likely to be catchable and/or edible. He pointed out the signs of various species on the forest floor and could differentiate among the droppings of birds and smaller mammals as if reading their signatures. He warned about dangers — the poisonous, tempting berries, the few larger creatures in the wood, themselves untamed, who would call them prey.

"Us? *Me?*" Harry said, shocked. He had stopped walking, trying to take in the concept that he could be viewed as a desirable lunch or dinner by some slavering, uncivilized creature.

"Yes, you. All of us. You need to remember," his father said, turning and taking his paw while Isaac walked beside them, "that foxes, badgers, weasels, ermine, raccoons, and a few others are the only creatures to have achieved this level of civilization. Didn't you learn this in school?"

"We learned it," Isaac said, "but they didn't tell us about

the other part. That we could be someone's dinner." He looked around. "Maybe we should go home."

"But aren't *we* doing the same thing?" Harry asked.

Dad stopped. "We are doing this for sport," he said seriously. "This is not the way we live our lives, you know that. Your mama shops at the market and we eat cooked, prepared foods at restaurants. What we are doing is called recreational hunting. It's perfectly acceptable as long as it's kept under control and is not part of an instinctive, thoughtless life behavior."

"But the prepared food was alive once. Aren't we just as bad as the animals who want to eat *us*?"

"Some things are not fair or logical, Harry," his father said and patted him on the head. "This is one of them. Now let's find ourselves some lunch."

They continued on the narrow path. Harry's thoughts about unfairness were swept away by another idea: that some *thing* out in the forest, covered with the same lovely summer sunshine, could be hunting for *him*, slinking silently through the woods, watching his every move. The thought made Harry tremble with fear and excitement. Maybe Isaac wasn't lying.

Ahead of them, Dad stopped, signaling silence with a severe glance and his paw to his mouth. Harry heard the rustle of leaves and twigs and, in a few minutes, saw a mouse family darting through the underbrush, their camouflage so effective they could barely be seen.

Dad gestured for Isaac to come closer. Isaac did, but when he saw the mice, he leaped forward. "I see them! I see them!" he shouted and pounced, but by then the mice and all their relatives had scampered madly away, leaving only the unsettled leaves and a darkened trail of overturned, sweet-smelling earth behind them.

"Patience, Isaac, my son, patience!" Dad said with kindness in his voice. "Don't just jump on it, whatever it is. *Wait.* Let your senses tell you the right moment to make your move. You still have your old instincts. Learn to listen to their voices."

Isaac nodded, embarrassed. "Sorry, Dad," he said.

Harry could hardly refrain from laughing. *I could have caught them all,* he thought. He poked Isaac when Dad wasn't looking and mouthed the word, "Baby!"

"Dad! Harry hit me!" Isaac said in his whiny voice.

"Harry, leave your brother alone. He's younger than you, and it's your job to look out for him. Hitting is not a part of that responsibility," Dad said without turning around.

"Yes, Dad," Harry said, and poked Isaac harder.

Isaac's face crumpled and he was about to howl in protest, when Dad stopped and gave them That Look. They were alongside a stream, hidden behind some shrubbery, while a family of voles slept peacefully in the dirt along the bank in front of them, barely two feet away. Harry could still remember the feeling. He had focused on the voles with such intensity that the smells and sights about him faded and became distant. The voles came into sharp focus, while around them the ground, the sky, and the stream became soft and blurred. All that existed were the voles, his own slow, measured breaths, and the pounding of his heart.

"*Now*, Harry!" Dad whispered, but Harry had already leaped and sunk his teeth into the neck of the largest vole, which barely had the opportunity to offer a protesting squeal before going limp in his mouth. As the others vanished into the brush, Harry took the vole out of his mouth and brought it over to Dad. The taste of hot blood and velvety skin lingered pleasantly.

"How was that, Dad? Was that all right?" he'd said, even though he knew it was more than all right.

"Wonderful, son," Dad said, with a generous pat on the back. He turned. "Did you see your brother, Isaac?"

Isaac was sitting under a tree with an odd look on his face. His sandy brown fur was rumpled, and he seemed pale. "I don't feel good," he said, and his lower lip trembled. "I want to go home. I want Mama."

"What's the matter now?" Harry said to Isaac. "Do you always have to ruin everything? Dad?" He turned to his father. "Do we have to go back?"

Dad was bending down to look at Isaac. "What's the matter, son?" he asked with tender concern. "Are you hurting? Did you eat some of those berries I warned you about?"

Isaac hesitated, then nodded.

Dad shook his head. "Let's go home," he said. "We can come back tomorrow." He picked up Isaac and held him in his arms all the way to the house, while Harry trotted alongside, his anger and disappointment a bitter taste in his mouth. All around him the forest breathed its tempting smells and sounds, but Harry could only focus on Isaac, who had spoiled the best day of his life.

They never went back. Isaac's illness had been catastrophic; he was bedridden for months. Mama kept a vigil at his bedside day and night. Dad became distant and distracted. Harry was left to his own devices, making his own meals, doing his homework at the kitchen table while Dad and Mama sat with Isaac and Mama sang him the old songs to help him sleep.

Isaac gradually recovered from the strange paralysis that had gripped him, but when he did his left leg was permanently weakened and he walked with a limp. Harry remembered tiptoeing into Isaac's bedroom — they had once shared it, but Harry had been moved out to avoid possible contagion, and had been sleeping on the living room couch. It was a winter afternoon when Dad had finally told him it was safe.

It had been so long since Harry had seen their room that

he was shocked at its familiarity — and at the changes. Isaac, looking very small and fragile, sat propped up in Harry's bed, which had been moved closer to the window, "so Isaac can see the sunshine," Mama explained, hovering nearby. Harry's precious collection of forty-nine perfectly oval black pebbles neatly arranged by size on his dresser had vanished, never to be found again, and his favorite toy, a raggedy stuffed mouse named Clarence, was nestled under Isaac's arm.

"Here's your big brother, Isaac, dear," said Mama. "Come here, Harry, and say hello to Isaac. He's finally feeling better." Mama reached out her paw to Harry to draw him close.

Before Harry could move, Isaac said in a weak voice, "I'm thirsty, Mama," and Mama quickly turned away from Harry and poured water into a glass from a pitcher that sat on a new nightstand near the bed. "Here, dearest," she said, holding the glass to his mouth. Isaac took the glass and drank one or two sips, then sighed and pushed her paw away. When Mama's back was turned, Isaac looked at Harry with a triumphant little smile and stuck out his tongue.

For a few moments, Harry was lost in thought, staring blankly into the silent woods. Then he sighed and washed the blood and gore from his paws and face with some clean snow. *There is no point in living in the past,* he thought. *Isaac has made his life, I have made mine. Isaac is the wealthy Managing Director of*

Foxboro, hobnobbing with the powerful and rich, never wondering where his next meal will come from. I live from day to day in a run-down apartment owing money to just about everyone. Mama and Dad are gone, and so is my inheritance.

But Dad left me his compass.

At midafternoon, Harry paused for a rest and cleared away the snow beneath a tall, bent pine. He sat down, bit off his gloves, undid the pouch, and pulled out the map with icy paws.

His plan had been to stop for a time at Inn the Forest, Isaac's disparaging evaluation notwithstanding. His brother's distaste somehow made the place even more appealing. Furthermore, he'd have the chance to take in some good meals — assuming, of course, that the Inn was well stocked — and hope for an end to the snow. A storm like this could not last forever. According to the map, the fortress was still far away. He could get there later in the week, look around, and return home just in time to collect the rest of the money. On the way he'd stop at the abandoned summer cottages that clustered near Elk Lake, where as a child he had vacationed with his family. It was a good plan. He pulled out the compass, checked it, and returned it to the pouch. Then he carefully folded the map and tucked it away.

As he walked with difficulty along the snow-covered path, he thought about Isaac's money. *Was I too willing to be his flunky? Should I be running errands for the brother I despise? Can*

Isaac be trusted to pay me when I return? Isaac was once again using his weak leg as an excuse to avoid anything difficult or inconvenient, just as he had his entire life. *I'll find a way to come out on top,* Harry thought confidently. *I just have to figure it out.*

After hours of climbing upward into the hills on the meandering trail, struggling through the underbrush when the path disappeared, backtracking and stumbling over brittle shrubs and fallen branches, he found what he'd been looking for: In a clearing stood a large, sturdy wooden building, somewhat rambling in shape. Over the years additions and extensions had extended the original squarish structure until it tentacled broadly over the snowy landscape. The door would open into the lobby of what he knew to be the shabby but friendly Inn the Forest, run by a badger. Sure enough, there was a carved sign on the door. Harry knocked loudly.

The peephole above the sign opened. A cold black eye gazed at him briefly, then the small window clicked closed. A deep voice growled at him from the other side of the door. "What do you want?"

The door creaked open. Harry's nose detected the pungent vestige of an earlier visit from a skunk, perhaps even several winters ago, and the stronger, slightly salty smell of raccoon.

"I want a room. May I come in?"

There was a shuffling noise and the door opened wider. A

huge creature loomed before him, now backlit by the lamps just inside the entryway.

It was one of the largest raccoons Harry had ever seen. Wearing faded overalls and a checked flannel shirt, the raccoon had substantial girth and was a good head taller than Harry. The creature's eyes were bright and alert behind the black mask of fur.

Harry's fatigue made him angry. "This is Inn the Forest, right? There is a vacancy, right? What happened to the badger?"

The raccoon looked at him sharply. "Now, now. Let's not get fleas up our socks! I'm the new owner, along with my partner. Yes, we have one vacancy, our last room. The place is packed." The raccoon peered at Harry suspiciously. "You aren't from the foxes up North, are you? Because if you are, you can just keep moving. I'll know if you're lying."

The air about them had become colder, and a breeze had picked up. Snow began to fall again in fine, powdery flakes.

"No, I'm not from the North," Harry lied. "Now may I please come in?" He tried to walk inside, but the raccoon shifted slightly to prevent Harry from getting closer.

"I don't believe you."

Harry was losing patience. "Look," he said. "I want a room. I'll pay in advance. Here." He reached into his pocket, fumbled for one of the large bills, and waved it.

The creature was silent for a moment, as if weighing the risks. "All right. I know I'll regret this." The raccoon turned away. "My name is Allison."

Harry followed her inside as a gust of wind slammed the door behind him.

4
Quentin: Possibly Very Dangerous

When Quentin arrived at the café the next morning, Zack was staring out the window at the gently falling snow, his naturally sad expression even more thoughtful and tense than usual. It was still early in the day and the café was chilly — he'd kept his black jacket on. *What's going on?* Quentin thought. He was about to ask, when Zack said, "How are you feeling? And how was guard duty?"

"I'm all right — still a little sore, though. Listen, you won't believe who my supervisor was."

"Who?"

"Wally! Remember him?"

"Of course I do. S.E. — old Small Ears! I thought he'd moved away."

"Me too."

"What's he like?"

Quentin thought about it. "A little heavier, but pretty much the same. Seeing him again brought it all back. I'm afraid I lost my head."

"What do you mean?"

Quentin picked up the menu, then put it down. "You remember Wally was never the ripest apple on the tree."

"That's an understatement."

"I decided to find ways to annoy him. He's so dense, I don't think he even realized what was happening. He aimed that bow at me at least five times — I was warm and toasty for the rest of my watch. Even the pain in my ribs went away."

"You really like to live on the edge! If Wally is a perimwall supervisor, he must be pretty important in the military establishment."

"I know."

"He could make trouble for you."

"True. I guess I don't care. For the moment." He paused. "I think."

"Well, at least you know your own mind," Zack said with a laugh. "All right, then, tell me what you did. I'm all ears."

"Very funny. I don't remember everything, but I can tell you it felt wonderful. I know I disguised my voice at least three different times. I spoke in a heavy north county dialect and then pretended I had a cold. I had a coughing fit every time I was about to say the password, which of course was wrong anyway. Once I sang it, and he couldn't decide if the password was valid because the guidelines didn't mention singing."

Zack had got caught up in the story and was chortling with delight. "That must have been satisfying. I wish I'd been there."

"Mind if I join you?" a voice said above them.

A very tall rabbit, deep chested and large about the middle, wearing a cap at a rakish angle, stood alongside the table.

"Frank! How great to see you!" Quentin said. "Of course, sit down." He pulled over a chair from a nearby table and gestured. "Do you know Zack? Zack, this is my old friend, Frank."

"My pleasure," Frank said. He shook Zack's paw warmly. "Thanks. I will join you, if you're sure it's all right." He pulled out the chair and sat down heavily. "It's great to see you too, Quentin. Of course it hasn't been that long, has it? Only a year, but it feels like ten." He picked up the menu. "It all looks good," he said. "I could eat a field of cabbage. In fact, I think I did, just yesterday!" He laughed and patted his stomach. "Enjoyed every bite."

"You do look a little . . . larger than when we last saw each other," Quentin agreed. There were other changes too. Frank's light gray fur was still mottled with irregular patches of brown and his hazel eyes were still warm and friendly, but there was a deep crease in the middle of his brow that had not been apparent a year ago. He seemed more . . . serious. "Frank and I spent a lot of time together his last year of Upper School. We met in the choir — two rather raucous tenors, wouldn't you say?"

"I prefer to think of us as enthusiastic," Frank said to Zack with a smile.

"Frank made a permanent connection right after he graduated," Quentin went on. "How is Mary?"

"Great, great. And look — we've just had our first." He patted several pockets and pulled out some small, flat pieces of wood on which several small portraits had been painted. He handed them to Quentin with obvious pride. "These are recent."

Quentin studied the paintings as Frank and Zack chatted. There were several pictures of four young bunnies; one, the smallest, looked like a miniature version of his father. Frank turned and pointed. "That one — Charlie — I'm afraid he's become my favorite, and not just because he looks like me! Very bright, amazing energy, very loving. Like his mother. I never really appreciated babies," he continued, "but it's completely different when they're yours."

Another single painting of a dark brown female with soft eyes and a quiet smile made Quentin look up. "Mary looks terrific," he said. "I always liked her." He handed the portraits back and Frank tucked them away carefully. "I can see your new life suits you."

"It does. What about you? Still playing the field, you rascal?"

Quentin nodded. "The field suits me fine, I'm happy to say."

"What about after graduation?"

"Too far away to think about," Quentin said. "Besides, these days, anything's possible." He glanced at Zack, who nodded in agreement.

"True. I heard you had your first guard duty last night. How did it go?"

"Bad news travels, eh?" said Quentin. "I was just telling Zack what a good time I had. Did I ever mention a rabbit named Wally who made my early school days so miserable?"

"Don't think so. But I've heard of him recently. Nasty creature, apparently. Go on."

Quentin related the story of the swimming hole and the nickname.

"Sounds like a rabbit who deserves some retribution," Frank said. "Not that I actually approve of that kind of thing. At least not publicly. I'm going to try to teach my children that most creatures can be reasoned with, and that kindness is more effective than a stick or a punch in the face. I wish I believed it! So what did you do?"

"Let me," said Zack.

Frank's hearty laugh when Zack finished was gratifying. "Brilliant, as usual, Quentin," he said. "You haven't changed a bit! But possibly very dangerous," he added, suddenly serious.

"Speaking of dangerous," Zack said, "I'm curious. How do you see the current situation?"

Frank shook his head. "Do you mind if I order first? I have a hard time talking politics on an empty stomach." He gestured to the waiter, and in a few minutes there was a large salad and two vegetable sandwiches in front of him. He began with the salad. "Mmm. The current situation. Let me be frank."

Quentin smiled. It was an old joke.

"I think something has to be done."

Quentin was surprised. Frank had never been interested in radical causes. He had been focused on what he'd called the four Fs — Food, Females, Frivolity, and Frank. The occasional rebellion on the part of the more activist students had found him on the sidelines, making funny, wry observations and providing the food when the crowd returned from wherever they'd been, hungry and tired. Like many big eaters, Frank had been a great cook.

Now Frank lowered his voice even more. "Can I trust you?" he said, looking first at Quentin, then at Zack.

"Of course," Quentin said, bemused. They all leaned closer.

"Well," Frank said, between mouthfuls of salad, "are you aware that many of those who have disappeared in the last few months were among the rabbits who questioned some of the government's recent decisions?"

"That can't be!" Quentin said.

Frank nodded. "It's true."

"Wait a minute," Quentin said. "These disappearances started in the spring. There were no dissidents then."

"Are you sure? I think . . ." Frank broke off as the diners at the next table exchanged looks.

"Maybe we should have this conversation another time," Quentin said, leaning back in his chair. There was no point in taking chances. "How about tonight, my place, before curfew. Do you have any plans, Zack?"

"Not really."

"Frank?"

"No . . . no plans."

"Fine." Quentin wrote down his address.

Frank started on his second sandwich. "I can understand why Wally bothers you so."

"I haven't told you the half of it, Frank — he used to beat me up every day. He'd wait for me after school and leap out from behind the hedges near the ball field. He told terrible lies to his friends about how my father died. He called me horrible names. He made my school days a living hell — and why?" Quentin leaned forward. "*Because he was stronger than I was and could get away with it,* that's why." He leaned back. "He's perfect for the military, in my opinion. They're all bullies."

Zack shook his head. "That's a big generalization."

"Really? What about coming home from the library?"

Zack turned to Frank and told him about their confrontation after curfew.

Frank put down his sandwich. "Nefarious? You *said* that?"

"Yes," Quentin replied, a little defensively. "It was a test of his intelligence. Unfortunately, the rabbit passed it."

Frank patted him on the shoulder. "Good old Quentin."

"For a moment I thought he might be all mouth and no teeth," Quentin went on. "Especially with that voice. But I was wrong."

Frank finished eating. "Scary."

"I know."

"Maybe you're right about Wally and that rabbit from the other night," Zack said to Quentin. "But couldn't there be *someone* in the military with a conscience?" He laughed at Quentin's expression. "No? You're tough, Q."

The door to the café opened and a cold blast of air rushed into the room. Quentin turned, along with several other diners who glanced briefly at the doorway. "Oh, gods," he said in a whisper. "It's Wally — and that rabbit is with him."

The two sat down at a reserved table near the fire. A waiter hurried over and bent down to take their order.

"Is he the one you were talking about?" Frank said. "I think that's Dan. I've been hearing about him too. He has a reputation for being ruthless. Not good."

Quentin turned to Zack. "Smart and ruthless, huh? Maybe joining the rebels is not such a crazy idea, after all."

Frank looked up sharply. "The rebels?"

"Never mind, Frank," Quentin said with an embarrassed laugh. "We've just been sunshining."

Zack was silent.

Frank turned. "Wally doesn't look evil from here," he said. "With all that white fur, he looks almost fatherly."

"Looks are deceiving," Quentin said, glancing in the same direction. "Especially in his case."

Wally said something to Dan, and they both looked at Quentin. Wally smiled.

Quentin froze. "Oh, gods. I know that smile. Pretend we're talking."

"We *are* talking."

Wally gave him a casual salute and mouthed the words "*Vole-hole.*" Quentin turned away. "Notice that? When Wally smiles, his eyes stay cold and serious. That's how I always knew he was planning something . . . and now he has an accomplice."

Frank glanced at the rabbits who sat at the table next to them, silently eating, and slapped a paw on the table. "This has been terrific." He stood up with difficulty and burped quietly. "Seeing you has made me nostalgic for the old days when I had no responsibilities and could . . ." He pulled out the small paintings and stared at them for a long moment. "What am I talking about?" he said softly. "This is the happiest time of my life." He cleared his throat, replaced the paintings, and tossed some money on the table. "Listen, I need to get home. Thanks for letting me join you. Quentin — I look forward to this evening." They shook paws all around and Frank walked slowly out of the café, not looking at Wally and Dan, who watched him with interest as he made his way to the door.

"This is really unsettling." Quentin caught the eye of the waiter and waved his paw in the air as if writing. The waiter nodded and brought the check in a few moments. Quentin got up, but Zack didn't move.

"So, Zack. What's going on?" Quentin asked, sitting down again. "I know there's something. Is it Dan and what happened the other night? I could see it in your face the moment I walked in."

"No, it's not just Dan." He sighed. "It's my upcoming guard duty."

Quentin searched for the right words. "It could be worse. It could be the draft."

"True, although that's surely next."

"And besides," Quentin continued, "it's not that bad. I did it, and I'm the one who hates physical exercise."

"It's not the physical part." Zack leaned forward and spoke in a passionate whisper. "There's something else going on.

67

Frank obviously thinks so too." He stood up. "Maybe we can come up with something tonight. Maybe he has a few ideas. . . ." Zack's face was grim.

"What do you mean, come up with something?"

Zack just shook his head.

By tacit agreement they left the café by a side door and walked around to the front, where they took shelter for a few moments on a wide porch with a deep overhanging roof and looked at the snowy landscape. They stood before another park, a large, open square in the exact center of Stonehaven. Quentin looked across the expanse of white, which in warm weather was a pleasantly green, landscaped space, with large trees, a small pond, and the occasional statue of a former leader. Now the benches were drifted or buried in snow; the statues wore white epaulettes, the pond was frozen solid. The white branches of the trees bent low to the ground. The snow fell in powdery flakes, covering the already buried roads and making white turbans of the distant rooftops of downtown.

"If it weren't so endlessly cold, it would be very beautiful," Zack said. His dark eyes were sad and his mouth turned down as if he'd eaten something bitter.

"The two things don't cancel each other out," Quentin said. "You're just worried. Listen, I've got some chores to do. Want to come along?"

Zack didn't respond.

"Come on," Quentin said, clapping his friend on the back. "You have nothing else planned."

They started down the road.

The Rabbittampers had been through and the walkways had been flattened, but they were becoming icy and maintaining balance was difficult. Ahead of them, rabbits walked slowly in twos and threes, bundled up in blue scarves and long coats, clutching mittened paws for balance. A few youngsters sledded down the icy streets without fear of interference.

Quentin and Zack were silent. All around them the snow fell straight down. Without a wind the air felt warmer. Quentin was thinking about the conversation over lunch: the charming pictures of Frank's family; their run-in with Dan, last seen seated next to Wally at the table near the fire; and Wally's icy smile. He shivered.

Then he felt a tap on his shoulder. Startled, he turned. Dan stood behind him, holding out an envelope. Standing next to him were four large rabbits in uniform, their faces grim and impassive. "We meet again," Dan said, in his odd, high voice. "What a coincidence!"

Quentin took the envelope, and Dan turned away, marching confidently on the slippery path. The others followed, four abreast, behind him.

Zack stared after them, then came closer. "What is it?" he said. "It looks official."

Quentin removed his mittens, tore open the envelope, and looked briefly at the contents.

"Ah," he said, trying to make light of it, but his heart sank. "The chubby, white paw of Wally falleth upon me. I've been drafted. Tomorrow at this time, I will be in the army."

5

Harry:
Inn the Forest

The lobby of Inn the Forest had not changed since Harry's last visit. The brightly lit interior only exaggerated the shabbiness of the furnishings: a worn, plaid couch; an oval, braided area rug, slightly askew on the dark wood floor; and the brown velvet armchairs, whose cushions held the permanent impression of many a large guest. Several raccoons sat or stood around the crackling hearth, warming paws in silence or conversing quietly. They looked up when Harry entered, and their conversations ceased. Some groups moved away, while others stared. A weasel, somewhat older than the others, sat in a chair by the fire, smoking a cigarette that reeked of sassafras and scribbling into a notebook. He looked up briefly as Harry entered and then returned to his writing.

Harry noted he was the only fox in the room.

Someone called from beneath the reception desk. "Who was that, sweetie? The mail carrier?" It was a voice with a pleasant, hoarse undertone, as if the creature had been laughing.

"No," Allison growled. "It's a fox. I told him he could have our last room."

There was a brief silence, and then a flustered figure emerged. Another raccoon, somewhat smaller, looked out at Harry, and the professional, welcoming smile faded almost immediately.

"Oh," she said. "You're not one of the foxes from up North, are you? We've had some of those. I don't consider myself an inhospitable creature, but those foxes were dreadful. Well, are you one of them?"

Harry lied again.

"Well, in that case, of course you can have a room. Where are my manners?" The raccoon opened a guest book and handed a pen to Harry. "My name is Becky. Allison and I are the new owners. Welcome to Inn the Forest."

Harry took the pen and signed the book. His stomach growled. "Do you have enough food here?" he asked. "The storm . . ."

"Yes," Becky replied, "we do, thanks to Allison's good planning and a bountiful early harvest. It's almost exclusively vegetarian, I should warn you, and not much variety, I have to admit. But our other guests seem pleased. Of course, nothing lasts forever," she said with a sigh. "We'll have to start thinking about a contingency plan soon if this terrible weather continues." It was more than Harry needed to know about the food, but Becky didn't notice his impatience. She took the pen from him and looked briefly at his name.

"Harry," she said with a smile. "We'll see you at dinner in about an hour."

"Follow me," said Allison curtly, and led him through the lobby, past the still-silent groups of guests, and down a long corridor toward the back, until she stopped in front of a door numbered 27. She reached into a deep pocket in her overalls and removed a large ring of keys, all of which looked exactly alike to Harry. Without hesitation, she picked one and opened the door. Allison lumbered around the room, lit the table lamp with a match she took from her pocket, then turned to Harry. "Becky always likes to see the goodness in creatures," she said. "But the foxes she mentioned were more than dreadful — they were despicable. It took us weeks to repair the damage. . . ." She shook her head. "Anyway, it always ends badly with foxes. Maybe you'll be different." She looked him up and down again. "Maybe not." She closed the door behind her.

Harry bolted it. The fox visitors must have been the scouts Isaac referred to. Considering the lowlifes Isaac associated with, it seemed more than likely. Harry placed his pouch on the battered table, took off his boots, and fell onto the bed.

The room was very much like one he had stayed in the last time — small and minimally furnished, with a vase of faded paper flowers perched at the corner of a small dresser. A multicolored rag rug at the foot of the bed was the only bright spot. Everything else was brown or gray, including the curtains and the bedspread. The earthy colors gave the room a warmth that belied the temperature. Harry could see his breath.

He dived under the blankets. For a few moments, his mind was blank as his body heat warmed him and his toes tingled. Yesterday he had been pacing his apartment, gnawing on a moldy sandwich and wondering when he'd have his next meal. Today he was considerably richer, having been paid by his disgusting brother to do something he'd been planning to do anyway.

Wait a minute. Harry sat up in bed. What a fool he was! Why bother to travel through this unpleasant weather to the fortress at all? There was food at the Inn. He could stay here, relax during the evening, hunt during the day if he liked, and return home at the appropriate time with a story he could invent without too much trouble.

As for the story, no explanation of what had happened to the scouts — that would be the first thing. Their disappearance would forever be a mystery. And as for the rabbits, suppose Harry told Isaac that there *were* no rabbits? That they had all died of a mysterious and contagious disease that had made them inedible? Or they had been decimated by a marauding band of feral wolves who had descended from the gods-know-where and vanished, their bellies full, leaving skin and bones and not much else behind? Or the rabbits were gone, perhaps migrated to a better climate — who could blame them? — leaving nothing but their burrows and the not-very-tasty aged and weak, who had quickly expired in the frigid weather? Harry could collect the balance of the payment — he would have fulfilled his part of the bargain, after all — and live comfortably for the rest of his life somewhere warm. Isaac and his friends would not discover the truth until Harry was far away and it was too late to do anything about it. Perhaps Isaac, unable to keep his promises, would be drummed out of Foxboro, humiliated, revealed to be the hypocritical manipulator he truly was. The snowstorm had to end sooner or later, other prey would return and multiply, the fox community would survive. The little children Isaac professed to care about would grow plump and happy.

Harry couldn't resist following this line of thought. Isaac would be living in exile, his resources depleted. Under cloak of darkness, a ragged and starving Isaac would search out Harry to beg for shelter. Harry would be living in luxury. . . . And if his lies were discovered? Isaac would be held accountable, not Harry. Isaac would be blamed for not having chosen a more reliable investigator. Even better. He fell back in bed, imagining himself embroidering a tale of the demise of the rabbits, and picturing Isaac's rapt expression as he swallowed every word.

. . . "I tell you, Isaac, it was the most horrifying sight
I have ever seen. Thousands of rabbits, dead and dying,

trapped behind the fortifications, covered with disgusting lumps and pustules and stinking of rotting flesh, even those who still lived. I don't think I'll ever be able to eat rabbit again."

Isaac shook his head. "What a tragic waste," he said. "How can I ever thank you for risking your life this way?"

"It was nothing, brother," Harry replied, holding out his paw as Isaac counted out the remaining five thousand. "Nothing."...

Harry smiled.

... "I tell you, Isaac, it was the most horrifying sight I have ever seen. The bones of thousands of rabbits, stripped bare, with only bloody skin and fur brutally shredded by the sharp teeth of the feral wolves. The survivors flung themselves about on sharp stones until they too were dead. I don't think I'll ever be able to eat rabbit again...."

Isaac shook his head. "Feral wolves! We can't go near their territory — the stories one hears! How can I thank you for taking such a risk?"

"It was nothing, brother, etc., etc."...

Satisfying. Very satisfying.

After a while, Harry got out of bed and picked up the pouch to go downstairs. Briefly he acknowledged that this was exactly the kind of deception Isaac himself would have tried, had their positions been reversed. *Yes,* he thought, *but I could die in this snowstorm, couldn't I? Don't I have a right to try to save my own life? Why should I lift a paw to help Isaac anyway? I hate him and he hates me. He deserves to be deceived.*

He walked into the bathroom, used the facilities, and ran some water, brushing the thick, reddish brown fur on his head and ears with damp paws. He looked briefly into the mirror, put his boots back on, turned out the lights, and made his way to the dining room, carefully locking the door behind him.

The knotty pine walls of the dark, dimly lit dining room were bare except for a very large painting of the Inn itself, silhouetted against an impossibly glowing sunset. In one corner a lone rat of indeterminate age, dressed all in gray, sat on a low stool and strummed songs on an ancient stringed instrument, barely in tune. Each table had been set with what appeared to be good-quality utensils and a pear-shaped vase of bright paper flowers. The low hum of conversation and the clink of silverware and glasses gave the room a pleasant, surprisingly intimate ambience.

Harry found the only vacant table, near the entry, and in a few moments Allison appeared before him. "You don't need to spend much time on the menu," she said, handing him a green piece of paper. "Not a lot there for one of your kind, I wouldn't think."

"Yes," Harry murmured. "The result of your good planning and a bountiful early harvest." In spite of Isaac's comment, he'd been anticipating a good meal at the Inn, where years ago he'd had some excellent *vole au vent*. He sighed and ordered the specialty of the day called *sans-mouse* and a glass of what he hoped was a drinkable red wine. He looked around.

There were approximately a dozen tables scattered about the room in a roughly defined semicircle around a crackling hearth. He noted a quiet family of ermine, a few fierce-looking older rats eating alone, and a youngish, bespectacled badger in tweeds, but the rest of the guests were raccoons, in twos and threes, of varying ages and gender combinations. When the wine came, he sniffed it cautiously and took a sip. *Sans-cabernet*.

Behind him, he heard a sound and looked up. It was the older weasel who had been reading in the entry lobby when Harry had arrived. Harry noticed — he could hardly help it — a gleam of gold at his wrist and a ring with a large stone that caught the light. The weasel, who carried a worn brief-case, looked around the room and, not finding an empty table, turned to Harry.

"Mind if I join you?" he asked. "There doesn't seem to be another spot anywhere." His voice was velvety smooth, like that of an actor, and he flashed a wide smile. Harry was searching for a polite way to say no when Becky appeared with his dinner.

"Oh," she said to Harry, as the weasel sat down — apparently his question was rhetorical — "thank you so much for being willing to share your table. I told Allison she was wrong about you." She set Harry's dinner in front of him. She turned to the weasel. "The usual?" she asked.

The weasel nodded and settled back into his chair.

Harry, ravenous, began to eat.

"My name is Gerard." The weasel held out his paw, but Harry ignored it, pretending not to see. Maybe if he was implacably rude Gerard would leave. He had just hit upon a way to combine the contagious disease and the feral wolves. The interruption was annoying.

The food turned out to be better than Harry expected, although, he had to acknowledge, his hunger surely influenced his judgment. When Gerard's food and wine came, he too began eating with considerable relish.

"Are you traveling on business or for pleasure?" Gerard inquired between mouthfuls.

Harry sipped his wine. "A little of both."

"Ah, the best kind of trip, don't you agree?" He didn't wait for a reply. "A balance. A little of this, a little of that. In my profession, creating a balanced life is not always easy. In fact, it's a challenge."

It was obvious Gerard was fishing, but Harry would not bite. He didn't care what Gerard's profession was and he wasn't going to ask. The silence between them grew.

Allison and Becky came in to clear the dishes from the other tables and then returned to stoke the fire. They left chatting in a low undertone, arm-in-arm. Shortly after that the rat stood up, said, "Thank you, everyone," in a gravelly voice to no one in particular, and left as well.

The weasel Gerard leaned back in his chair, reached into his pocket, pulled out a pack of sassafras cigarettes and proceeded to light one in an annoyingly deliberate and self-conscious way. The aroma filled the room.

"I'm an actor by profession . . . ," Gerard said through the smoke, which he at least had the decency to exhale away from the table, ". . . although I confess I am . . . between engagements at the moment." He coughed and inhaled again. "As I was saying, finding a balance between the drama of the stage and the more humdrum reality of the day to day can be quite difficult. At least it was for me. One can become addicted to the theater — the attention, the applause. Don't you agree?" He looked intently at Harry. "Have you ever tried acting?"

"Gods, no," Harry replied, feeling pleased that he had guessed so well about Gerard, who now reminded him of Isaac in his political mode. Was it the phony smile, the forced camaraderie? Politicians, actors — both pretended to be something they were not, while the gullible audience only applauded and demanded an encore. Of the two professions, Harry preferred politicians. At least you didn't have to buy a ticket to see them perform. But one way or another, he reflected, you did end up paying.

"I was an actor for much of my life," Gerard was saying. "Started quite young — ran away from home, joined a group of traveling players — a familiar story — and have been working at my craft ever since. Or at least I was until recently." He sipped his wine and looked away.

"Mmm," said Harry, hoping his lack of interest would discourage the revelation of more details.

No such luck.

"You see, the troupe I was with disbanded — dissension in the ranks, you might say," the weasel continued. "Constant arguments about what plays to perform, who would take which parts, agreements broken, gossip, backstabbing . . . I expected theater people to be more . . . honest, more idealistic, more devoted to the calling, so to speak. I didn't expect politics."

Harry looked up. "That seems naïve, if you don't mind my saying so."

"Perhaps," Gerard replied. "But sometimes I think I'd give anything to be that innocent again. . . ." He stared into space for a moment, then shook his head. "Well! This delightful wine has put me in a sentimental mood, it seems. How do you know about politics? Are you by any chance connected to the dark and mysterious world of government bureaucracy? Foxboro, perhaps?"

Harry nodded and regretted it immediately. *Why should this stranger know where I live?* But it was too late. "No, I'm not involved in government, thank the gods," he said curtly.

"Ah." Gerard exhaled a cloud of blue smoke and leaned forward with interest. "Interesting. So you *are* from up North, after all. I live in Foxboro myself, on the outskirts of the city. What did you say your name was?"

"I didn't. It's Harry."

Gerard held out his paw again. "Glad to meet you, Harry."

They shook briefly. Gerard returned to his wine. "I have . . . acquaintances in your community."

Harry's senses began to tingle. "Oh? Anyone I might know?"

"Probably not," Gerard replied. He patted his mouth with a napkin and stubbed out his cigarette on the edge of his plate. "Performing arts — you know, musicians, theater people, that sort of thing." He seemed eager to change the subject. "Don't worry — I won't mention your . . . evasion . . . to the ladies." He chuckled, then grew serious. "I've been here for a while and I heard about the four foxes. They were scouts, I'm guessing. Are you the fifth, may I ask? You don't seem like the others."

"In what way am I different?"

"Oh, well, they were apparently very crude, each of them. Loud, vulgar creatures — drank beer, and quite a bit of it — cooked food in their rooms, although what they found to prepare — and where they found it — I hesitate to say. Apparently the aroma was extraordinary! Many guests complained and left, demanding a refund. Treated the ladies rather badly too. Sneaked out without paying. I understand they vandalized their rooms, as well. A reprehensible lot, most definitely."

"That's not my style," Harry said, and started to leave.

"I heard they were traveling to the fortress," Gerard said as Harry stood. "I don't suppose you've heard any of the rumors about the place?"

Harry slowly sat down. "I've heard some. What have *you* heard?"

Gerard lit another cigarette and lowered his voice, even though the dining room had virtually emptied. "I've heard the rabbits become enchanted in the full moon and dance on the fortification walls. That anyone who comes close is put under a spell and forced to fly eternally, without rest, like an owl in the dark. Others say they've heard music coming from within, and a wild keening and wailing, and a drumming. They tell of ghastly rituals being enacted, always in darkness." Gerard's voice fell to a whisper. "I heard that the bodies of three of those foxes were found outside the wall, horribly mutilated, as if powerful, vengeful beasts had viciously hacked them to pieces. The fourth has . . . never been found."

So that's what Isaac didn't tell me, Harry thought. It wasn't only that the scouts had not returned. They'd been killed, and by a force that was inexplicably cruel and violent. Harry shivered. The dining room seemed suddenly dark and very cold.

Gerard leaned back in his chair and inhaled, looking just a little self-satisfied.

Ah. The actor.

"Powerful, vengeful beasts, eh?" Harry said. "Feral wolves, perhaps?"

"Possibly," said Gerard, nodding seriously. "Possibly. What do you think?"

"I think you have mastered your craft. I don't believe a word of it. We're talking about rabbits. Rabbits! They are mindless prey and have been since the beginning of time. They are no different from the voles or mice or possum or squirrels or any of the others we have always hunted and eaten. It's preposterous to believe that rabbits — enchanted or not — are capable of such things!"

Gerard did not protest. "I see you don't frighten easily," he said with a slight nod of approval. "Still, we can't be certain which parts of the stories are true and which are the embellishments of an imaginative mind in a snow-locked burrow nearby. And you *are* heading in that direction, aren't you?" He indicated the back of Harry's chair. "Your leather pouch could be filled with supplies for an extensive journey. Except for those empty cabins not far from here, there's nothing else around for miles. It's the only possible destination. The other guests are just weekenders, mostly. It's quite clear you are traveling with a purpose."

Harry did not respond immediately. His mind had returned to Gerard's earlier comment about having friends in the Fox community. At home, the performing arts organizations were very small and consisted almost entirely of amateur singers and players recruited from the political parties to perform at campaign events and fund-raisers. There was, in fact, hardly an activity in Foxboro that was *not*, directly or indirectly, connected to the political structure. Even if he lived on the periphery of the city, Gerard must know Isaac.

In other words, the weasel was lying.

Harry recalled standing on the snowy, deserted street with Isaac. "I wouldn't stop at Inn the Forest if I were you," he'd said, making it all the more likely that Harry would do exactly that. Knowing that Gerard would be there, waiting for him, *because Isaac had sent him*. But why? Harry took a moment to compose himself.

"Yes," he said cautiously. "I am heading south, but I haven't decided when I'll be leaving."

"Ah. I see."

"Why do you ask?"

"I was planning . . . to head in that direction tomorrow," Gerard replied. "I'm . . . tired of these woods. It's time to move on, and I would like some company. Perhaps we could make the journey together."

"No, thanks. I prefer to travel alone."

"Are you sure? The weather is terrible and will probably continue. I've been a little apprehensive about it myself. A slip on an icy path, a broken bone, the cold — better to have a companion under such circumstances, don't you agree? Why not give it some thought?" Gerard stood up. "Thank you for sharing your table."

Harry stood up too. "I'll let you know," he said.

Gerard's footsteps echoed in the empty room.

Harry sat down again, trying to put the pieces together. It seemed Gerard was working for his brother, sent to spy on Harry, perhaps to be sure he didn't spend the money and return with a false but plausible story to explain the disappearance of the scouts. That was why Gerard wanted to travel with him.

Instead of relaxing for a few days at the Inn, Harry would be continuing through the snow with the irritatingly phony Gerard watching his every move. It was outrageous.

"Damn it! Isaac should have trusted me," Harry said aloud. "I'm his brother!"

He would have to formulate a new plan, one that would take into account the presence of Gerard and his function as a spy. A spy can be given wrong information, misled. Gerard could not be on guard all the time. He was older and clearly less agile. Perhaps Harry could lose him in the forest.

Harry had to be sure about Gerard. He left the dining room and walked quietly down the hall toward the lobby. There was the weasel, seated in front of the fire, elbows on his brief-case, talking to the badger. He seemed to be telling the poor fellow his life story. Harry felt certain Gerard would be there for quite a while. He turned and walked back down the hall until he came to Gerard's room. On a hunch, Harry tried his own room key in the lock. The door opened easily. *Allison, you sly boots,* he thought. He went inside.

It had stopped snowing and a gibbous moon shone brightly on the snow-covered forest, reflecting a silvery light through the window and making a surprisingly bright, oblong patch on the bare floor. Everything in the room seemed outlined in silver — the bed, the table, the lamp — and the large carpetbag that lay half open on the unmade bed. Harry rummaged through it with a practiced paw, returning each item to its original place. He didn't know what he was looking for — a sign, an indication of certain proof that Isaac had sent Gerard — and then his paw closed on something.

The stairs creaked. "Where's my key?" said Gerard's voice. "Oh. Found it!" The latch clicked.

"Damn!" Harry breathed. He flattened himself against the wall as Gerard walked into the room, groped his way to the bathroom, and closed the door.

Harry hurried to the window to look at the object in his paw: a paper envelope imprinted with the letters *FB* and stuffed with bills. A note inside read: "Remember: I trust you." — I.F. It was Isaac's handwriting.

Harry hastily returned the envelope and the note to the carpetbag. In a moment, he was back in his own room, breathing hard. He lit the lamp and closed the shade. The envelope had come from FoxBank, the note from Isaac. It couldn't be more clear.

Gerard was a spy.

6
Quentin:
Mouse Courage

Quentin sat in his living room and stared into the crackling fire. He'd left Zack abruptly a few hours earlier to make his way home, his chores forgotten. Zack had offered to come along, but Quentin had said no. "I'll be all right," he'd told Zack. "Really. I'll be fine."

He'd poured himself a large glass of *plumbo*, the recently forbidden beverage that he and Zack had managed to get from an underground source, and was almost finished with the first glass.

Drafted. This changed everything. He was absolutely certain he could not join the army. He could barely stand the discomforts of guard duty — what would the real military be like?

Quentin got up and paced the floor, then parted the curtains and stared out the tall window. The light was fading fast, and the wind now blew with periodic violence that rattled the panes and caused the building to rumble, as if in the midst of a thunderstorm. Snow and sleet blew against the glass, sounding like handfuls of tiny gravel. He was glad to be indoors.

He closed the curtains and resumed his pacing, then stopped to stare blankly at the books, neatly arranged in alphabetical order by author, that lined the room. Quentin reached for more *plumbo*, then retrieved some matches from the kitchen and lit a dozen candles, flooding the room with a flickering, warm light. It didn't help.

There was a pounding at the front door.

"Q! Let me in! It's Zack! Q!"

"Coming! I'm coming." Quentin put the glass down and walked to the door unsteadily. It took him a moment to negotiate the lock. Zack pushed his way past him, blown by the wind.

"It's freezing out there," Zack said. "Another terrible night." He slipped out of his jacket, tucked his mittens into his pockets, and, rubbing his paws together, walked over to the fire. He looked at Quentin. "How are you doing?"

"Oh, I'm great, just great. Want some *plumbo*? I've been working my way through this bottle and there's more in the cabinet."

"I'd love some. We're going to need more if this weather keeps up — and even if it doesn't. Is Frank here yet?"

"No. I'm surprised. It's almost curfew and he's usually on time."

Zack followed Quentin into the kitchen. Quentin poured the clear liquid into a tall glass, splashing some on the surface of the table. He wiped up the spill with a paw and licked it, refilled his own glass to the brim, and drank deeply. The liquid burned deliciously in his throat, and the fragrant combination of berries and fermented rhubarb left a lingering tartness on his tongue.

Back in the living room, Quentin raised his glass. "Long ears and long life," he said gloomily.

Zack clinked his glass with Quentin's. "Friendship. Long may it wave." He swallowed. "So, how are you, really?"

Quentin shook his head. "Terrible! I didn't realize how much I was dreading this." He gulped down the *plumbo* and looked around for the bottle. Returning from the kitchen, he tilted it to his mouth, finished the last few swallows, and wiped his mouth on his sleeve.

"Never seen you do that before," Zack said in surprise.

"Never been drafted before."

Quentin sat down and leaned back in his chair, holding the empty bottle on his lap. The room was spinning gently around him. He closed his eyes.

Zack, who was sitting opposite him, leaned forward. "Listen, Q. There's something I have to tell you."

"What?"

Zack reached into a pocket and held out a piece of paper. "I have guard duty tomorrow night."

Quentin opened his eyes and put the bottle down. "You're

joking. Let me see that." He glanced at the notice and handed it back to Zack. "I bet Wally's behind this. Or Dan."

"It crossed my mind."

"It's too coincidental. And it's not even your turn yet. They've just started on the *R*s." Quentin sat back in the chair. "What a mess." He closed his eyes again. "I should never have provoked him. It's all my fault."

"Don't blame yourself. I'm sure my sarcastic comments to Dan the other night didn't help. Listen, Q, don't go to sleep. We need to talk about this."

"Not sleeping. Resting my eyes," Quentin mumbled. "What's there to talk about? We're doomed."

"I don't think so. Look at me!"

Quentin looked. Zack was standing in front of him. "You are to be inducted into the military and I have guard duty — both on the same night. This is more than a coincidence. This could be an opportunity!"

"What do you mean? Oh. I see. You're going to try to leave so you don't have to get up there on the wall. I had a feeling that was it."

"Not just me. You — the two of us — maybe the three of us!"

"*What?*" Quentin stood up and made his way unsteadily to the bookshelves. He shook his head. "Zack, wait. I can't just leave. It's out of the question. What about school? Don't you want to finish . . . ? And . . ." The thought occurred to him. "What about all the others who will have to serve? What about trying to protect Stonehaven? You heard what those rabbits said the other night! Maybe there's a good reason for the draft and guard duty. We have to do something, don't we? And why should others have to risk their lives and not us?"

"Hold on!" Zack put his glass down and walked over to Quentin. "The others who have been called can follow their conscience, if they choose. I need to follow mine. And besides . . ." He put his paws on Quentin's shoulders and looked him straight in the eye. "You *know* you've been thinking about it." He stopped. "Do you *really* want to be on the same side as Wally?"

Quentin was silent. It would be just like lower school, only much, much worse. "I'd rather die."

"What?"

"I'd rather die than be on the same side as Wally," Quentin said emphatically. "I mean it."

"Well, then . . . ?"

"But just leaving everything . . ."

There was a pounding at the door again. Quentin opened it to a blast of freezing wind and snow. Frank stood in the doorway, without a coat or scarf.

"Quentin! Help me! Let me in!" He fell heavily against Quentin, who staggered back. Zack jumped to his feet and the two rabbits led Frank into the living room. Quentin dashed into the bedroom, returning with a blanket; Zack ran back and pushed the door closed.

Frank fell into a chair, shivering. His fur was soaked from the snow and matted about his face, which was a mask of grief.

"Here. Try this." Zack offered him his glass of *plumbo*, and Frank took it, trembling.

"They're gone," Frank said, his voice breaking. "They're gone." He handed the glass to Zack and buried his head in his paws.

"Who?" Quentin asked.

"Mary and my children," he said in a muffled voice. "They're gone." He broke into deep sobs.

"For the gods' sake, what happened?" Quentin touched Frank's shoulder gently. "Frank. Talk to us."

Frank lifted his head, his eyes red. "After I left you, I didn't go home right away. I stopped at the bakery to pick up some apple turnovers — my little Charlie loves to nibble on them — and it was cold, so I sat for a while with some hot tea and a few muffins. By the time I left the shop, it was late. Oh, gods, why did I stop? Maybe if I'd been home I could have prevented this!"

Zack went into the kitchen and returned with another bottle.

"It was just like all the other disappearances," Frank went on. "The door was open; there was no sign of struggle. I called their names, to tell them I was home, but there was no answer. I ran upstairs, I looked in every room — even the root cellar. Gone, just gone. I've been wandering through the streets, I went to the park. . . ." He slumped over in the chair and covered his face.

Zack filled their glasses. "Drink more of this," he said to Frank.

"Thanks." He looked up and wiped his eyes. "I *have* to find them. If they're alive they'll be terrified. If not . . . I must know what's happened to them. I can't live the rest of my life without knowing."

"Of course, of course," Quentin murmured, his mind numb. Frank walked over to the fire, still wrapped in the blue blanket. Zack and Quentin exchanged looks.

"I wish there were something we could do to help," Zack said. "But I have guard duty tomorrow night, and Quentin's been drafted. He has to report tomorrow, as well. We were just talking about it. We think Wally may be behind the whole thing."

Frank turned, looking distracted. "Drafted? *And* guard duty? I knew that Wally creature would get even, Quentin. I'm sorry. That's a tough break."

"I was saying I see it as an opportunity," Zack began cautiously.

"I don't follow." Frank walked to the window and pulled

the curtain back. "It's so cold out there," he murmured. "I hope Mary had time to find her hat and mittens, and to get the babies into their little boots. Charlie always needed more help. . . ." He broke off and buried his head in his paws again.

"Maybe this isn't a good time," Quentin said, gesturing to Zack. "We need to help find Frank's family. This other matter can wait."

"*No, it can't,*" Zack mouthed the words to Quentin, who just shook his head.

"Frank, what can we do?" Quentin said. "Tell us."

Frank lifted his head. "There might be something."

"Really? What?"

"What did you mean by 'an opportunity'?" Frank asked Zack.

"I was saying we could leave Stonehaven tomorrow evening," Zack began, looking at Quentin, "just before Q is scheduled to appear at the induction office downtown and before I appear at my tower on the perimwall. We could sneak past the curfew guards and supervisors, find some path into the forest, and . . ." He grew silent as Frank turned away again.

The wind whooshed outside the windows, and the panes rattled.

"Wait a minute," Quentin said after a moment. "Evading the draft or guard duty is a criminal offense. If we're caught we could be thrown in prison for the rest of our lives. Have you thought of that? And if we did manage to get out, what would we do for food? What about shelter? And where are we supposed to be going? The nearest Newrabbit colony is at least three weeks away — and that's in good weather."

"I was assuming we would *not* get caught, obviously," Zack said somewhat defensively. "And I was hoping we'd find . . . a cave or something. And we could bring food to last us for a while."

"Maybe we'd learn to love tree bark and dead roots," Quentin said. "This is crazy. And by the way," he added sarcastically, "how are we supposed to escape? By jumping off the perimwall?"

"As a matter of fact, yes. By jumping. Why?"

"For the gods' sake, Zack, I was joking! Forget it," Quentin said, horrified. "I won't do that. As I said before, we are doomed."

"What other way is there? Strolling out the entry gate in the middle of the night while the guards wave good-bye? What do you think, Frank?"

Frank took out a pocket handkerchief and blew his nose, then turned to face them. "I've got to get out there and find my Mary and my children," he said. "Whatever we do, we can't waste any time! I'll tell you what I know and then you can decide." He took a deep breath. "It was no coincidence that we met at the café today. I was looking for you."

"Why?" Zack asked. "And why the restaurant? Why not come here?"

"I wanted a neutral place in case I was followed," Frank said. "I needed to be sure I could trust you — both of you." He dropped the blanket on the couch and sat down. "I've been in touch with the rebels."

Quentin walked unsteadily to the leather chair. "The *rebels*?"

"Yes," Frank said. "I've met with them twice. I'm sure that's why my family has disappeared. I'm probably on a dissident list . . . it's what I was telling you about this morning. I should have been more careful. I should have . . ." He looked at Quentin. "I'm not a violent creature, you know that. I've never knowingly hurt anyone in my life. But I swear I'll kill whoever's responsible if I find out they've . . ."

"But why come to me?" Quentin asked.

"You're the smartest rabbit I know," Frank said, "and the most rational. I thought you could help me sort it all out."

Quentin's mind was reeling. I must stop drinking, he told himself, but the *plumbo* seemed essential to understanding the turmoil around him, even as it was increasing his confusion. He poured himself another glass and offered one to Frank. He thought about the exchange with Wally on the perimwall. Why was I so childish? Why do the most innocent mistakes always have the most terrible consequences? My life, which has been so orderly and predictable, has veered off course, like those pine cones that float calmly on a quiet, lazy river and then suddenly tumble and disappear in the thunder of a raging waterfall.

"Thanks," he said, closing his eyes. "But to tell you the truth, I'm not feeling very smart or rational at the moment."

"Why did the rebels contact you?" Zack asked Frank. "And how?"

"They're former residents, at least one of them was," he replied. "They were given a day pass through the gate. Anyway, it's not predators who are taking our families. The rebels say they have evidence that . . . our own government may be behind it all. They wanted me to join them because they need a larger force if they are going to be able to fight this. That's why I was trying to find you."

"You were planning to leave your family?" Zack said, surprised.

Frank nodded. "Yes, just for a short time, until we could find out more. I never made a definite commitment, though," he said. "I wanted to be sure Mary and the children would be safe." He shook his head. "Gods, what have I done!"

"Go back a bit," Zack said slowly. "You're saying that the government gets rid of those who object to its repressive measures . . . which it has instituted to protect us from the strange disappearances . . . for which it is responsible? Sorry, Frank. This can't be right. It makes no sense."

"I know. I agree. But the rebels say they have proof. They just don't know why. I think they *do* know but . . ." His voice broke. "It's too terrible. They're not saying."

"I can't believe the Leader is involved in something like this," Quentin said, opening his eyes and sitting up.

Zack looked at him incredulously.

"Oh, all right," Quentin said. "Although why it's unreasonable to expect our own government to have our best interests at heart —" He sighed. "I want to help," he said to Frank after a moment of silence. "What can we do?"

"I think we should leave tomorrow, just as I said," Zack replied before Frank could respond. "Except now we'll be able to connect with the rebels, who can provide us with food and shelter. No tree bark and dead roots, Q, at least not for the moment," he added. "If we're careful we won't get caught. They can help us find Mary and the children. Right, Frank?"

"I don't know," Frank said. "Waiting until tomorrow night . . . ?" He walked back to the window. "But I can't do this myself, either. I can hardly see straight. What do you think, Quentin?"

This is probably the most important decision of my life, Quentin thought fuzzily. *He weighed his options: exchange security and predictability, the things I most rely on in my life to make me happy, for risk and the unknown, and jump off the wall. Or be drafted and become part of the military elite, always watching my back because Small Ears would certainly do everything he could to destroy me. Is this the way I want to spend my life, fighting Wally? And what about helping Frank, an old friend?*

I am between a wolf and a weasel.

Quentin swallowed a large gulp of *plumbo*, and the room began to swim again. What about the wall — could he jump? Never. But how could he admit to Zack and Frank that he was terrified, that he'd rather face a thousand starving foxes and wolves, alone and unarmed, than jump from the wall into the dark? He couldn't, not when they were willing to risk their lives to do the right thing.

He took a deep breath. "All right," he said, hoping his voice showed conviction. "We'll go together. I'll leave with you, tomorrow."

"Good decision, Q," Zack said, obviously relieved. "Frank, you can stay with me tonight."

Frank stood up. "I'm grateful to you both." He held out a paw. "Thank you."

"Maybe the *plumbo* has given you mouse courage," Zack said to Quentin, "the courage of the timid."

Quentin thought about it. "Beware the courage of the timid," he said quietly.

"You realize that once we leave, we may not be able to come back," Frank said.

"Yes." Quentin stood, wavered, and held out his glass.

Frank and Zack did the same.

"May the gods be kind," Frank said, his voice breaking.

"Yes," Quentin said. "And to mouse courage."

They clinked glasses and downed the contents in one gulp.

7

Harry:
Remember: I Trust You

When Harry went downstairs for breakfast at around midmorning, he saw the dining room had been transformed. One very large, long table had been set up horizontally across the room, and the early rising guests were already seated. A buffet, which Harry had not noticed the night before, stood against one wall, loaded with toasts, jams, preserved fruits and vegetables, and several different kinds of hot beverages. The fire spat and crackled in the hearth, and the light through the snow-spattered windows was pale and slanted. There was a murmur of conversation in the room; one or two raccoons looked up as he entered and then returned to their plates. At the farthest end of the table sat Gerard, looking fresh and rested, engrossed in conversation with the badger of the previous evening.

"Harry!" called Gerard, gesturing. "Over here! I've saved a spot for you."

Wonderful, thought Harry. *The surveillance continues.* He forced a smile and made his way to the end of the table. "Good morning," he said with a nod.

"Harry, meet Elton. We've been chatting about our journey to the Southeast. Elton's in sales."

Elton the badger wore a brown tweed jacket with patches at the elbows. His eyeglasses had thick lenses and gave him a studious, bookish air. He leaned across the table. "Harry," he said, and held out his paw. His voice was low-pitched, and he spoke in the odd shorthand characteristic of his species.

"*Our* journey to the Southeast" did not escape Harry's notice. He decided to take up the challenge. "Yes," he said, "our journey. We should plan to start immediately."

Gerard smiled broadly. "Excellent, excellent. Oh, Harry, try the acorn toast. It's delicious."

"I will." Harry went to the sideboard and piled his plate high, then poured himself what looked like hot fruit juice and returned to his seat. "What do you sell, Elton?"

Elton was carefully scraping syrup from the bottom of his very clean plate, his face very close to the surface. He didn't look up. "Tools. Art supplies. You?"

That was a good question. "How's business these days?" Harry said quickly, digging into his breakfast. "This weather must make it difficult to be traveling with samples."

"Catalog mostly." Elton looked up. "You?" he repeated.

"My good friend Harry is . . . an investigator," said Gerard, with a sly look at Harry. "He investigates things."

"Going Southeast?" Elton asked, peering over his glasses.

"Yes," Gerard said. "We are."

"Cabins?"

"Yes, I believe we were planning to stop there," Gerard said with a questioning look at Harry, who nodded curtly.

"Join you. Company." Elton squinted at the sideboard. "More," he said, and pushed back his chair.

"Join you? What is he talking about?" Harry said as Elton made his way to the food. "He's not coming along. *He* may like company, but I don't."

"I agree," Gerard said, his brow furrowed. "But what excuse can we give? The weather is terrible, and apparently we are all going in the same direction."

"I don't care."

Elton returned with another full plate and a mug of steaming liquid. He seated himself, carefully and methodically attacked the breakfast, eating slowly but without stopping, except for a periodic sip from the mug. Harry took in his glasses, his intense concentration, and the expression of deep satisfaction he seemed to take from the meal.

Mama would have said anyone who enjoyed food that much couldn't be too bad.

"Tools. Could help," Elton said, picking up the conversation as if he'd never left.

Gerard cleared his throat. "Harry and I were just discussing that," he said. "Thank you for your offer, but we prefer to go on alone."

"Why?"

There was an uncomfortable silence. Harry had to acknowledge that he had no answer. "I just do," he said curtly.

Elton looked at Gerard. "You?"

"I'm afraid I must agree with my good friend Harry," he said. "Perhaps another time."

Elton finished his breakfast without speaking. "Perhaps," he said, nodding to Harry and Gerard. He walked out of the dining room.

"Well, that was awkward," Gerard said. "You know," he went on after a moment, "it might not be a bad idea to have him along."

"What?"

"Think about it. For one thing, he certainly won't overwhelm us with conversation. And he could be useful. Badgers are famous for their stubbornness. I've been thinking he could come in handy were we to meet with any unexpected resistance."

"Resistance? From rabbits? What are you talking about?"

"Slip of the tongue, old fellow. I didn't mean resistance *as such*." Gerard seemed uncomfortable. "I should have said 'unexpected *occurrences*.' You yourself mentioned feral wolves, for example. What with this weather and the rumors about the rabbits, one never knows."

Harry munched on the acorn toast. "If you want to travel with him, that's fine. I'll go on alone."

"No, no," said Gerard. "You're right. We don't need him." He stood up and stretched. "I'll ask the ladies to prepare us some food for the trip."

A short while later, when Harry walked into the lobby, Gerard was already there, his tapestry carpetbag bulging, his briefcase under his arm. Bundled in a fur coat and a hat with earflaps, the fur side inward, he could barely raise a paw in greeting.

"Allison has checked your room," Becky said to Harry in her musical voice, "and she says it's all right. No damage, no vandalism. I hope you'll come again," she added. "We so rarely have foxes here. I mean, decent ones." She held out a paw. "Thank you for staying at Inn the Forest."

Gerard went to the front door and turned in Becky's direction. "Farewell, good innkeeper," he said with a dramatic bow, whose effect was somewhat diminished by the earflaps, "and thank you for the delicious repast you have prepared for us."

"You're most welcome," Becky said, looking pleased. "It's the least we can do for one of our most loyal guests. Will we be seeing you next week?"

"I'm . . . not sure. In any case, I look forward to partaking of your gracious hospitality once again, whenever that might be." He glanced briefly at Harry and added drily, "Oh, and please extend my thanks to your partner, the warm and charming Allison."

Becky, detecting no irony, laughed with delight and said, "You always say that, Mr. Gerard. But I certainly will."

Harry opened the door and they stepped out into the gray-white world. He was stunned to see Elton, wrapped and bandaged in scarves and a heavy coat of uncertain origin, squinting into the distance, his glasses nearly covered with partially melted snow, his sample case and pack alongside him.

Gerard looked at Harry. "Well," he said. "This is a surprise."

Elton lifted the heavy backpack to his shoulders and turned to Harry. "Ready?"

Harry shrugged. He couldn't prevent the badger from taking the same road at the same time. "I travel quickly and I don't like to waste time."

Elton nodded. "Understood."

They started off into the forest. The path was buried in soft, new-fallen snow that had been mounded in little hills by the wind; they pushed against it with every step.

Harry's irritation gave him energy, and he was soon far ahead of Gerard and Elton. *Good.* He needed to think.

He had not slept terribly well. His mind kept returning to

Gerard and the note he'd found in Gerard's carpetbag: *"Remember: I trust you."* The confidence, the certainty! The faith in someone obviously not the least bit trustworthy. But Isaac was no fool. Surely, he'd seen through the weasel's deceptive nature as easily as Harry. Then why the note? What was going on? What was Isaac up to? Harry turned it over in his mind, but could come up with nothing.

He breathed in the cold air and looked back. Behind him, he could see the small shapes of Gerard and Elton moving toward him; beyond them, the Inn was gray-brown in the distance, its strange, sprawling additions nearly buried in the snow-laden woods around it, the smoke from several chimneys barely visible against the white sky. Harry's tracks were slowly filling with snow; in a short time they would vanish. It was very quiet. He took his pouch from his shoulder and rested it on the ground, where it sank gently into the crusted snow cover and quickly became covered with wet, white flakes.

After a while, Gerard and Elton approached. Gerard was breathing hard. They threw down their bundles and the weasel sat heavily, leaning against a boulder.

"Tired already?" Harry said. "We'll never reach the cabins before dark at this rate."

"Need help," said Elton. He rummaged in his pack and withdrew a small hatchet in a worn leather sheath. He walked off to their right and soon disappeared into the snowy forest.

They heard him thrashing through the brush for a few minutes. Then it was silent.

"I'm beginning to think this may work out," Gerard said, breathing more regularly now. "He's a good listener. A rare quality these days, don't you agree?" He reached into his carpetbag, pulled out a small silver box and removed a cigarette and some matches. He lit up and inhaled deeply, dropping the match into the snow, where it sizzled briefly. The aroma of sassafras leaves filled the air.

"I suppose."

Gerard looked at him closely. "What's on your mind, Harry?" he asked. "Something bothering you?"

You *are bothering me,* Harry thought. *You and* "Remember: I trust you."

"You'd have more stamina if you gave that up," Harry said, ignoring the question and nodding toward the cigarette.

Gerard gave him a sharp look and then quickly smiled. "You are of course correct, my friend," he said agreeably, inhaling deeply again. "It was a habit I acquired during my career on the stage. Always good to have something to do with one's paws instead of just standing there like a stick. Besides, there are so few pleasures one can actually count on in this life, don't you agree?" He gazed into the woods. "What *can* he be up to?"

They waited in silence. Gerard smoked and flicked ashes

into the snow, his eyes closed. The aroma of sassafras was intense.

Harry stood and looked up. The falling snow was endless, the cold pervasive. "You know," he said angrily, "*this* is why I travel alone. I could have been halfway to the cabins by now!" He turned to Gerard. "If he isn't here within the next two minutes I am going on ahead. You can catch up to me."

Gerard opened his eyes. "I share your impatience, but that's probably a good idea," he said. "I like the way you think, Harry. We'll follow your trail and be right behind you. You can start a fire when you arrive. Here . . ." He reached into his carpetbag and pulled out a large wrapped package. "The ladies prepared this for us. You'll need it. There's more — I can share with Elton."

Harry was surprised and then immediately suspicious. He had expected resistance or some kind of protest from Gerard. Instead, the weasel had agreed to his idea — too quickly. Did he *want* Harry to travel alone? But how could he spy on him if they didn't travel together? Or was this an effort to throw him off the track?

The package was too large to fit into his pouch, so he tucked it under his arm. "I'm going, then," he said.

"Good," said Gerard, raising himself with difficulty and brushing himself off. "I'll explain to Elton. We'll see you . . . wait! I hear something."

There was a thrashing in the distance. In a few minutes, Elton emerged from the woods carrying three stout sticks and handed one to Harry and one to Gerard. "Here," he said. He put the hatchet into his backpack.

Harry suddenly remembered Isaac's folded walking stick. He pulled it out of his pocket and opened it up. "I have this," he said, "but I'm sure Gerard will find his helpful." He handed his stick back to Elton, who tossed it into the woods.

"Indeed I will, and I'm not too proud to say so. Thank you, Elton."

Elton nodded briefly in response, then took Isaac's folding stick from Harry's paw and examined it. "Fine work," he said, turning it over in his paws. He handed it back. "Sell lots."

"It doesn't belong to me," Harry said. "It was borrowed."

Gerard was walking slowly in a circle, testing his stick. "Excellent, excellent. By the way," he said, turning to Elton, "Harry was just leaving."

Elton looked up.

"I'll wait for both of you at the cabins," Harry said. "I used to spend summers there when I was young. Look for me in the building along the lake, the farthest from the main road."

"Ah, a return to the magical land of childhood," Gerard said. "No wonder you're impatient to leave. I would be too. In fact, I *am*. Unfortunately, I'm not as fast on my feet as I used to be and my progress will be slower than I would like." He sighed. "We do our best."

"It's not nostalgia," Harry said, barely able to contain his annoyance. "We still have some distance to go, and I prefer not to travel at night. We'll need some place to rest."

"Good plan," Gerard said. "Don't you agree, Elton?"

Elton nodded.

"Well, see you soon, then," Gerard said, leaning down to pick up his things. Elton did the same.

Harry turned and started out briskly. The walking stick provided excellent stability even on the snowy path, and in a short while he was nearly a mile away.

All around him the forest was white and silent except for the regular, muffled thump of the walking stick and the soft *shush* of the falling snow. Occasionally a tree branch snapped and fell, but even that sound was distant. The gray sky seemed low to the ground, as if the horizon were at his feet.

Harry breathed deep sighs, inhaling the cold air with relish. He felt as though an enormous burden had been lifted from his shoulders — even his pouch seemed lighter. After a while, he stopped and consulted the map, making a small adjustment in his direction. Toward midafternoon he stopped again and unwrapped part of the meal the raccoons had provided.

He sat, leaning against a tree, and munched on the mushroom-and-potato sandwich. In the back of his mind there were questions, puzzles. The more he thought about it, the more he found the unanswered questions intolerable. There was only one solution: Confront Gerard with what he knew and demand an explanation. The presence of Elton would be inconvenient, but Harry felt confident he could find a way to handle it. Gerard would either lie or tell the truth, but Harry would know the difference. It would be almost entertaining to watch Gerard attempt to fabricate a story, undoubtedly some long, detailed narrative, delivered in the weasel's characteristically cheerful manner and ending with "Don't you agree?" *No, I don't agree,* Harry thought. *Whatever you say, whatever you make up,* I don't agree.

Harry gathered his belongings, picked up the walking stick, and headed toward the cabins. In a short time, he would have his answers.

8
Quentin:
A Trap

The cold hit Quentin's face with a force that made his eyes tear. He reached with a mittened paw to tighten the scarf around his neck and with the other closed the door to his apartment firmly. As he fumbled with the lock, the key slid from his paw and fell to the ground, disappearing into the snow. "Damn!" Should he look for it? There was no time — he was late. *Late! I have never been late for anything in my life — and now my first time is going to be my last.*

He had slept for fourteen hours in what he realized was a kind of drunken coma, and now he was AWOL. They would be coming after him at any moment to take him to prison. *I have to get to the perimwall,* Quentin thought. *Damn plumbo. Damn the key. Damn everything.* He left the key and turned down the street. *I'm not coming back anyway. Maybe.*

He looked around and saw no one — of course. It was after curfew. For a moment, the dark, empty streets before him, blanketed in white, looked safe and peaceful. Then the glare of the flickering street lamps on the snow nearly blinded him, and his head pounded with every beat of his heart. *I don't need to wait for the military police. This hangover is going to kill me.*

He had been planning to take an indirect route to the wall and double back occasionally in order to confuse anyone who might have decided to follow him. It was too late for that now. The direct route would be more dangerous because he'd have to avoid the unpredictable curfew patrols — would Dan be among them? — but in the end it would be faster. *Maybe I can make up some time.*

Quentin had often commented that whoever had built the fortress had been careful, as well as smart, about defense. The old perimeter wall began on a cliff high above the river, which ran along the edge of the compound and formed an additional barrier that took up about half of the western side of the community. Tower 1 was located at the northwesternmost corner; the towers and the wall continued around the roughly rectangular fortress, with the towers evenly spaced. All he had to do was turn right out the door, walk a few blocks, and make another right. It shouldn't be too difficult, even at this late hour.

He began by trotting down the street, but the satchel he'd packed thudded heavily against his back and he couldn't keep up the pace for long. He switched shoulders, but soon decided to carry it and slowed to a walk, trying to save his energy. In a few moments, his paws began to sting with the cold in spite of his mittens.

Quentin found he was grateful for the dark between the lampposts as he tried to watch for the guards. The enormity of the risk he was taking slowly dawned on him. *Maybe I should at least try to concoct a story to explain why I'm here,* he thought — just in case. But his mind was fuzzy and his head ached. He could come up with nothing.

As he half walked, half trotted through the snow, he went over last night's conversation with Frank and Zack. He had agreed, hoping his reluctance was not too obvious, to meet Frank and Zack at the entrance to Tower 33, where Zack had guard duty. But they had been expecting him at dusk. *Now,* he thought, *suppose they have already jumped? How long will they wait for me? And how will I know if they're waiting, or if they've given up and have gone ahead without me? Or if they've been caught and taken away for questioning — or worse? Suppose I jump and find myself alone in the forest? We should have agreed on some kind of signal, some way of letting me know they are down there in the dark!* But if they had, he couldn't remember what it was. In desperation last night, he'd asked Frank — casually, of course — if he had heard anything about the tunnels that were rumored to exist under the perimwall, but apparently no one knew where they began or where they ended. It had been Quentin's last hope.

He stopped at the sound of muffled footsteps. Was he being followed? He turned slowly and searched the dimly lit streets in all directions. There was no one. Why hadn't the military police found him by now? The turning made his dizziness worse and he staggered, barely able to recover his balance.

"I'm not drunk," Quentin muttered into the darkness. "I just have a monumental hangover. There *is* a difference."

It's been a long time since I've been out at night, alone, he thought. *Now I know why.* The darkness and the quiet streets were terrifying: The wind sighing in the firs below the fortress could be heard even from this distance; the shadows, the shapes of familiar benches and buildings were suddenly strange and ominously threatening. Then there was the unnatural silence when the wind was still and nothing moved, and the whole world seemed to be waiting for the one violent act that would . . .

The sound of footsteps stopped him again. He shrunk into the shadows and pressed himself against the cold stone wall of a building as the sound came closer.

"Who goes there?" a youthful voice asked, and Quentin could hear the fear behind the challenge. This was not Dan. The curfew guard stepped cautiously toward him. Quentin didn't breathe. Holding a torch aloft, the youth peered into the darkness, but the search was halfhearted. *He doesn't really want to find anything,* Quentin thought. *I know how he feels.* He could almost hear the guard's sigh of relief as he turned and walked away, his boots crunching in the snow. In a few moments, the guard had vanished into the night.

Quentin let out a long breath and slid slowly to the ground against the wall. He was drenched with perspiration inside his jacket and he began to shiver. He crossed his arms, tucked his paws beneath his armpits, hoping for warmth, and looked around.

He seemed to be in some sort of alley between large buildings. Here, far from the inhabited and familiar streets, the Rabbittampers apparently had visited once, perhaps weeks ago, and never returned; the ground was soft with snow that had acquired a crisp coating of frost. There were no homes now, only warehouses for food storage that loomed above him, windowless and stark, like prisons.

A sharp ache in his stomach reminded him that he had eaten nothing since last night. He opened the satchel and felt around in the dark until his paw closed on the familiar shape of a veggie bar. Pulling it out, he tore off the wrapping and chomped down on its salty sweetness, the saliva pouring into his mouth and dribbling down his chin. He reached for another and then another, then buried the crumpled rice-paper wrappers in the soft snow. *Littering. Just one of the many laws I will have broken by the time this day is over.*

He leaned over and opened the satchel again. *Why is this so heavy?* He'd taken some dried fruit, a few packaged vegetables, and his last bottle of *plumbo*, wrapped in a heavy sweater. What do you take when you may not be returning, ever? The travel

119

advisors never talked about it. His pockets were heavy too, with a few more veggie bars and a small book. On an impulse he had gone to his bookcase and found an old childhood favorite: *Rabbit Heroes for All Times.* Zack would have a good laugh at that.

He heaved himself to his feet. Now, thankfully, the street lamps were farther and farther apart, and for long stretches he walked in near darkness, the only sound the crunch of his footsteps and the occasional *whoosh* of wind that blew the soft snow against his face.

The perimwall finally loomed in the distance.

Suddenly he heard something behind him again — another curfew guard? So soon? His heart pounded, and the simultaneous pain in his head was almost blinding.

Quentin turned, but could see nothing except the empty streets, the glittering snow, and the dark shapes of the buildings. He picked up the satchel, slung it onto his back this time, and started to walk again, more quickly.

In a few minutes, he began to run heavily toward the wall. It was farther away than it looked and Quentin lunged toward it, panting. The satchel thumped on his back; he slipped it off his shoulders and grasped it in his paw. Reaching the wall at last, he squinted at the numbers that were painted above the small entry doors at ground level. According to his mental map, he should be right in front of Tower 33.

He looked up — 22.

No! It can't be! He stopped and, trying to catch his breath, reconstructed his actions. The dropped key had distracted him. He had gone too far in the wrong direction. *Damn!* Feeling dizzy, he started to run back, but the snow alongside the wall was deep and he stumbled several times, catching himself and struggling to regain his stride. As his heart pounded, so did his head. He searched the wall ahead for a sign of Frank, but could see nothing. He looked up and gasped. Ahead of him the entry door said 18.

He had turned the wrong way.

Now panicky and barely able to breathe, Quentin ran alongside the wall, staggering with the weight of his burden. He reached inside his satchel, grabbed the bottle and the sweater and tossed them into the snow. Good-bye, *plumbo*.

Snow blowing off the top of the wall stung his face as he continued on, but he'd used up every last bit of energy and could hardly move beyond a fast walk. He was worn out. Quentin's face and paws were very cold, but inside his jacket the perspiration poured down his back. He stopped more and more frequently to lean against the wall and catch his breath. Periodically he squinted up at the faded numbers painted on the small doors that led to the interior staircases, which in turn led up to the top of the wall and the guard path. The numbers were going up. He was almost there, thank the gods. He stopped when he heard footsteps crunching softly in the distance behind him. When he turned, he had a fleeting glimpse of four large figures holding torches far away and a tall, thin rabbit in what looked like a military uniform who quickly vanished into the night.

Dan.

Touching the wall to keep himself steady, Quentin walked slowly, close to exhaustion. *I can't go much farther,* he thought, peering into the dim light for Frank's familiar shape. Then he saw him, crouched against the wall, bundled up against the cold in a blue-gray coat that almost disappeared in the darkness.

"Frank!" Quentin whispered loudly.

"Where have you been? Do you know how dangerous this is?" Frank's breath puffed in front of his face as Quentin stumbled toward him.

"I'm sorry. Fell asleep. Too much *plumbo.* I'm sorry." He gasped. "I'm being . . . followed. It's Dan. And . . . some others." The running footsteps were much closer.

"I hear them," Frank said. He pulled out a pocket watch and tried to read its face. Then he tapped softly on the wooden door to the interior tower staircase, his ear to the wall. "I don't understand why Zack hasn't responded," he said. "He told me he'd come to the door every half hour, or else he'd leave it unlocked." He jiggled the handle, turning it right and left, but it did not give.

Then from behind the door they heard a voice. "Quentin? Frank? Is that you?" Zack's voice was low and urgent.

"Zack? Where have you been?" Frank said angrily.

"I'm sorry. I couldn't get down here before this. I'm being watched," Zack whispered. "I'm supposed to be up on the wall right now."

"I've been spotted too," Quentin said, still breathing hard. "It's Dan and some others. Open the door, Zack!"

"I'm trying. It's jammed. You won't believe who's got my tower — Wally!" The handle moved slightly. "He hasn't taken his eyes off me for a second. Damn this thing! I think the lock's rusted. I could barely get through this door when I reported. Give me a minute — I'll be right back."

"Zack! Don't go away! What are you doing?" Frank whispered, and Quentin could see he was tempted to pound loudly on the door. There was silence from the other side. Quentin rubbed his mittened paws together, shivering. He looked around him and could see nothing moving, no sign of life. It was suddenly very quiet again. *This isn't good,* he thought. *What are they up to?*

After what seemed like long time, Quentin heard a clicking from behind the door. "I had to find a tool in my pack," Zack said. "Wally's disappeared, at least for the moment. Sorry this took so long." More rattling and scraping sounds coming from the door handle.

"Did you say Wally was in the tower?" Quentin asked.

"Yes. I . . ." There was a faint clattering sound. "Damn! I dropped it. Give me a minute."

Wally in the tower, Dan on the ground — they'd been set up. Guard duty and the draft for two friends on the same night. Friends who'd been overheard complaining about the government, perhaps; friends who'd been seen with Frank. It probably hadn't helped that Quentin had mocked Wally on the perimwall, or that Zack had confronted Dan. It was a trap, and they had walked right into it. Now Wally had enough evidence to bring to the Leader. Quentin, Zack, and Frank would be sent to prison for life for attempting to avoid military service, for collusion, treason, and any other charges Wally and Dan could invent. Old Small Ears would have the last laugh after all. "Zack! Hurry, for the gods' sake!"

"I think I've got it," Zack said. "Just one more . . . Hey!" Quentin heard a thump and the sound of scuffling. More thumps and a groan, then the sound of something heavy falling against the door.

"Zack! Are you all right? Open the door!" Frank cried. He leaned on the door, kicking it and pushing against it with all his strength. "Zack! Zack! *Open the door!*" There was no answer, and the scuffling and pounding had stopped.

Suddenly, an arrow whirred past Quentin's ears and *whumped* into the snow close to where he and Frank stood.

Another followed, and another. He could hear shouts and Dan's high voice, and the sound of running on three sides of him, coming closer and closer.

They're shooting at us! Quentin thought in amazement. *I can't believe it. We will be killed like prey.* He felt a rising anger. *No! Not here, and not by Dan!*

Then there was a rain of arrows, just as the tower door opened slightly. An arrow pierced Quentin's shoulder and the pain shot down his arm.

"Weasels!" he cried, and with a last desperate effort, he and Frank pushed their way inside and fell into the darkness.

9

Harry:
Badger Checkers

arry arrived at the cabins by dusk. He'd been able to maintain a steady pace trudging along the snowy path with the help of Isaac's walking stick, and soon he could see the vaguely dark shapes of the cabins in the distance. Many years ago this had been a summer vacation spot for wealthy families who rented the cabins from an aging, irascible fox. Harry remembered the last time he was here with his parents, shortly after Isaac had recovered. They had swum in the lake and watched the stars circle the heavens at night while Mama read to them and Dad pointed out the constellations.

But the fox, a widower, had died without heirs, and no one had bought the property or maintained the cabins, which had fallen into serious disrepair. Now, rumor had it, they were notorious for their use as a refuge by vagrants and lowlifes. That didn't bother Harry.

There were nine cabins, settled in a clearing and arranged in a very large, roughly shaped triangle, about thirty steps apart, not far from the frozen Elk Lake, with one point of the triangle close to the woods. Only four cabins faced the water, set back about a hundred steps — Harry and Isaac had counted — from the water's edge, and these were the most coveted.

Harry approached from what had been the main road and looked around. The cabins were built of logs, with slanted roofs and small chimneys, all now blanketed in snow. Each had had a porch with a swing or chairs made of rough twigs that poked you when you sat on them without the cushions, he recalled now, and each cabin door was painted a different color. Harry's family had stayed in Green, the farthest cabin facing the lake.

The light was fading, and he was tired. His pouch had become heavier with each step, and with dusk had come a damp and freezing chill that promised more snow. Harry found the last cabin just as darkness fell.

He used the walking stick to clear away the path before him and stepped cautiously up to the porch. There was no way to know if the steps had rotted, or if they were there at all. With a gloved paw, he brushed away the snow that clung to the door.

"Anyone here?" he called. There was no answer. He pushed the door slowly. It gave with a slight creak. "Anyone here?" he repeated. When there was no response, he pushed harder on the door, which creaked some more as he walked inside.

He dropped his pouch and reached for the matches he knew were in a small pocket near the top. He struck one and looked around.

The cabin was much smaller than he remembered, and it was damp and cold. The main room was square, with a small alcove for a bare minimum of kitchen equipment, and there was a bathroom in a small building outside in the back. There had been bunk beds, and a separate, smaller room off to the side, where his parents had slept. As a child, Harry had loved the idea of sleeping in the kitchen, although there had been the predictable fight about the bunk bed and who would get the top. In the end it had been Harry, but only because Mama would not allow Isaac to try to climb the ladder with his weakened leg.

"Isaac needs to save his strength," she had said, tucking him in, and the triumph that Harry had felt at having secured the top bunk instantly soured. He had climbed nimbly up to the top, but felt no pleasure even at his ability to lie on his back and barely touch the ceiling with all four paws. Besides, on warm summer nights it was hot, and the first few times when he awoke in the middle of the night to use the bathroom, he bumped his head. Isaac slept soundly below. Harry shoved him *hard* as he climbed back up, but Isaac didn't stir. It wasn't fair.

Six large, fat candles, burnt low, sat on the counter, and he lit them with his match. The room brightened. Now Harry saw in the flickering light that the bunk bed still stood against the wall near the kitchen alcove. A worn plaid blanket lay crumpled on the lower bed, and an ancient rocker, its woven seat shredded, stood silently in a corner. Harry didn't remember a rocker. He walked into the adjoining bedroom, which was empty. The floor was gritty with dirt and bark, tracked in from the forest, and the shriveled droppings of small animals. Back in the kitchen area, a dented black pot encrusted with many ancient meals sat near the hearth, alongside a rusty kettle.

Clearly the cabin had been used frequently, although not in a while; the ashes, stirred slightly by the rush of air that swept down the chimney, were cold. He pushed the blanket aside and sat down on the bed, feeling the mattress sag beneath him, then opened his sack and dug out the remains of the meal Gerard had offered — two more sandwiches and some dried fruit. When Harry finished eating, he stepped outside to scoop some snow into the black pot. He held it over the candle and when the snow melted, he drank deeply. Cold and rusty.

How long would it be before Gerard and Elton arrived? Reluctantly Harry walked back outside into the freezing night and wiped away the snow from the window that faced the road. Inside, he placed one of the lit candles on the window ledge, where the flame flickered slightly in the draft.

He moved his pouch to lean against the door after he bolted it from the inside, folded the walking stick, and tucked it into his coat pocket. He went out the back door to use the deteriorating outhouse and found a large pile of dry wood stashed under the cabin. In a few minutes, he'd lit a fire and the room began to warm. Pulling the rocking chair over to the hearth, he folded the blanket on the seat and watched the fire spit and crackle. He took off his boots and stretched out his feet. Shadows leaped across the rough, brown walls and ceiling. *Time to make a plan.*

Harry went to his pouch, pulled out his map, and brought it over to the candles, holding it close to his face in the dim light. It was impossible to know how long it would take to reach the fortress. Since there was no road, he'd have to make his way through the dense underbrush of the forest in what would surely be another series of storms and find whatever food and shelter he could. Still, he had almost two weeks to get there and back. It shouldn't take *that* long. He folded the map and put it back into the pouch, planning to leave the cabins in the morning.

But what to do about Gerard? And what of Elton? Could he be a part of Isaac's devious plan? Harry had to know. He'd simply ask Gerard, perhaps circuitously at first. Then, depending on the weasel's response, he'd question him more closely.

"My brother, Isaac, thinks highly of you," Harry would say. It would be a statement, not a question that Gerard could avoid answering. Gerard would look surprised, then try to disguise his reaction by elaborately lighting a cigarette.

"Indeed."

"Your work for him has been so consistently excellent," Harry would continue. *"You must be gratified to know he trusts you with such delicate matters."*

"So you know all about it," Gerard would respond. *"Funny that Isaac never mentioned he'd told you. Don't you agree?"*

Harry could go no further. He had not the slightest idea what Gerard's relationship was to Isaac, or what Elton's relationship was to Gerard, and the more he tried to imagine the conversation, the more it went in circles, with Harry probing, Gerard evading, and Elton replying in infuriating monosyllables.

Much later there was a knock at the door.

Harry, who had been dozing in front of the fire, leaped up from the rocker. *Good,* he thought. *I'm ready. They will be exhausted and cold; I have eaten, rested, and am refreshed. There will be a certain amount of verbal sparring, but now that I know Gerard is definitely working for Isaac, and Gerard doesn't know that I know, I have the advantage. Elton will probably lose interest and go to sleep; I can question him later. By the end of this evening I will know where I stand.*

But Elton stood at the door, alone. "Where is Gerard?" Harry asked as he let the badger in. Elton was carrying a small lantern lit by a candle that flickered behind its protective glass. He looked tired; his spectacles were nearly covered with frozen snow.

"Turned back. Hurt knee. Try tomorrow." He slipped the backpack off his shoulders and dropped it and the sample case against the far wall.

"Tomorrow? Where will we meet him?"

Elton shook his head. "Didn't say." He looked at Harry, searching his face through his spectacles, which had now fogged over and were covered with moisture. "Problem?"

Harry was furious but tried not to show it. "No. Not a problem." Only an opportunity lost, perhaps not to come again. Then he understood. This must be part of a larger plan, something that had been in the works for a while. Gerard wasn't spying on Harry. There was something else, there had to be. He'd never intended to come to the cabins. He needed to carry out the errand he'd agreed to do for Isaac. Harry had played right into his paws.

Now Harry would be spending time with Elton, trying to make conversation, if you could call it that. He'd have to find out if Elton was a part of this scheme. And the confrontation with Gerard he'd been anticipating would have to wait.

Elton inspected the cabin and noted the facilities in the back. When he returned, he reached into his large satchel, removed a small whisk broom, and attached a short wooden handle. In a few minutes, he had swept the floor of both rooms clean. Then he opened the door and briskly brushed the pile of dirt and crumbled dead leaves onto the porch before dismantling the broom and returning it to the satchel. Pulling a sandwich out of his pack, he sat down in front of the fire, then went outside and returned to melt some snow in the pot, as Harry had done. He knelt again in front of the fire and held out his paws, rubbing them.

"Good fire."

Harry had watched Elton distractedly, his mind racing. He *had* to know what Gerard was up to. But there was a good chance he'd never see the weasel again. He would never know what that note was all about.

Into the long silence, Elton said, "What now?"

"What? What do you mean?" Harry had almost forgotten the badger was sitting beside him.

Elton reached into his pack and pulled out a small leather pouch. He gestured to Harry and they sat down on the floor. Elton carefully emptied the pouch in front of them.

"Don't tell me you believe in this stuff!" Harry said. On the floor in a neat pile were about two dozen small shells and several smooth stones of different dark colors. There was one small translucent quartz crystal and a larger one, blood red.

Elton looked up. "Why not?"

Harry was disgusted. Fortune-telling was a fraud.

Elton pointed to the stones. "Pick."

"No, not me."

"Pick."

Harry stood up. "No. I don't want to. I don't believe in it."

"Pick."

The fire was dying and the room had cooled. Harry walked out the back door and returned with more firewood. He built up the fire again and when it was spitting and snapping, turned back to Elton, who sat, unmoving, on the floor, looking at the stones and shells. Elton looked up. "Pick."

The stubbornness of the badgers.

"All right," Harry said with a sigh of impatience. He picked up a smooth, dark stone, almost a perfect oval, recalling for a moment his long-lost collection. "This one."

Elton nodded. "Ask question." He removed his spectacles and wiped them on his pants, then carefully replaced them. "Shake." He lay back on the floor, his head on his bulky pack, and closed his eyes. "Throw. No hurry."

Harry stuffed the stones and the shells back into the leather pouch. It was very soft and thin, and he could feel the edges of the shells inside as he squeezed the pouch in his paw.

Think of a question. Fine.

What is the connection between Isaac and Gerard?

He untied the pouch and shook it violently, dropping the stones and shells onto the floor with a clatter.

The shells scattered across the floor and the oval, black stone rolled into the darkness and hit the wall. The blood red crystal, smaller and more jagged, continued to tumble until it stopped, touching the black.

Elton sat up and peered over his spectacles.

"This is nonsense," Harry said. "I don't believe in moochy-poochy stuff."

"Not moochy-poochy." The badger looked up, offended.

"Well, then, what's the answer to my question?"

Elton was silent for a moment. "Not good."

"Just tell me, for the gods' sake."

Elton pointed to the two stones against the wall. "Danger. Close to you. Path you follow. Dead end." He started to gather up the scattered stones and shells.

"What danger? What dead end? Is that all?"

Elton nodded, his face expressionless.

This is nonsense, Harry thought. "The only thing close to me is you, Elton," he said, scooping up the distant stones and handing them over.

"Not me."

Harry looked at Elton's calm, bespectacled face. *I believe him,* he thought. "And besides, it didn't answer my question."

"Sure?" He took the stones and shells from Harry. "My turn."

"Which piece is yours?"

Elton held up the translucent quartz. He put everything

back into the pouch and held it in his paws for a moment, his eyes closed. Then he smoothed a spot on the floor, shook the pouch, untied the leather cord, and poured out the contents in front of him.

This time the shells formed an irregular circle on the floor; a few appeared to radiate from the center. Harry's black stone had stopped next to the translucent quartz near the center of the circle; the red had rolled far off into the darkness along with some other shells.

"What did you ask?" *What urgent question could Elton need to have answered?* Harry thought. *Will I sleep soundly tonight? Will my customers place big orders? Will I ever speak in complete sentences?*

"Weather," Elton said. He looked at the floor for a moment, then pointed to the circle. "Sun tomorrow." He collected the shells and stones, put the pouch back into his sack, and turned to Harry. "Need sleep. You?" He gestured to the top bunk.

Harry had no idea if there was even a mattress there. He climbed up and saw that it was in the same condition as the one below. "Yes," he said. "I'll take the top."

In a few minutes they had doused the candles. The cabin was very dark, the fire slowly dying once more. Elton had placed his pack beneath the bed after withdrawing from it a pair of soft, faded red slippers and a matching nightcap, both of which he donned with obvious relief and pleasure. He wrapped his coat around him, carefully placed his spectacles on the floor next to his bed within easy reach in the dark, and fell asleep almost immediately. His snores, quiet and rhythmical, had an odd buzzing quality, as if he were a bee or a fly.

Harry climbed to the top bunk, taking the brown blanket with him and keeping his coat on. He had put his boots back on because of the cold. Did he even *own* a pair of slippers? He decided to buy some as soon as he returned home — lined with rabbit fur, in different colors, one for each day of the week. With the money he'd have, he could buy a dozen pairs if he wanted to.

He thought about the stones and Elton's words. Where could the danger come from? Isaac? Of course, Isaac — Harry had always suspected his brother was capable of anything. But Isaac was miles away. Gerard? More likely.

Harry stared up at the ceiling, close to his head, his eyes now accustomed to the dark. The mattress was small and too soft. He noted he could now touch the ceiling, which was laced with spiderwebs, with his elbows and his knees.

The sound of dripping water awakened him the next morning. Harry opened his eyes and saw the cabin filled with sunlight, the snow melting from the windows, and Elton standing in the open doorway.

Sun?

He leaped down from the bunk bed and joined Elton at the door. The air was warm, and the sound of dripping, running water was everywhere. The snow melted from the trees, which now glistened as if their branches were covered with glass, and the icicles that had formed from the roof of the cabin dripped regularly onto the deep snow beneath, leaving small, deep pockmarks. The shadow of the cabin in the morning light was purple-blue. It was a long time since Harry had even *seen* a shadow outdoors.

Down the road in the distance he could see the other cabins clearly; the field in the center of the large, rough triangle of the encampment was still deep in snow; behind them, the jagged profile of the pines and firs, dark greenish black against the bright blue sky, was clear and sharply outlined.

"Stones right," Elton growled. "Nice day."

Harry took a deep breath of the warm air. "You can say that again."

Elton looked puzzled. "Stones right. Nice day."

Harry laughed, ignoring the comment about the stones. Pointing out the likelihood of coincidence was not going to get him anywhere. "Yes, it is."

Elton closed the door with apparent reluctance. "Hungry," he said. He'd already dressed in his walking boots and several heavy sweaters; the slippers and nightcap were nowhere to be seen.

"So am I. Anything left?" he asked, pointing to Elton's pack beneath the bed.

"No."

"We'll have to hunt, then."

Elton nodded.

In a few minutes, they were outdoors again, Elton carrying a small tool that looked like a hammer with a head made of stone, Harry with just an empty sack he'd found beneath the bed. Elton had had an extra cap with a visor, which made walking through the blinding snow-covered field much easier, and Harry had accepted it with a grunt of thanks.

They agreed to separate and meet back at the cabin by noon. Harry looked up at the bright blue sky. He had about an hour to find food and return. Elton started in the direction of the other cabins along the lake, working his way back to the main road. Harry decided to try the near arm of the triangle, heading away from the lake and toward the woods behind the clearing.

That last summer with his family he had explored these cabins and the woods on his own many times. Inevitably Isaac would be lounging pathetically on the porch swing, as he did almost every day, lovingly attended to by Mama.

Now, as he walked slowly through the snow, Harry thought, *I could have accepted my role as the older, stronger sibling, protectively caring for my fragile, sick brother — if Isaac had been a different kind of fox. Mama and I could have taken care of him together. Dad would have come to me for advice on how to handle Isaac's mental state; they would have turned to me for guidance.*

... "Harry," his mother said. "I'm concerned about your brother. He doesn't seem to be eating. Do you know what could be bothering him?"

"Perhaps he's just tired, Mama. Let me try to feed him. I'll tell him a story to distract him."

"My darling child!" Mama replied. "How could we manage without you?" She turned to Dad. "Don't we have an unusually kind and caring son?"

"I'm so proud of you," Dad said. "But you need to go out and play. We can take care of Isaac."

"No, no," Harry said. "Let me do it. I don't care about playing with friends. My brother's health is much more important."

Dad and Mama hugged him, and Mama kissed him tenderly.

"No one could ask for a finer son," Mama said. . . .

Harry approached a cabin, deserted and blanketed in snow, with icicles dripping from the roof. He walked around the back, peering beneath the foundation where wood was normally stored. Holding on to the sack, he got down on all fours and crept slowly toward the base of the building.

Sure enough, he picked up the scent of mouse. It was very strong, which suggested a colony, perhaps several, living together under the cabin for warmth and shelter, foraging for smaller bugs and whatever dead vegetation could be found. They wouldn't be fat but they'd be alive, and if there were enough of them, they would be filling.

Harry was slender enough to crawl under the cabin, which he did slowly and silently. Some snow had drifted around the perimeter but it was otherwise dry. When his eyes became accustomed to the dark, he saw what he was looking for: dozens of bony adults and a number of their young, equally thin, all asleep. He pounced on the adults, breaking their necks with his paws; the babies squealed and ran; some in their panic ran toward him, which made it easy to kill them. Harry simply swept the dead and dying into the sack. When he crawled out from under the cabin it was bulging and lumpy with the dead mice; blood began to soak through the thin burlap, and the slightly bitter scent of fresh-killed mouse made his stomach growl in anticipation.

Should he eat one now? Why not? He was very hungry; the scent was very strong, and it was impossible to imagine when he might eat again. Sharing with Elton would mean less food for Harry. Elton could take care of himself.

Harry reached into the sack and pulled out one mouse after another. The first mouthful, still quite warm, was incredibly good. Had he forgotten how much he'd always enjoyed mouse?

They were so delicious that by the time he reached the bottom of the sack he was gulping them down whole. *That's the thing about mice,* he thought. *You can't eat just one.*

Suddenly, he choked. Harry coughed and gagged until the tears ran down his face, trying to swallow a bone that had lodged horizontally in his windpipe. He doubled over, reached for some snow, and filled his mouth. The melting snow cooled his throat and gave him something to swallow, and in a few moments he could breathe again. He wiped his face and mouth with snow and finished the last few mice, this time chewing slowly. He sighed with satisfaction.

Harry buried the bloodstained sack in a snowdrift and trotted back to the green cabin. He'd explain to Elton that he'd been unable to capture the mice, which had escaped from under the cabin into a dozen small and inaccessible holes in the flooring, leaving him with nothing. He'd pretend to be hungry and frustrated. *Maybe Elton will have something to share — in which case,* Harry thought, *I will eat again.*

On his way back to the cabin, Harry felt the air become cool, then cold. He looked up. Large gray clouds floated in front of the sun, which was now a shiny white disk in the overcast sky. In a few minutes it disappeared completely; the quickly moving clouds, blowing in from across the lake, were darker gray, and the horizon vanished. It smelled like snow.

Elton was already inside, having made a fire. He'd thrown some brown and surprisingly fragrant leaves into the iron pot, which he had scrubbed clean, along with some melted snow, and was in the process of chopping several dark and intimidating root vegetables — Harry hoped they were vegetables — with his hatchet. Elton gestured to the limp gray bodies on the countertop.

"Vole," he said. "You?"

"Good work," Harry said. "I found some the other day on my way to the Inn. Tasty." He tried to look discouraged. "Unfortunately, I was not as successful just now. " He explained about the mice.

Elton looked him up and down from behind his spectacles. "Too bad. Sack?" he asked.

Harry thought quickly. "Oh. Must have dropped it on the way back. I'll look for it later."

Elton skinned and gutted the voles deftly and dropped them into the pot along with the vegetables, then placed it on the fire in the hearth, where it teetered unsteadily.

The badger wiped his hands on his shirt and walked over to his pack. He reached in and withdrew a small, flat piece of wood hinged in the middle like a book, opened it, and placed it on the floor.

What now?

It was a checkerboard, the squares faded to gray and rose.

"You like games, don't you?" Harry said.

"Pass time. You play?" Elton asked. He opened a small wooden box and carefully placed a number of oddly shaped objects on the floor.

"I think so," said Harry, reluctantly. "But what are those?"

"Badger checkers. Easy."

Elton explained the game. "Rules change," he said. "Three moves. Change back."

"But changing rules means no rules," Harry said, beginning to be interested. "Why not just call it what it is — cheating?"

Elton shook his head. "Not cheating. Players choose."

"You mean they decide whether to change the rules or not?"

"Yes. Sometimes."

The badger finished talking and then walked over to the pot. He lifted the lid and sniffed the bubbling contents. "Not bad," he said.

He returned to the checkerboard and set up the pieces. Harry was intrigued. A game with rules that kept changing? *Sometimes?* How would you win a game like that?

They played in silence and Harry watched Elton closely, looking for clues. At one point, when Elton jumped several of Harry's pieces, including an especially interesting feathered pine cone, Harry said, "Wait! When I did that you said, 'Not allowed.' What's going on?"

Elton growled, "Badger rules. Like mice. Hard to swallow." He glanced at Harry and walked away to check the pot in the hearth again. "Saw you," he said, without turning around.

Damn! "Look, Elton," he began, "I did find a few mice, but only a few. It didn't seem worth it to bring them back."

"Understood."

Harry stomped to the door and stood on the porch, watching the sky darken and breathing in the smell of imminent snow. He reached down, packed a snowball with his paws, and threw it in the direction of the frozen lake. *My life was so much simpler when I was alone.* He threw another snowball. *Well, it can be that way again.* He went inside.

Elton had taken the pot from the hearth and placed it on the floor near the checkerboard. The contents bubbled. He offered Harry a large ladle-like spoon from his pack and took another one for himself. "Share," Elton said.

"Are you sure? As you so tactfully pointed out, I have already eaten."

"Not tactful," Elton said. "Honest." His eyes behind his spectacles became icy. "Share," he said again, more firmly. "Badgers share."

Harry gave in. There was no point arguing with a badger.

Besides, it wasn't as if there had been a *huge* quantity of mice. "If you insist."

In a few minutes, Elton scraped the bottom of the pot, then turned it upside down and drank from it, after first offering it to Harry, who declined. A neat pile of vole bones lay on the floor beside Elton; Harry's were scattered. Elton put the all the bones in the pot and brought it to the hearth.

Harry felt the need to change the subject. "So, Elton," he said, "do you have a family?"

Elton turned. "Family?"

"Yes. A mate? Brothers and sisters? Children?"

Elton walked back to where Harry was sitting, cross-legged, on the floor. "Brother only."

"What's he like?"

"Like?" Elton looked puzzled. "Badger. Like me."

"No, I mean, what kind of creature is he?"

Elton sat down opposite Harry. "Older. Smarter. Bigger. Faster." Elton seemed to be thinking. "Big talker."

"For a badger, you mean."

"Yes."

"Do you get along?"

"Get along?"

"Do you like him? Do you get along? Do you trust him?"

Elton didn't answer right away. "At first, no. Jealous."

"Jealous? Why?"

"Older. Smarter. Bigger. Faster."

"What happened?"

Elton stretched out his short legs in their worn, brown boots.

"Hard to say. You?"

"Yes," Harry replied. "Unfortunately, I do have a brother."

"Get along?"

"No."

"Why?"

Younger. Phonier. Richer. Meaner. "Hard to say."

The two sat silently for a moment. "I don't know what your plans are," Harry said, changing the subject again, "but I'd like to move on to the fortifications today. I could get a few hours in before dark."

Elton turned to him. "Go tomorrow," he said. "Snow soon."

"Snow every day."

"Go tomorrow."

"I don't agree. I'll leave now and hope to make some progress by tomorrow morning." He got up to put his things together.

"Play again," Elton said, gesturing to the checkerboard. "You win, leave now. I win, go together. Tomorrow."

Will I never be rid of him? Harry thought. "All right. But if I win, I leave *by myself*, now. If you win, we'll see."

"See?"

"Yes."

"I win. Go together," Elton said, giving Harry that stubborn stare.

"Fine, fine." *Let's get this over with,* Harry thought. *I can still catch a few hours of daylight.*

Elton reset the board.

It was early evening before Harry won his first game of badger checkers. He had watched through six games, losing each one, as Elton attacked ("Ho!"), set traps ("Ho!"), took his playing pieces ("Ho!"), *returned* his playing pieces ("Ho!"), and defeated him by a wide margin ("Ho!").

Harry hated to lose. Today, perhaps because of the mice, he especially hated to lose to Elton. "Another game," he'd said after his first one, giving up on his plans. Elton had defeated him in more ways than one.

In the beginning, Harry drummed impatiently on the floor as Elton spent a lot of time preparing for each move. Finally, by the end of the seventh game, Harry understood. The winning strategy was to play conventionally for a while, and then, when your opponent least expected it, change the rules. Of course, when both players did that the game became almost impossible to follow. Bluffing, making distracting noises and gestures, and keeping a straight face while making errors (change of rules? or a deliberate effort to throw your opponent off track?) were techniques Elton had clearly mastered.

In one game, Harry noticed that Elton yawned loudly and scratched his head just before he made an unexpected rules change. A few times, Elton ignored an obvious opportunity and allowed Harry to advance into dangerous territory. No sooner was Harry feeling elated and confident about his success than Elton's next move decimated his defense. Toward the end of the seventh game, there were only a few pieces left on the board and Harry was cornered. It was Elton's move; Harry began to cough — a dry, hacking cough that seemed to come from deep in his chest. He doubled over and his eyes teared.

"Problem?" Elton asked, looking up with concern.

"I'm fine," Harry managed to choke out. "Sorry."

Elton made his move.

With a triumphant shout, Harry jumped his feathered pine cone over Elton's bundle of twigs.

"Ho! Double ho! I won!" After six straight humiliating defeats, it felt very, very good. He clapped his paws, stood up, and stretched.

Elton held out a paw and they shook. "Learn fast."

"Yes," Harry said with a satisfied smile. "I do."

He walked to the window. It was dark, and the faint light

from the cabin window illuminated the ground. Harry could see the snow, falling in thick, fat flakes, straight down. There was no wind. The tracks he'd made returning from the cabin had filled up with snow; the path he and Elton had made to the door had already disappeared. He turned back to the fire.

Elton sat on the lower bunk mattress, his nightcap already on his head. "Harry," he said as he fell back on the mattress. "Good coughing." In a few minutes, he was asleep on the bottom bunk, buzzing.

Harry picked up the checker pieces and moved them slowly around the board. Badger checkers. He thought about inventing Harry the Fox checkers. There would be rules, but they would never change: go my own way, depend on no one, eat when I can, get revenge on my brother. *A good game — a game I can win.*

He yawned. Sleep tempted him: The cabin was still warm; the hot food was comforting in his stomach; the brief moment of cold he'd felt looking out at the snow had made him shiver. The falling snow began to blow against the windows, and Harry could sense the temperature dropping.

He put the checker pieces and the board near Elton's pack, climbed up to the top bunk, and pulled his coat and the blanket around him. The fire slowly died; the cabin grew dark.

He thought about the "message" from the moochy-poochy

stones. Dead end. What could that mean? That it was futile to try to discover the connection between Gerard and Isaac? What path was he following that could lead to nowhere? *I knew there was a reason I hated those things,* he thought. *They make no sense, and it's a waste of time to try to figure them out.* He closed his eyes and tried to sleep.

10
Gerard: Declining Is Not an Option

Six months earlier, on a late spring morning, Gerard the weasel had awakened earlier than usual. He lay in bed for a moment, breathing in the fragrant air that drifted through the open window. Spring! A time for poets. What was that line from *The Wanderer*? *"Now the . . .* something . . . *morning / Glows upon the misty hills / And shows her flowered apron to the waiting sky." Lovely,* he thought. *That ermine really knew how to write. But you'd think having declaimed those lines a hundred times or more, I could remember the entire speech.* He'd begun to notice that essential words and phrases from his acting past were vanishing from his memory like . . . like . . . *dew in the sunshine,* as a matter of fact. He reached for a pencil and paper near his bed and jotted down his inspiration. A poem was coming — he could feel it.

He had dressed hastily, sipped some cold tea he'd left on the table from the night before, and started out on his regular morning walk. The spring air was fresh and sweet and already warm enough so that he regretted his jacket, and the sun through the newly leafed trees created a pleasing light in the woods on either side of the trail that led into Wildwood Forest. There was an eager, innocent green to the larches, he thought, and the evergreens were tipped — no, *gilded* — with the pale yellow of new growth.

He walked at a leisurely pace on the familiar path, feeling a surge of well-being. His most recent project had been gratifyingly successful: A prosperous rat had asked him to investigate and report on the activities of a competitor. "No sabotage, please, and no destruction," the rat had said from behind his enormous desk. "I just want information."

Gerard had spent a week studying at the Foxboro Public Library and had picked up enough construction jargon to present himself as a consultant. "I'll need access to the company's files, of course," he'd said to Howard, the competitor, a genial older rat with a doting wife and no children, and the rat had obliged.

"I've been looking for a fellow like you," Howard had said. "Someone I can trust. A rarity in this world."

Gerard had been invited to the rat's home and had eaten several spectacularly good meals amid much laughter and warm conviviality. He'd made his report within a month and had been handsomely paid.

The older rat would shortly be out of business.

Now I can relax a bit and actually write some poetry, he thought, *instead of just contemplating the possibilities.* He reached into his jacket pocket, found a pencil and a small pad, and sat down on a damp tree stump at the side of the trail. He stared at the paper and jotted a few notes: dappled light, gilded trees . . . *I walk among the dappled trees / The morning sun, the* . . . something . . . *breeze.* That might work. He folded the paper neatly, put it back into his pocket, and reached for a cigarette, thinking he'd return to the poem later. For now, it was more pleasant to breathe the air, listen to the birds, and soak up the warm sun.

In a short while he heard an odd, irregular step approaching on the path. Coming toward him was a fox walking with the help of a cane, which, Gerard could see as he came closer, was made of expensive mahogany and tipped in silver. The fox was handsome for his species, with a powerful upper body, and well dressed. There was a look of cunning — he was a fox, after all — and confident authority that told Gerard, who prided himself on his ability to read character with little evidence, that this fox was accustomed to having his way.

The fox stopped in front of him and asked, "Are you Gerard? My name is Isaac — perhaps you've heard of me."

Of course! The Managing Director of Foxboro, known for his shady dealings and for his ability to manipulate the press, although the former had never been proved. Now Gerard understood the attitude of authority, the aura of power and privilege. He tamped out the cigarette in the damp soil and rubbed it with his boot. He stood. "Yes, I'm Gerard, and of course I know who you are."

Isaac nodded curtly. "I need to talk to you. Can we walk?"

"Certainly." Gerard returned to the path and walked on Isaac's left, the side with the cane.

"Do you mind?" Isaac said with some irritation, gesturing.

Gerard moved to his other side. "Sorry." So the fox was sensitive about his disability. Clearly his left leg was not as strong as his right. An injury? A childhood illness, perhaps?

"What can I do for you?" Gerard asked after a moment of silence.

Isaac did not respond immediately.

Gerard looked around. Although he sensed a business proposition in the offing, he almost wished it weren't so. The world was beautiful right now, and he wanted to soak it up with all his senses.

"I know the kind of work you do," Isaac said suddenly. "I need someone like yourself to handle a delicate matter for me. But I must know I can trust you." He stopped walking and turned to face Gerard, looking him squarely in the eye. "Well?"

"Ah," said Gerard, thinking of the older rat. "Someone to trust," he said smoothly. "A rarity in the world, don't you agree?"

Isaac sighed impatiently. "Obviously. That's why I asked."

"Trust is my business, or shall I say it's my single most

effective tool of the trade. I wouldn't have achieved my reputation and my success if I hadn't been trustworthy." He paused. "I don't suppose you want references."

"I don't need them," Isaac said, continuing on the path. "I'll pay well," he added. "Generously."

"Oh?"

"I'll tell you this much for now," Isaac said as he turned to leave. "I've been contacted, in the flesh, by a rabbit who offered an . . . arrangement."

"*What?* A rabbit? That's impossible!" Gerard exclaimed.

Isaac looked at him with narrowed eyes. "No, it's not." It was a statement not to be argued with. "My place, tomorrow evening. Do not breathe a word of this to anyone. I have ways of finding out if you do." He reached into a pocket and pulled out a business card. "Here. Shall we say midnight? That way I can be sure you won't be seen." He disappeared around a turn of the trail.

Gerard stood watching him with his mouth agape.

Contacted by a rabbit who talked? Was the Managing Director insane? The conversation was so disturbing for so many reasons that he found he could no longer focus on the beautiful morning. He walked for a while on the path, but tripped several times and once actually fell, scraping his elbow. He picked himself up and looked around. Had anyone seen? The woods were silent. *I need to go home,* he thought finally.

He turned around and quickly walked back to his house and went inside, locking the door.

Gerard dropped into his easy chair and mopped his brow with a silken handkerchief. If it was true that Isaac Fox had actually met a rabbit who could speak . . . He tried to imagine what that would be like, talking to one's food and having it respond. It would be as if a piece of cheese or a bunch of grapes or a vole had stood up on one's plate and said good morning. What next? Talking furniture? Conversations with trees? It was ridiculous. The fox must be hallucinating.

He walked to the small ice chest that sat in the corner of his kitchen and opened it up, moving the straw out of the way to uncover the contents: a bat and a dozen frogs, each still whole and neatly folded around itself like a small package, stiff and silent. The bat stared at him with open, sightless eyes, its sharp little teeth bared in a frozen death-smile. Beneath the bat and the frogs were layers of frozen vole and squirrel, a number of vegetable sandwiches, several eggs, frozen berries, a snake, and dozens of tender earthworms hardened into a glistening, frosty mass, like a misshapen ball of thick, brown string.

Gerard looked at the bat. "Hello," he whispered, and immediately felt the utter fool. He covered the ice with the straw and slammed the chest closed.

He returned to his chair and lit another cigarette. *I haven't eaten rabbit in ages.* Food of all sorts had been so plentiful in

Foxboro he'd never given it any thought, until just recently, when he'd come across a particularly tempting recipe in an old cookbook. *Rabbit!* he'd thought. *It's been years since I've tasted rabbit. But there were none to be found in the Foxboro markets.*

He'd spoken to his local grocer, who specialized in delicacies of particular interest to the small weasel population that lived on the outskirts of the city. "My dear fellow," Gerard had said to the slightly seedy weasel with bushy eyebrows and a scar on his chin. "Surely it's not possible that the rabbit supply has vanished forever. You seem to be the kind of weasel who could get his paws on anything. Isn't there something you can do? Price is no object," he added, thinking about the recipe and his sudden craving for braised rabbit with fresh mushrooms and garlic.

The proprietor, wearing a plaid cap and a soiled green apron, wiped his paws on his front and stepped from behind the counter. "There ain't no rabbits nowhere," he said emphatically. "There ain't been no stinking rabbits for a long time, except maybe inside that old fortress on the other side of Wildwood. But even the black market ain't never been able to get none. Believe me, I've tried," he added, with a nudge of his elbow into Gerard's shoulder, from which Gerard slightly recoiled. "There ain't no one like me, Martin, for finding your illegal liquor or your hard-to-get imported tobacco." He winked. "About the rabbits, though — it ain't just us, sir, believe you me. Nobody ain't got no rabbit, nowhere. Nobody never had no rabbit since I can't remember. Nobody can't never get no rabbit, neither."

"Did you say tobacco?"

They completed the transaction in a small, filthy back room that also, apparently, served as Martin's living quarters. Gerard, dismayed by the weasel's grammar, appalled by his accommodations, pleased with his respectful tone, and delighted to find a source for his much-sought-after sassafras tobacco leaves, had put the matter of rabbit availability and the tempting recipe out of mind.

Now, it seems, I am about to be involved with rabbits in a very different way.

He reached into his pocket and found the piece of paper on which he had written. "*I walk among the dappled trees / The morning sun, the . . .* something . . . *breeze.*" He would save it exactly as it was, a memento of a time of innocence, a time when the world was an orderly and predictable place, before he had been told that rabbits could talk.

Isaac came to the door with a lantern in one paw and his cane in the other. "Come in." Gerard followed him inside, and the heavy wooden door closed solidly behind him. Isaac locked it. "Follow me."

Gerard had made a trial run to Isaac's mansion during the day, to be sure he could find it in the dark, and to get a sense of how the fox lived. He'd glimpsed the home of the Managing Director only from a distance. Now he saw the mansion was enormous; a long path led to the front door; no other homes existed nearby. The house was situated on a hill overlooking the town and Wildwood Forest; the view was spectacular but Gerard noticed no chairs or tables outside, and the shutters were closed, even on this beautiful spring afternoon. No flowers bloomed; no trees blossomed, no grass — just gravel, neatly raked and edged with scalloped metal of no recognizable color. Two young foxes in uniform looked at him with calculated indifference as he stood at the foot of the path.

There was no sign of them when he approached the mansion that night.

Isaac and Gerard walked down a wide hallway, dimly lit and lined on both sides with large mirrors in elaborate frames that reflected their images to infinity. Their footsteps and Isaac's cane made a sharp tattoo on the dark wood floor. Isaac opened another door and Gerard saw a library; a fire crackled in the hearth, which was at least four times his height and framed in marble; books lined the walls from the floor to the very high ceiling on three sides of the room. There were no windows.

"Sit."

Two chairs had been placed in front of the fire, one large and comfortable looking, the other smaller and made of wood.

Isaac took the larger chair, leaned his cane against the arm, and put the lantern on a large table at his side. He rested his left leg on an ottoman that was perfectly positioned in front of him. Gerard settled uncomfortably in the wooden chair, noticing that it was also just a bit lower than the other, like a seat for a child. *A tired technique,* Gerard thought, *but a familiar one. Many a scene designer had manipulated scale on the stage for dramatic effect.*

I am not that easily intimidated.

"Let's dispense with the preliminaries," Isaac said abruptly. "As I told you yesterday, I received a message from a rabbit requesting a meeting with me. It was sent from the warren inside the abandoned fortress to the south."

"A message?" Gerard said. "Now you're saying they can write as well as speak? How can that be? They don't have the brainpower. They're prey!"

"By which you mean they are not self-aware," Isaac said mildly. "I believed that once myself. Nevertheless."

"How do you know this was not some kind of trick? Why would a rabbit want to meet with a fox? Can you prove the message was actually from a . . . rabbit?" He had to control himself to keep from laughing, the idea was so ludicrous.

"Because I met the rabbit who wrote it."

Gerard leaned back in the chair. "I don't believe it."

Isaac stopped. "I will, for the moment, ignore the implication that I am lying," he said coldly. "We need to get this over with. Please try not to interrupt me."

"May I ask a question?"

"Never *mind* your questions," Isaac said. "They are not important."

"If I am to work for you," Gerard began, "I need to know . . ."

"*Never mind* that."

Gerard sighed. "Can you get to the point, then? I'd like to get home before daylight."

Isaac ignored him. "The rabbit's name was Dan."

"It had a *name*?"

"Yes, it had a name. Dan came to see me very late one night disguised as a fox — very effectively too, I might add. Completely fooled the guards, who thought he was one of my constituents."

"Couldn't you smell rabbit?"

"That was the odd thing. It looked like a fox but smelled like a skunk. It apologized for the odor and said something about a surprise attack in the dark. The scent was nearly overpowering — you can imagine. I was ready to turn it away."

"Why didn't you?"

"My first impression was that this was a fox who had had an unfortunate confrontation. He was rather tall and thin and wore a hooded cape and dark boots. He carried a traditional lantern and spoke in a high-pitched, nasal voice. I saw in the light that his nostrils were stuffed with cotton, probably — I realized later — so that *my* predator scent wouldn't overpower *him*. His speech was accented to my ear because — I'm guessing on this — they speak a dialect of our language. Southern, I'd say."

"You opened the door to a stranger in the middle of the night?" Gerard said, doubt in his voice. "A stranger who had just had a run-in with some skunks?"

"Yes. He said he had some important business to discuss with me, a proposition that would make me wealthy beyond imagining. Naturally, in spite of the horrific odor, I was curious."

"Naturally."

Isaac had invited the fox inside and had lit a fire. "He sat there, right where you are sitting now," Isaac said, gesturing.

Gerard tried to imagine the scene, but he couldn't get his mind around it. *A rabbit disguised as a fox.*

"At what point did . . . Dan . . . reveal his true identity?"

"He sat for a while without saying anything. I tried to breathe through my mouth. Then he said I would have to promise to sit in my chair without moving while he explained. He handed me a small parcel, heavily wrapped in several layers of mouse skin and bound with cord. 'Take this someplace private,' he said, 'and open it. Then we can talk.' I did. When I came back into the room, the rabbit was smiling — and so was I."

"What was in the parcel?" Gerard asked.

"Wait here," Isaac said. He walked out of the room and left Gerard in front of the fire.

Gerard got up from the chair and began to pace, admiring the fox's professional sense of timing. The story was bizarre. Gerard had always been able to spot a liar — being one himself — but he could see no sign in Isaac that the fox was inventing this tale. It was just weird enough to be true.

He walked around and looked more closely at the books, perfectly and elegantly bound. But there was something wrong — what was it? *Ah!* The books had been painted on the wall with extraordinary skill, complete with shadows, the occasional worn or tattered spine; here and there, a book rested at an angle, supporting a tilting row of other titles. "Remarkable," he murmured, distracted for the moment. He looked closer and noticed a very thin vertical line crossing two shelves, and a minute brass hinge — no, two. A safe, perhaps? He turned quickly at the sound of Isaac's approach.

Isaac balanced a tray with glasses and a bottle on one paw, his cane in the other.

"Let me," Gerard said, surprised by the hospitable gesture, but Isaac's expression on hearing his offer silenced him. Gerard watched, unmoving, as the fox put the tray down, shoved the lantern out of the way, sat heavily in his chair, placed his cane alongside, raised his leg to the ottoman, and reached for a glass. "Here," Isaac said. "You're going to need this."

Gerard returned to his seat and took the glass. "I was admiring your library," he said. "Excellent work."

Isaac looked at him sharply. "It impresses the near-sighted."

"Indeed."

"Where was I?"

"The heavily wrapped package."

"I'll get to that." Isaac poured the wine. "I promised the rabbit I would not move from my chair no matter what he said or did. Then he slowly slipped the hood from his head and I saw in the light that he was wearing a fox mask over his face. At the same time I saw the ears — they were rabbit ears! — and then he removed the mask. It was a rabbit, a rather odd-looking one, with a large, circular bald spot at the back of its head and long fur growing down the side of its face. Most unattractive. It wiped its face with its mittened paws and breathed deeply through its mouth. I had the feeling it was trying not to show panic."

"So he doused himself with skunk to prevent you and your guards from devouring him on the spot? What did you do? What were you thinking?" Gerard gulped the wine in his glass and held it out for a refill.

Isaac obliged, then leaned forward. "You're the only one who knows about this," he said. "Remember you swore an oath of secrecy."

"I remember," Gerard said. "Who would believe it anyway?"

For a moment he saw the arrogant veneer vanish. "I couldn't think of anything," Isaac said. "My mind had stopped functioning. I think at some point I actually pinched myself to see if I might be dreaming." Isaac's eyes were wide with recalled astonishment, and his voice, which had been cold and impersonal, became warm with amazement.

"Well," Gerard said. "What did . . . Dan . . . want? And what does all this have to do with me?"

Isaac leaned back in his chair, his guard back up, the coldness returned to his voice. "I'll tell you. As you may know, there is a rabbit colony within the walls of the old fortress on the far side of Wildwood."

Gerard started to speak, but Isaac held up a paw.

"Wait," he said. "You'll get your answers. Yes," he went on, "there's an administration, a government, a city. That crumbling fortress wall is now reinforced and guarded. They are thinking of setting up a military structure for defense. According to Dan, the new government, of which he claims to be the Leader, plans to eliminate dissent, spy on the rabbit population, and dismantle the minority press. By sowing distrust and suspicion in the community, he hopes to provide enough distraction so that no one will notice that he and his cohorts are enriching themselves by executing the plan I am about to reveal to you. In short," he said with a touch of admiration in his voice, "the rabbits are civilized.

"A fluke," Isaac continued, responding to Gerard's disbelieving expression. "It's the only way to explain it. One rabbit is born and is aware. This rabbit naturally mates with another like itself; they produce sentient offspring. The older species dies out — having been killed for food, probably by us, as a matter of fact — and those remaining are the new kind, of which Dan is obviously one. He, in turn, is assisted by a rabbit called Wally." Isaac finished his wine and poured another glass. "They actually seem to be quite intelligent! When I asked Dan how he knew he could communicate with a fox, he said he'd found it hard to believe that rabbits could be the only sentient beings in the universe. He took a chance. Quite a courageous act, when you think about it."

Gerard nodded. "Yes. But I'm guessing he figured the outcome — whatever that might be — would be worth the risk."

Isaac looked at Gerard appraisingly. "Right. As you will now discover. Some time ago, these sentient rabbits found the fortress and decided to create a community behind its walls.

The remote location and the difficulty of breaking through its barriers have made it . . . inconvenient, to say the least."

Gerard lit a cigarette. *All right,* he thought. *I'm beginning to believe it.* "Are you going to tell me what was in the package?"

"Yes, eventually. You've noticed, I'm sure, that it's been years since we've had a supply of edible rabbits."

"As a matter of fact, I was thinking about it just recently. But of course we've never needed rabbit — food has always been so plentiful. Most of the younger population have grown up without ever having tasted it."

"Exactly." Isaac put his glass down and lifted himself out of the chair. He reached for his cane and limped over to the fireplace, staring into the fire. "All that is about to change," he said. "Dan offered to provide me with a limited number of healthy, well-fed rabbits for food on a regular basis. Alive or recently killed, as I wish. In turn he wants gold, lots of it, to trade for weapons. He mentioned a flourishing black market in some new and better technologies that will eventually make bows and arrows obsolete."

"And what will they do with those weapons?"

"They will use them to defend the compound from other predators, he says, and perhaps from any rabbit insurgents who may decide to question the status quo. In the meantime," Isaac said, turning to Gerard with a brief smile, "I will have rabbits."

168

Gerard stood up. "But you can't use a sentient creature for food! It's disgusting. And it's against the law."

"Do you think I give a damn about the law? What kind of idiot are you! Rabbit is rabbit. Whether it *talks* or *reads* or *thinks* or *sings* is completely *irrelevant!*" Isaac snarled, pounding the floor with his cane at each word. "What matters to me is that I can have a constant supply of excellent rabbit — which has not been available for years! — and that I will be the sole supplier. The wealthy elite of Foxboro will pay generously for the privilege of tasting rabbit again. In exchange, I gave Dan my word that I would pay in gold and promised we would not attack the fortress under any circumstances, no matter how tempting the opportunities might be." He paused. "The foolish rabbit believed me."

Gerard decided to try another tack. "But they could use these new weapons against foxes, couldn't they? And weasels?" he said, as an afterthought.

Isaac turned to him. "Damn it!" he shouted furiously. He lifted his cane and banged it against the table, which wobbled and tilted over with a crash, spilling the wine. "If they break their part of the bargain and try to use these weapons against us, I will organize the entire fox population for miles around, *and* the wolves, *and* the coyotes, and any other predators we can find, and we will scale the fortress wall and destroy them, fancy technology or not! They know we can do it — I said as much to this Dan creature — and I made it very clear!"

"Why not scale it now?"

Isaac threw him a look of utter contempt. "You *are* a fool. Why go to the trouble when I can have the food delivered to my doorstep? Besides, do you think I'm stupid enough to share this windfall with a bunch of ignorant wolves and coyotes? When I have the chance to become wealthy beyond imagining?"

"All right, all right," Gerard said. "Calm down."

Isaac lifted his glass to his mouth and tilted it back to finish the contents. "This arrangement," he continued more quietly, "would have to be a secret, obviously. No one must know that we have an agreement with the rabbit administration, or that the rabbits even *have* an administration." Isaac stood up and walked over to Gerard. He looked him in the eye. "If you tell anyone, or reveal the nature of this conversation in any way, I will find out and I will have you killed, and I will kill whoever you confide in. Not to put too fine a point on it." He turned away again. "I will not be stopped."

"Yes. I know your reputation. What do you want me to do?"

"I want you to facilitate the exchange."

"What do you mean?"

"I want you to meet Dan or Wally or whoever is going to handle this, pick up the rabbits — recently killed, I think, would be easier, don't you? — and bring them to me or to a place or authority I will designate. A while ago I sent some trusted foxes to handle this for me."

"What happened?"

Isaac turned to Gerard suddenly. "They were killed, quite brutally, all but one, who returned, mortally wounded, and judging by the story he told, obviously maddened by the experience."

"What story?"

"Never mind," Isaac said. "This is dangerous work. I need someone who is smarter than they were."

Gerard thought about it. "Who killed the other three? Surely not the rabbits!"

"Not *the* rabbits. Others, perhaps — *if* you believe the mad creature's story about rebels — and I don't. The details aren't important," he said abruptly. "This is not exactly the straight-forward business arrangement you are used to. But I'm sure you can handle it."

"Why choose me?"

"I've been observing you — and your career — for quite some time. You're smarter than most of your kind and you know how to disguise your true motives. You look out for your own interests — qualities of character that make you perfect for this assignment."

"I'm flattered," Gerard said, although he found himself

somewhat disconcerted at this blunt evaluation. "But I think I'll decline your offer. There are other ways to make a living."

"Declining is not an option," Isaac said, and Gerard, seeing the fox's expression, realized with a sinking feeling that he had no choice. "Besides, I will pay you well enough so that you never have to work again. You can spend the rest of your life drinking tea and writing poetry, since that seems to be what pleases you."

Gerard looked up. *How did he know about the poetry?*

"As I said, I've been observing you for quite a while," Isaac said with a grim smile. "You will also deliver the gold payment to Dan and Wally," he went on. "You need to do this without being noticed or detained by anyone. I will pay you ten percent of the income I receive from selling the rabbits here."

"Twenty," said Gerard, his mind numb. "And I want a percentage of what you pay the rabbits. I don't want to wait until you sell anything. Pay me up front."

Isaac looked at him with disgust mixed with grudging respect. "You drive a hard bargain. All right. And if you prove yourself up to this, I'll throw in one rabbit from each exchange. At the prices I plan to charge, that's quite a decent offer. Rabbits have been as rare as mouse feathers. They will make us both rich."

"No need," Gerard said. "I prefer cash."

Isaac shrugged. "Whatever suits you. Once you have a

system established, I may join you, as the spirit moves me. Just to be sure things are going . . . smoothly."

"Fine."

"You can meet Dan near Inn the Forest. I'll give you a map. Apparently there's a tunnel — that's all I know." He walked over to the library door and held it open.

What kind of monsters would sell their own kind for food? Gerard thought as he made his way down the mirrored hall, Isaac at his side.

"You can start tomorrow," Isaac said, opening the front door. A sliver of moon lit the path ahead.

Gerard turned to him. "The package?"

"Oh, yes, the package. I won't go into details," Isaac said. "But I can tell you this —" He leaned closer and whispered into Gerard's ear. "When I roasted it with onions and garlic the next day . . . it was delicious." He licked his chops noisily and closed the door behind Gerard.

11

Quentin:
Rabbit Heroes for All Times

It was a few moments before Quentin's eyes adjusted to the dim light from the small, flickering torch fixed to the stone wall of the tower, several feet above his head. He and Frank had fallen inside the tower door and Quentin had landed on his side on top of something — or someone. The someone was Wally, sprawled face down and unconscious on the floor. He took up much of the space between the door and the bottom of the spiral staircase that led to the tower and the perimwall several stories above them. Next to Wally lay Zack, who began to groan softly.

Frank had tripped over Wally and had fallen, and now he made no effort to get to his feet. "That was much worse than what I expected," he said. "I should have known it was a trap."

Quentin dropped his satchel and started to remove his jacket.

"You're hurt!" Frank said, standing. "Let me see." There was blood all over the inside of Quentin's sleeve, and his shirt was wet with it. Frank reached into his pack and pulled out a long cotton strip of bandage. He turned Quentin into the light. "It's just a flesh wound. It probably hurts, though."

Quentin nodded. "It does." He was surprised at his own calm. It was as if he had entered another world when he pushed his way into the tower room. It was like a dream.

Frank dabbed at Quentin's shoulder and proceeded to wind the bandage expertly around his upper arm.

"You come prepared," Quentin said. "Thanks! All I brought were some snacks and my last bottle of *plumbo*, which I dropped in the snow. Oh. And a book. You can see which of us was thinking ahead. It wasn't me."

"Did I hear you say you brought a book?" Zack said, getting up and rubbing his head. "Quentin, you amaze me. Were you planning to catch up on your reading?"

Before Quentin could respond, there was a pounding on the door behind them, and shouting. They could hear Dan's high voice. "They're going to have trouble getting through," Zack said. "It's an automatic lock. That's one reason I couldn't open it. It's rusted."

Quentin looked at Wally. "What did you hit him with?"

Zack picked up a large stone from beside him on the floor and looked both pleased and dismayed. "I brought it just in case. It was so heavy I almost regretted it, until he clobbered me with that." He pointed to a large wooden club that lay on the floor near Wally.

"Wish I'd been here," Quentin said.

"I know. I had just enough strength to hit him before I lost consciousness."

"He could come to at any moment," Frank said, glancing at Wally's prone body. As if on cue, Wally stirred and moaned.

"Let's get out of here," Frank said.

Zack quickly climbed a few steps and reached for the torch. The spiral staircase was narrow and turned on itself over and over; the torch cast large, dancing shadows against the rough stone, and Frank and Quentin's footsteps echoed as they made their way to the top. By the time they reached the door, Quentin was breathing heavily again and pulling himself up by the handrail.

Zack stopped. "This is it," he said, turning to Quentin and Frank. He was breathing hard too. "Frank? Any thoughts?"

"Yes," Frank said, panting. "We'll drop our packs over the wall first. I think we should jump separately. That way, if one of us is injured the others can help."

"Injured?" Quentin looked at him.

"Well, the ground should be soft. But there are no guarantees."

Zack nodded.

"Then, Zack, you jump. Try to aim your body away from the wall and toward the woods. It shouldn't be too hard a landing — as I said, I'm certain there's nothing there but several feet of soft snow. Quentin will jump next, and I'll jump right after. We'll look for shelter in the woods, and when the rebels find us we can try to find my Mary and the children first thing in the morning. How does that sound?"

Zack nodded. "Fine." He started to open the door, then turned back to Quentin. "You're afraid of heights, aren't you."

"Yes. Ever since that day at the pond." It was a relief to admit it.

"You are?" Frank looked surprised. "Why didn't you say so?"

"It wouldn't have made any difference," Quentin said with a sigh of resignation. "You yourself said there's no other way."

"I'm sorry," Frank said. "I wish I could help."

Zack pushed the door open and, when they were safely on the path, placed the stone in front of it. He doused the torch.

Quentin expected shouts or a rain of arrows, but there was nothing but an eerie silence. The light from the tower above them made the snow-covered path sparkle; the skies had cleared and a bright, full moon rode high in the sky above them. Its face looked down on him, its expression unreadable.

Zack dropped his pack over the edge, without looking down. Quentin waited to hear it land. *Gods, how far down* is *the ground?* he thought, as the seconds seemed to tick by. *Thump.*

There was a shout. Ahead, on the path in the distance, several rabbits in uniform, armed with bows and arrows and carrying torches, were running toward them, having climbed the stairs from the next tower. Another shout far behind them, and Quentin saw one or two more rabbits in military gray, more arrows.

"Look out!" Frank shouted, and they ducked as an arrow thunked into the snowy path.

Zack stepped up to the low railing that bordered the pathway and stood looking down. He turned for a moment to Quentin and whispered, "Mouse courage!" He jumped. The sound of his landing was muffled by the shouts of the rabbits coming toward them and the pounding of Quentin's own heartbeat in his ears. Was Zack all right? He wouldn't find out until he landed beside him.

Frank reached down, picked up Quentin's satchel, and dropped it over the side. "You're next," he said. "You can do it! But for the gods' sake, hurry! They're getting closer!"

Quentin felt the panic rising in him. His heart pounded and he could feel the perspiration trickle down the backs of his legs.

Another arrow thunked into the path, closer this time.

There was the sound of the door being shoved against the stone. Behind them a voice growled, "You won't escape, Vole-hole! Don't even try it!"

Quentin turned to see Wally's thick, stupid face, streaked with blood from an ugly gash on his temple, peering from behind the partly opened door. His cold eyes were red with rage, and he leaned with all his might against the weight of the stone. "You're going to rot in jail for the rest of your life!"

"*Now!*" Frank shouted to Quentin.

Quentin turned to the woods and took a deep breath. He crossed his paws over his chest, closed his eyes, and jumped.

He fell, plummeting through space, thinking, *Ohgodsohgodsoh* as the cold air rushed against his face and ears, and then landed with surprising gentleness in a snowbank that immediately buried him up to his knees. He struggled to regain his balance and saw his pack a few feet away, resting in a deep hole made by the impact. *I did it! I did it!* he thought and then, for a fleeting, irrational second, wanted to jump again.

A few moments later, there was a heavy *thump* nearby. Frank had landed and was struggling to reach his pack. A hail of arrows rained down on them and there were shouts from the wall above. Zack had landed on his back, deep in snow, not too far from Quentin. Arrows zinged around them, but the tower light provided little illumination to the distant ground and the moon was now partly hidden by dark clouds, filled with snow. It was clear Wally and the others could not see well enough to find a target.

Quentin made his way to Zack. In a few minutes, Frank joined them, dragging the packs. In the dim light the three friends embraced.

"Q! Are you all right?" Zack's sad brown eyes were anxious. "That couldn't have been easy."

"I'm fine," Quentin said, the good feeling already fading; he felt more exhausted than he'd ever been in his life.

They struggled through the snow. The light from the tower grew faint; the shouts of Wally and Dan and the others were far away. In a short while, they were at the edge of Wildwood Forest, illuminated only by the moon, hidden, then revealed, then hidden again behind the increasingly dense clouds.

The three rabbits walked abreast into the woods, silent. Quentin's wounded arm throbbed and he began to shake and sweat so much he could no longer carry his satchel. He stopped walking as Frank and Zack continued ahead. At one point Zack turned and waved encouragingly. Quentin raised his good arm in response. He'd catch up when he could. Now his knees shook and he dropped to the ground.

He leaned against a tree and retched.

Then it was over; his head cleared, his heart stopped pounding. He scooped up some snow and washed his face, then put more snow in his mouth and swallowed the cold, pure water as it melted.

Something tight inside him uncurled. *I'm ready*, he thought.

Frank and Zack stopped beneath a snow-covered fallen tree on a low hill. How had they gotten so far ahead? Zack brushed snow away from the ground while Frank unpacked two small blankets and what looked like some packages, probably food.

Suddenly, as Quentin watched, three large rabbits wearing heavy boots and jackets and carrying clubs leaped out from behind the trees and grabbed Frank and Zack, roughly tying their paws behind their back and throwing them to the ground. Quentin could hear Frank's voice, protesting, and Zack, explaining, and the curt responses of the large rabbits.

Quentin couldn't move. Were these Wally's forces, already mobilized to prevent their escape? They didn't appear to be in uniform. Could they be the rebels? But then why take Zack and Frank prisoner? He watched in horror as the three rabbits lifted Frank and Zack to their feet and pushed them forward. In a few moments they had vanished into the woods.

It was very quiet. Stunned, Quentin walked slowly toward the fallen tree and saw that Frank and Zack had left their packs, partially opened, on the ground. Their tracks led into the forest and disappeared in the darkness.

I should go after them, Quentin thought. *I could follow them and try to find a way to save them. They would do it for me.*

He started into the woods, following the deep footprints in front of him. After a while, as the darkness closed in, he stopped. *Wait. Does this make sense?* The trail was now almost impossible to see; the night had grown colder and he realized he was starving. *I'll never find them in the dark, anyway.* He turned back to the clearing where the half-opened packs sat silent, waiting.

I'll look for them first thing in the morning, he thought. *Right now I need shelter and I need food.*

Now he wished he'd paid more attention when his friends had talked about camping on summer vacations. Knowing how to build a fire or find water — information he'd decided he'd never need — would certainly have been helpful right now.

Wait a moment. It can't be that difficult, he told himself. *Use your head.*

He looked around and gathered some large fallen branches, shaking them free of snow with his good arm, and piled them up against the tree, forming a basic shelter. He dragged the packs, blankets, and packages of food and tried to stow them neatly underneath it. Breathing hard, he finished clearing the ground of snow as best he could, sat down on an unfolded blanket, and wrapped the other one about his shoulders. He leaned back against the fallen log. Then he took off his mittens and opened one of the food packets — it was an enormous eggplant-and-dried-tomato-sandwich — and wolfed it down.

Probably I should ration the food. He rummaged inside Frank's pack again, finding amidst the sandwiches, bandages, and matches, two small packages, fragrant with cinnamon. Apple turnovers! *I'll save them,* Quentin thought, although his mouth watered. *If we find Charlie, we can give them to him.*

I mean, when.

He closed his eyes.

When he opened them it was morning and a pale light filled the sky. Quentin stood up and stretched. He'd slept in the same seated position with his head on his bent knees the entire night. His back ached and his injured arm was stiff.

All around him, the forest was silent and white. The tracks of the rabbits and Frank and Zack had long since disappeared in the light dusting of snow that had fallen during the night. Quentin seemed to be in a small clearing of sorts, carpeted with ivy and ground cover but with few shrubs. Only the tall firs stood guard in an irregular semicircle around him. If he had to be lost, this was as good a place as any.

Lost! I'm not lost. Frank and Zack will come and get me, either by themselves or by directing the rebels — if that's who those goons were. I'll just wait for them. I certainly can't go back to Stonehaven. I've probably broken every law we have! Maybe the rebels will find me before Wally and Dan organize a search party.

Why haven't they done that?

Of course, I'm assuming that Frank and Zack are still alive.

But maybe they're dead, or suffering in some way, beaten or imprisoned, trying to prevent their captors from finding out about me!

Quentin's mind filled with images so terrifying he cried out, "No!" his voice muffled in the snow-filled woods.

Suppose they never come back. What will I do?

I am not going to think things like that. They are fine and I will be fine too. I have food, shelter, and blankets. I have matches, and I can make a fire if I have to. They'll come back for me. It's just a question of time.

He sat down again and reached inside Frank's pack, devoured another sandwich and then carefully removed every item from Zack's satchel searching for — there it is! A bottle of *plumbo* and a corkscrew. Good old Zack!

Quentin opened the bottle and tilted it above his head. The tartness burned, and in a few moments he was quite warm. He recorked the bottle, wrapped it carefully, and sat back, looking around.

Gods, I'm all alone.

Something poked him in the side; he looked down at his pocket and saw *Rabbit Heroes for All Times.*

He pulled out the book, its cover worn and pages yellowed. Inside, on the flyleaf, was the enormous, crooked *Q* where as a toddler he'd attempted to write his name with a blue crayon.

He began to read the familiar introduction: *"Although many think that rabbits are timid and easily frightened, the fact is that we have been known throughout history for our bravery and courage under the most difficult circumstances. Here are some stories of the bravest of the brave."*

Quentin lifted his head. It was beginning to snow. The sky was a light gray; the profile of the fir trees sharply outlined against it. There was not a sound.

He put the book aside and covered his face with his paws.

12

Gerard:
Nice Clothes

Gerard rose early after a sleepless night. The conversation with Isaac had replayed itself in his dreams, and at one point he'd awakened and walked restlessly about his apartment, smoking, unable to calm down. For some reason, he kept seeing the painted bookshelves and the almost invisible safe — *like a stage set, a façade of civility,* he thought — covering a blank wall and disguising the hidden container for the gold Isaac would collect from the trade in sentient rabbits. *With my assistance. And there's not a thing I can do about it.*

A while later he picked up a quantity of boxed, gold coins from Isaac and fitted them neatly into a briefcase, along with a large, empty burlap sack. Isaac had met him at the door and handed him the heavy box.

"Remember — I trust you," he said, "and I'll know if you betray me."

Gerard nodded. "Yes."

But after walking through Wildwood on a beautiful day, Gerard felt his equilibrium returning. *This is no different from any other assignment I have ever accepted,* he told himself as he trudged along the quiet path. *Have I not handled uncomfortable situations before? It's merely a job, a role to play. I see this now as a question of attitude. The right attitude can enable a minor character to steal a scene — as I know, perhaps, better than most,* he thought with a smile. *The wrong attitude can cause stage fright and memory lapses. Besides, I have no choice. Might as well make the best of it.*

He tried not to think about Isaac's last words.

When Gerard finally arrived at Inn the Forest, it was dusk. The innkeeper greeted him with a grudging hospitality; her partner, however, was friendlier and more welcoming. The food turned out to be quite good. *I can stop here on a regular basis,* he thought, as he sat in a comfortably worn leather chair in the lobby, smoking. *This is going to be easier than I expected.*

The next morning he left the Inn early, carefully hiding the briefcase at the bottom of his overnight bag and piling his change of clothes on top of it. Then he started down one of the overgrown paths, following the map Isaac had given him. Gerard soon found himself in a clearing, looking up at the enormous firs, the lovely light and the sweet scent of spring woodland flowers all around him. This was too delightful to ignore. He sat down on a rock and patted his pockets, found a pencil and a piece of paper, leaned on his knee, and gnawed the end of the pencil thoughtfully.

Birds are singing, he wrote,

Time is winging

Quickly flies the newborn day,

Sun is shining

Insects flying . . .

Flying and shining, Gerard thought. *Hmmm. I can do better. But I do like the sound of* "quickly flies the newborn day." *Archaic yet . . . appealing.* For a moment he sat gazing into the woods.

He became aware of an odd scent. Then he heard footsteps crunching on the forest floor behind him. Gerard stood and turned as a rabbit, dressed in a gray uniform, walked toward him. The rabbit was thin and hatless, and he had a knife tucked into his belt. There was that odd bald circle at the top of his head and long fur at the side of his face. *There are cures for mange,* Gerard thought fleetingly. *Why not avail yourself of them?*

The strange smell was rabbit-like, he thought, but with a difference. This scent held no attraction, no mouthwatering promise. It was an identifier, the way one would recognize the presence of a lilac or a rotten egg — or raccoon or rat, for that matter: duly noted, but not tempted to ingest. How could this be? If rabbits didn't smell like food, why would they be of any interest to the foxes? Perhaps Isaac knew that once rabbit meat

188

was sautéed with onions and oil and a white wine sauce no one would notice.

Gerard found he was breathing with difficulty. Yet at the same time it surprised him that the creature who was negotiating with a weasel should be so unprepossessing. Didn't the rabbits have a more formidable representative? Someone who might intimidate by his sheer size or demeanor? (But could a rabbit of *any* size intimidate?) Gerard hastily put the pencil and paper back into his pocket. *He's going to speak next,* Gerard thought. *What will that be like?*

The rabbit stopped some distance away and looked at Gerard.

"You know who I am?" it said in a high, almost female voice.

Did they all talk this way, like preadolescents? Why not! Anything was possible.

"I assume you are the rabbit named Dan," Gerard replied, after clearing his throat. He reached into another jacket pocket and pulled out a small cigarette case. Stage business. Something to do while he tried to remember his lines. He was pleased to see his paws did not shake. Gerard lit the cigarette and the comforting aroma of sassafras filled the clearing.

"Yes. I am Dan, and you are . . . ?"

"Gerard," he said, consciously making his voice one or two levels deeper than normal. *How embarrassing to have such a voice,* he thought. *But how perfect on the stage in a female role!* "You do not smell like prey."

"And I do not detect a predator scent," Dan said with obvious surprise.

So mutual self-awareness has neutralized the prey-predator bond, Gerard thought. *I've never thought about it, but of course it's true. Among all the sentient creatures I know, there are none who interest me as food, and vice versa, although surely this was not the case for my ancient ancestors. Interesting.* Dan didn't need to douse himself with skunk the night he visited Isaac after all. But how could he have known that? He'd never spoken to a fox.

Dan seemed to be thinking the same thing. "That will make this easier," he murmured. "Follow me." He walked farther into the forest and in a short while stopped. Gerard looked up and saw the wall of the fortress looming in the distance. Dan turned onto a narrow path for a few moments. He appeared to be looking for something. "Ah," he said. "Here it is."

He had stopped in front of the opening of a small cave, almost hidden by the thick foliage and underbrush that grew around it. Dan gestured to Gerard, and the two walked inside the shallow entry. The rabbit brushed away the sand and forest debris from the floor and revealed a roughly hewn round stone, almost flush with the surface. He reached for a short, sturdy oak branch with a chiseled point that rested against the side of the cave and, with some effort, pried up the stone.

Gerard stubbed out his cigarette and peered into the dark space beneath. "I see some steps. Is this the tunnel Isaac mentioned?"

"Yes. It begins on the other side of the fortress wall. No one knows about it except . . . a few of us. Here is where the product will be delivered."

"And I assume this is where you want to receive payment?"

"Correct. I assume you would prefer to transport . . . inanimate . . . product?"

The rabbit's face was blandly unreadable.

"Inanimate product!" Gerard exclaimed. "What a remarkable euphemism!"

Dan looked at him coldly. "You are taking money to transport freshly killed rabbits to serve as food for a limited number of wealthy foxes, in clear violation of the law; rabbits who can talk, think, read, work — who are in many respects not that different from you," he said. "You are hardly in a position to feel superior to me. What euphemism do you employ to ease *your* conscience?"

Touché, Gerard thought. *Still, I'm not knowingly serving up my own kind into the ovens and sauté pans of enemy gourmands. I am merely a facilitator.* But all he said was, "Let's not

191

quibble about morality. You have your reasons, I have mine. Don't you agree?"

Dan did not answer and turned away. "I will meet you here at midnight on the appointed evening. If you bring a lantern you should have no trouble finding the cave. I've drawn a map, just in case." He handed Gerard a folded piece of paper. "We will deliver no more than two or three . . . at a time."

"'We'?"

"My . . . assistant, a rabbit named Wally. You will probably need help in transporting the product back to Foxboro. Find someone you can trust and pay him well."

Martin, Gerard thought, recalling the greasy apron and the ugly plaid cap. *He'd be perfect.*

"And if you're not here?"

"I'll be here. We'll be picking up the gold you are going to be bringing, remember?"

"Ah. The gold, of course."

"Any questions?"

"Yes. What weapons are you going to buy with the gold, and from whom?"

Dan laughed. "Do you really think I'm going to answer that?" He pulled a candle from his pocket, lit it with a match, and climbed down into the dark tunnel, taking the oak staff with him, and closing the lid from the inside.

Gerard retraced his steps and returned to the Inn. It wasn't until much later that he thought about food, but found, once he sat down to eat, that he had no appetite. Instead he spent the evening drinking red wine in the lobby, smoking cigarettes, and staring into the fire.

A few nights later, Martin sat beside him in the Inn the Forest dining room, studying the map, his bushy brows furrowed in concentration,

"It don't look too far from here," he said, following the route with a stubby, unmanicured paw.

"It isn't," Gerard said. Martin had ordered beer and was finishing his second, gulping from the bottle and wiping his mouth on a ragged sleeve.

Gerard looked away. He'd paid Martin well and had promised him more. The weasel, seeing a financial advantage, had turned over the operation of his store to a distant relative and promised to devote himself entirely to Gerard's service. He seemed trustworthy enough, in that he obviously needed money, and when Gerard had mentioned that there was a connection to Isaac — without being too specific — Martin gasped.

"Isaac?" he breathed. "The same Isaac who runs Foxboro?"

"Yes. I see you've heard of him."

"Ain't everyone?"

"So you understand what can happen to you if you talk about this."

Martin nodded. "It ain't necessary to spell it out none." He counted the gold coins Gerard had dropped into his paw. "I ain't never saying nothing to nobody."

"Good. Then we have a deal."

"Deal." They shook on it. Gerard wiped his paw on his trousers.

Gerard had persuaded Becky to lend him a duplicate key to the front door, explaining he would be out late and didn't want to disturb her.

"How thoughtful," Becky had exclaimed, without questioning where he would be going. "Of course you may have a key. You have an honest face, Mr. Gerard. I know I can trust you."

Interesting how everyone says that, Gerard thought. He bowed. "And so you can, my dear Miss Becky," he said, taking the key from her outstretched paw. "And so you can."

Martin had arrived at the Inn shortly before dinner with a tattered suitcase and a small wheelbarrow but, as previously agreed, had provided no explanation to the innkeepers. Becky, sensing his unwillingness to discuss it, had simply offered storage space for the wheelbarrow inside a toolshed at the back of the main building.

Much later, when the fire in the hearth had burned to cinders, Gerard and Martin left the Inn. The front door opened silently on well-oiled hinges; the air was dry and mild. Gerard met Martin emerging from the shed with the wheelbarrow and dropped the sack with the gold coins into it. He walked ahead, swinging the lantern.

When they reached the entry to the cave, Gerard checked his dented, tarnished pocket watch under the lantern light. "We're a few minutes early," he said. Martin rested the wheelbarrow on the ground and probed the cave entry with the lantern. Gerard lit a cigarette and looked at the starry sky. *Let's get this over with.*

At the sound of stone grating on stone, he stubbed out the cigarette and sighed with relief. Martin stood near him with the lantern, and they watched as the circular stone on the floor of the cave slowly moved. Gerard could see a dim light flickering against the walls of the tunnel, then Dan's face and his arm, holding a small lantern. In a moment the rabbit was standing before them, pulling a sack behind him. Gerard heard heavy breathing and cursing.

"Damn it!" a growly voice said. "Why are they so damn heavy?"

"Push!" Dan squeaked.

"What in the gods' names do you think I'm doing?" the deep voice replied. Dan heaved the large blue burlap sack tied with a rough cord onto the floor and reached a paw into the tunnel.

"Here. Can you see the steps?"

"I see them," the voice replied. "And I don't need your help."

Another rabbit, this one larger, with what appeared to be prematurely white fur and cold blue eyes, lifted himself with difficulty out of the tunnel. He wore a gray military uniform, snug around the middle, that gave the impression he had been stuffed into it, like a sausage. Wally, the assistant.

"Gods!" Martin gasped. "It's true." He backed up against the cave wall and slid to the ground, breathing rapidly through his mouth.

The large rabbit turned to Dan. "You were right," he said "They *can* talk! And they don't have the predator stink."

"Yes, yes," Dan said impatiently. "Now can we get on with this, Wally?"

Wally thrust his face into Dan's, and Dan backed up. "You have a problem with something, little baby-voice? Just remember — this may have been your idea, but without my muscle to set it in motion you would still be a small-time thief, stealing wood from the community lumberyard and cheating widows out of their life savings."

Dan moved aside. "You don't frighten me. I can always find someone to take your place — and your gold."

"Just try it." Wally raised a huge paw over his head and moved closer to Dan.

"Please, please!" Gerard said, lifting the sack out of the

wheelbarrow. "We're wasting time. Here." He offered it to Dan, who grabbed it and hefted it appreciatively.

"We need to count this," he said, and handed it to Wally, who sat down with the sack. He moved the lantern close and started to count the gold coins, stacking them in neat piles before him. At one point he looked up. "There's dinner," he said to Gerard, pointing to the blue sack on the cave floor. "Enjoy."

Dan caught Gerard's eye, then looked away.

Gerard gestured to Martin, who leaped to his feet and heaved the burlap sack into the wheelbarrow. "Maybe there ain't nothing in it," he whispered to Gerard. "Maybe we should check to see what's inside."

"You do it."

Martin undid the cord and opened the sack, then lifted the lantern and peered into it. He turned to Gerard and nodded. "Two adults, one small one. No blood. Nice clothes," he added as he retied the heavy cord.

Still clothed? What kind of barbarians *were* these creatures?

"It's all here," Wally interrupted, getting up from the floor and replacing the coins in the sack. "Let's go."

Dan walked over to Gerard. "In the future, we don't have to have these discussions. A simple exchange of . . . *prod-uct* . . . will be all that's required. That and counting the gold, of course," he added.

"Of course."

"Stop talking to them," Wally said. "They're weasels."

Wally took the sack of gold and stepped down into the tunnel. Dan followed with the lantern. Gerard leaned down, touched his arm briefly, and had the small satisfaction of seeing Dan jump. "Next time," he said softly, "no clothes."

"Sensitive, are we?" Dan said with a short laugh.

"No clothes," Gerard repeated firmly.

"We'll see."

Gerard turned away. When he turned back, Dan and Wally had disappeared into the tunnel and the stone was being scraped back into place.

"Here." Gerard reached into his pocket and dropped two more coins into Martin's outstretched paw. "Do your job."

"Right." Martin started slowly down the path with the wheelbarrow and its contents. Gerard followed, holding the lantern. "One thing I don't understand," Martin said, turning back to him. "I seen those rabbits, but I don't got no appetite for them. That ain't never happened to me before. Of course, I ain't never seen no rabbit talkin' and not wearin' no clothes before, neither. Maybe that's it?"

Gerard did not reply.

They parted company at the front door of the Inn. Martin was to continue on the road through the night and meet one of the guards at the gate to Isaac's mansion. The guard would take the contents of the wheelbarrow to Isaac; Martin would go home and sleep and later in the week would return to the Inn with the wheelbarrow.

Gerard would spend a few days at the Inn and at some point return to Foxboro, pick up the gold from Isaac — no one trusted Martin with that task — and meet Martin at the Inn for the next exchange.

"Don't waste any time," Gerard said, as he handed Martin the lantern. "I'm going to be seeing Isaac. He'll know if you followed instructions."

"I don't never waste no time," Martin said cheerfully. "Not when there's gold in my pocket and more to come." He disappeared down the path.

Gerard lit another cigarette and stood silently at the entry to the Inn. He'd already been paid handsomely and could see a future of luxury and freedom: a new, larger living space, a gold watch and fob, a ring he'd seen in a store window and admired wistfully. Birthday presents for his nephews. His sad and disappointing departure from the theater company could be put behind him forever, and while his fellow actors scraped out a living performing the classics for the unappreciative masses, Gerard would be living well, never having to worry about his next meal, or cigarettes, or nice clothes.

Clothes.

They were wearing clothes.

13
Harry:
A Way to Win

Harry tossed and turned on the upper bunk bed for hours. Elton's regular snoring had become an irritant instead of a soporific, and Harry was restless. *I'm wasting time,* he thought. *Why not leave now? I could be at the fortress by the end of the day tomorrow. I'll find Gerard, confront him with what I know, and get the answers I need. If I take Elton's lantern, traveling in the dark will be easier. He probably has another one collapsed inside his sample case.*

Harry jumped down and lit one of the stubby, fat candles. He packed his things in the flickering darkness, keeping the map and the compass close to the top. Then he picked up the lantern and unfolded Isaac's walking stick, blew out the candle, and left the cabin, closing the door quietly behind him.

On the porch, Harry struck a match and lit the lantern. The night was calm and not very cold; the snow had stopped. He started walking along the lake and soon found the main road, where he turned south.

It felt good to be alone again. The time with Elton had

been diverting: throwing moochy-poochy stones, playing —
and winning — badger checkers, but now Harry was focused on
his mission. He trotted along the path, the lantern swinging, the
walking stick thumping. The floor of the forest on either side of
him, periodically illuminated by moonlight, looked strangely
magical; the firs were dark against the starry sky. Harry doused
the lantern.

He had been on the road for some time when he smelled
rabbit in the distance, although there was something odd about
the scent. What was it? He broke into a run and in a short while
heard something rolling and bumping on the hard-packed
snow ahead of him, accompanied by a voice, singing. The
strange scent became stronger.

Harry stepped off the road into the trees.

Coming around a bend in the road was a weasel, pushing a
heavy wheelbarrow with a lantern dangling from one of its
arms. He drank regularly from a bottle he kept in his jacket.

"Gold in my pocket and more to come," he sang in a boozy
baritone and thumped on the handle. "Gold in my *pocket*" — he
held a long high note — "and more" — *thump thump* — "much
more" — *thumpity thump thump thump* "to come!" He stopped
to chug-a-lug.

The weasel dropped the wheelbarrow and sat down heavily
alongside it. In the lantern light Harry could see a worn, plaid

cap and a tattered jacket. The creature's face was hidden by the cap's visor, but when he tilted the bottle to gulp the contents, Harry saw a flash of bushy eyebrows and a scar on his chin.

What is a weasel doing alone at night, pushing a wheelbarrow and singing about gold in his pocket?

Harry stepped onto the path.

The weasel started. "Oops," he said, hastily stuffing the bottle into a deep pocket and leaping unsteadily to his feet. "Who's that?" He squinted into the dark. "You ain't never plannin' to rob me none, I hope. I ain't got nothin' on me but what's in this 'barrow, and that ain't for takin'.'" Then he seemed to remember his song. "Those words didn't never mean nothin'," he added hastily. "I ain't got no gold. Honest. No gold."

The weasel took a step closer. "Oh, it's *you*, sir! Mr. Gerard told me you might be joinin' us to see the operation. He ain't never said when, though."

Mr. Gerard? How is he involved in this?

"Well, I can tell you, Mr. Isaac," the weasel went on. "It's smooth. Smooth as an otter's behind. We ain't never had no trouble with them stinkin' rabbits."

Harry just nodded. The less he said, the more he'd find out, and he had a feeling he was about to find out everything.

The weasel whipped off his cap. "I'm Martin," he said

with a deferential nod. "I seen you in Foxboro, but we ain't never met. I deliver the product to one of your guards, sir."

"Right," Harry said, trying to approximate Isaac's snarl. "And you've been doing this for a while, correct?"

"Since the spring, sir. Ain't that when you hired Mr. Gerard? Ain't that when he hired me?"

This was it. This was the connection he'd been looking for. But what is this product he keeps talking about? Harry turned his attention to the wheelbarrow. "Well, what have you got there?" he asked gruffly.

Martin gestured. "Same as always. Ain't nothin' different. Wanna look?"

Leaning on the walking stick, Harry remembered to limp over to the 'barrow. Martin stood alongside it; Harry could sense his nervousness. The weasel reached in and fumbled with the drawstring that tied a burlap sack. He opened the sack, reached for the bottom, and shook it roughly, dumping the contents onto the snow-covered road.

Three rabbits, a middle-aged male and two adolescents, tumbled out into the moonlight, and all dead, judging by the look of them, killed within the last twenty-four hours. There was no blood; all three had been strangled.

Harry was shocked. Three rabbits but only the strange scent — how was that possible? It was rabbit, certainly, but there was nothing *delicious* about it, nothing tempting. Even more surprising, the rabbits were wearing clothes. The male wore boots and trousers of a heavy, woven material; the adolescents also wore shirts and boots. Why would anyone put clothes on a rabbit? "What's this?" Harry asked, gesturing to the clothes.

"What? Oh. Ain't that the way we always deliver 'em?" Martin replied. "Don't never remember no shipment that didn't have no clothes. Mr. Gerard wasn't happy none, the first time he seen it. Seems it don't matter none to him no more, though."

"Right," Harry said again with a curt nod. *I'll figure it out later,* he thought. In the meantime, he was about to find out how Gerard and Isaac were connected. "Where is Gerard?"

"Oh, he ain't nowhere," Martin replied with a shrug, laboriously stuffing the rabbits back into the sack and tying it tightly. "Not doin' nothin' but sleepin' in his bed at the Inn while I make my delivery, as per usual. He won't be doin' nothin' except meetin' with you to pick up more gold. Then in a few days we ain't doin' nothin' but collectin' the next shipment. Just doin' what we always done."

"Very well," Harry said gruffly. "Stop wasting time, then, and keep moving. Wait!" Harry stopped the wheelbarrow with his walking stick. "I'll take one of those." He reached in, opened the sack, and pulled out the large male. He was hungry, although there was nothing in the rabbit scent that tempted him. Maybe they would taste good anyway. After all, could Harry the Fox walk away from a 'barrow full of rabbits? Wouldn't he regret it tomorrow? Weren't they fresh killed? It had been years since he'd eaten rabbit! He grabbed it by the ears and started to drag it away.

"Stop!"

Martin had pulled himself up to his full height and was staring at Harry. He held a stubby knife and was walking toward him unsteadily, his paw shaking. "I'm sorry, sir," Martin said, his voice quavering, "but I can't never let you do that."

"What did you say?"

The weasel seemed to shrink into himself. "I can't never let you do that. I have a contract, ain't I? Ain't I deliverin' a specifical amount of the stinkin' product to the guards at your front gate? Ain't there a number written right here?" He fumbled for a piece of paper in his pocket with his free paw. "If I don't deliver no product, I ain't never gettin' no money. And probably worse."

"But those rabbits are mine! Whether I get them now or later makes no difference. Have you forgotten who I *am*?" Harry said, experiencing a moment of genuine outrage. Pretending to be Isaac was easier than he expected. He turned toward Martin, his walking stick raised.

Martin cowered, his paws protecting his head, and dropped the knife. "Please don't kill me, sir," he said, his voice a high-pitched whine. "Please. I ain't doing nothin' but my job." He fell to his knees and began to weep. "Don't kill me!"

Harry stopped. He suddenly recalled John, the fox who'd asked Isaac for an extension on his loan when he and Isaac had gone to the bank. The image of the bloody cane returned and he put the walking stick down.

"All right. Listen, Martin," he said in his normal voice, "I'm not Isaac. I'm Harry, his brother. Tell me what this is all about and . . . I won't say anything to Mr. Gerard about the bottle in your jacket pocket."

Martin fell back on the road. "You ain't Mr. Isaac?" He wiped his nose on his sleeve. "You ain't going to kill me?"

"No, I'm not going to kill you." Harry returned the rabbit to the wheelbarrow.

"I thought for sure you was Mr. Isaac," Martin said, squinting at Harry suspiciously. "You look like him. You sound like him." He stuffed the rabbit back into the sack. "You got a stick." He nodded toward it. "But you ain't him?"

"No."

Martin turned away. "You *say* you ain't," he said under his breath. "And I say *maybe* I believe you." He took out the bottle and drank from it deeply.

Harry ignored him and pointed to the wheelbarrow. "I don't like the way these rabbits smell," he said, trying to move things along. "They have no scent at all, not in the regular way. What's going on?"

"I swore to Mr. Gerard I wouldn't never say nothin' to nobody. I could get into trouble." Then he saw Harry's face.

Martin told Harry everything he knew.

Harry was stunned. "Are you saying Wally and Dan are *rabbits*? Talking? Thinking? And that the whole colony is like them?"

"Hard to believe, ain't it?" Martin said, nodding sympathetically.

"You're making this up!"

"I swear to you, Mr. Harry. I ain't making nothing up. I couldn't."

"What you're telling me is impossible. Rabbits are prey — they are *food*. Food doesn't talk and wear clothes. It doesn't trade for gold. How stupid do you think I am?"

"Just listen. I'm sayin' I ain't never seen nothin' like it, neither. First time ain't I almost fainted? Even now, it still don't make no sense to me."

"Dan . . . Wally — they're selling their own kind to be . . . eaten as food . . . in exchange for gold? That's disgusting," Harry said. "It's against natural law to eat any creature that can think and speak — and it's illegal in every culture I've ever heard about. Besides, sentient creatures don't smell like food." *That explains these rabbits. And I almost ate one anyway.* He swallowed hard; just the thought of it made him gag.

Martin nodded. "You're right, Mr. Harry," he said, nodding vigorously again. "You are so right. You definitely ain't wrong about that!" He'd found another bottle in a different pocket after tossing the empty one into the forest. He offered it to Harry, who shook his head.

"What is Isaac doing with them?"

Martin shrugged and opened the bottle. "Maybe Mr. Gerard knows, but he ain't telling me nothin'. But you know what, Mr. Harry? Old Martin here knows." He tapped his head, hard. "I ain't stupid. He ain't doin' nothin' but sellin' them to his rich friends for food. Ain't I been to his house at night? Ain't I seen the lights and smelled the smells?" He smacked his lips. "There ain't no one who knows where the rabbits come from," he said, starting to laugh and sounding like a barking dog. "*Harf, harf!* But I do. *Harf, harf, harf!*" He slapped his knee. "I know where they come from! *Harf, harf!*" He drank deeply from the bottle and wiped his mouth on his sleeve.

"When is the next . . . shipment?" Harry asked.

"In a few days. You ain't going to do nothing to stop this, are you?" Martin asked, looking alarmed.

"Why should I stop it? It's none of my business," Harry said, standing up. "You have nothing to worry about, Martin. I'll keep your secret."

Martin scrambled to his feet. "Thank you, Mr. Harry. Now you need to swear you won't tell nobody neither."

What an idiot. Isn't that what 'I'll keep your secret' means? But Harry said, "I swear." They shook on it.

"I need to get movin'," Martin said. "I ain't never been late before and I ain't goin' to start now. Good-bye, Mr. Harry."

Harry reached into his jacket pocket. "Martin," he said. "Can *you* keep a secret?" He held out one of the large bills Isaac had given him.

Martin nodded.

"You didn't see me and we didn't talk." He handed the bill to the weasel.

Martin nodded again, looking at the bill. His face was serious. "I ain't never seen you and we ain't never talked. Never seen you. Ain't never talked. You can count on me." He tucked the bill away in his pocket, lifted the end of the wheelbarrow, and continued toward Foxboro.

Harry started down the road again and then stopped. *If Isaac knows about the rabbits, then why did he send me to the fortress to investigate? As for Gerard, he obviously never had any intention of meeting me at the cabins. He went to this cave Martin mentioned to facilitate another exchange of "product." Disgusting. There's nothing wrong with his knee. He had to make up something to tell Elton.*

The encounter with Martin had slowed Harry's progress, but in other ways had greatly enhanced it. *Now I understand what "Remember: I trust you" means. Isaac must be making a fortune selling the rabbits for food. The money he'd be paying this Wally and Dan would be a pittance compared to what he was collecting. That's why he had so much money in the bank!*

I should have asked for more.

His mind raced. Who had killed the other fox scouts Isaac had mentioned — Wally and Dan? Harry laughed out loud. Foxes killed by rabbits had to be someone's idea of a joke. Ridiculous. And the "irregularities" Isaac had referred to, the promises he'd had to make — were they connected to this trade in sentient creatures?

Could he believe *anything* Isaac had told him?

Harry stopped in his tracks again. *Of course. In addition to being disgusting, Isaac's plan was a criminal act with serious consequences. All I need is proof.*

I have found a way to win at Harry the Fox checkers.

... "I swear it's true, Your Honor. I saw for myself and heard the story of this morally reprehensible trade. I had no choice but to bring the matter to the proper authorities."

The High Judge was impressed. "You are a remarkable fox, and an upstanding citizen," he said.

"Not even fraternal loyalty prevented you from doing your duty."

"No, Your Honor." Harry bowed his head modestly. "My utter devotion to a high moral code was stronger than the deep, abiding love I felt for my brother. I had no choice."

"The Court commends you, Harry." The High Judge, normally austere and reserved, smiled, reached down from the bench, and shook Harry's paw. The full gallery of spectators rose to its feet and cheered.

The Judge turned to Isaac. "Have you anything to say for yourself, you despicable creature?"

"Only that I never understood what a fine fox my brother Harry is," Isaac said in a low voice, "and how in every way he is superior to me." Then Isaac, his head bowed in shame, was led away in chains, to serve a life sentence in prison. . . .

Harry couldn't help himself. He did a little dance on the snowy road. *I can bring him down,* he thought exultantly, *and I can look good in the process.*

14
Harry:
So It's True

Harry walked the path with unflagging energy, his conversation with Martin ringing in his ears. He decided to return to the Inn to confront Gerard, perhaps inquire innocently about his knee. Then Harry could tell him what he knew; Gerard would deny his involvement, of course, but Harry would persist. After that . . . he'd wait and see. And there was no rush to get home, either. *Let Isaac think that his plan to get me out of town for two weeks, for whatever reason, has been successful. I can still return early and go straight to the High Court. Whatever Isaac is cooking up,* he thought with a grim laugh, *will disintegrate once the Court brings him into custody. As for the rest of the money Isaac owes me, I'll just collect it before I turn him in. A double victory.*

The day dawned clear and cold, but by midmorning it had started to snow again. Harry hardly noticed. The conversation with Martin had been stunning.

It wasn't only Gerard's connection with Isaac, although that knowledge provided Harry with unending satisfaction.

No. It was the idea of rabbits who could talk and think and wear clothes. *I still can't imagine having a conversation with one. What would we talk about, anyway? The weather? What could we possibly have in common?*

After a while he reached a point where the road turned toward the south; by late afternoon the sky was gray, and the snow fell in a steady curtain before him. As Harry walked along, he became aware of that odd rabbit scent again. He stopped. It couldn't be Martin and his wheelbarrow. The weasel would be close to Foxboro by now, making his delivery to Isaac's guards. The scent could not be coming from the fortress — he was too far from there, wasn't he? — and there was no wind to carry it this distance. He walked cautiously toward a large, rocky outcropping where the scent seemed strongest, and peered around it.

In a small clearing, he saw a rabbit wearing a jacket and boots, sitting under a roughly built lean-to and surrounded by several open packs and a small book. The snow fell silently over the scene. The rabbit sat with its head in its paws, a blanket wrapped around its shoulders.

"Oh, gods," it said, and its voice was muffled. "Oh, gods."

So it's true! Harry thought. The shock of hearing the rabbit speak made his heart beat faster. He turned away and scooped up some soft snow and rubbed it on his face. The cold was startling; he shook his head to clear it, then turned back. The creature was still there, only now it stood up, wrapped the blanket more tightly around its shoulders, and started to pace.

"It had to be the rebels and they have to have figured out by now that they made a mistake," it muttered, and Harry noted its foreign-sounding accent. The rabbit ran a paw over its eyes. "Gods! I'm talking to myself! Another day and night like this and I'll be completely out of my mind." The rabbit sat down again. "If I go off looking for Zack and Frank, I'll just get lost and they'll never find me. I have to stay here and wait — but where *are* they?" It opened the book, then slammed it closed and rested its head on its paws again.

Harry stepped into the clearing. "Who are you?"

The rabbit, startled at the sound of Harry's voice, jumped and peered through the falling snow. "A fox! You can talk!" It staggered back against the fallen tree. "Why didn't I pick up your scent? I must be dreaming! Whatever you are, don't come near me," he said, reaching behind the nearest pack for a large, heavy stick. "I'll defend myself, I swear it!"

Harry didn't move. Dan or Wally would not have been surprised to hear him speak. Then who was this one? The rabbit had long, delicate ears and didn't look terribly strong, but Harry recognized the defensive posture of a desperate creature and knew from experience what strength could lie behind it. "You don't need to worry," he said. "You don't smell like food."

The rabbit clutched the stick more tightly. "Who are you? What do you want? Oh, I know what you want, don't answer that."

Harry didn't move. "My name is Harry, and I told you," he replied with irritation. "You don't smell edible. And besides, it's against the law."

"Law? You have *laws*?"

"Surely you know there's a law against using a sentient creature for food. You *appear* to qualify."

"I know the law! What do you think I am? But you're a fox," the rabbit said. "Just because you don't smell like one and know how to talk doesn't mean you'll obey the law. Why should I trust you?"

Very true, thought Harry. "I don't have to justify myself to anyone, certainly not to a rabbit," he said scornfully. "You just proved *my* point. Just because you can speak doesn't mean you can think."

The clearing was growing darker; Harry lit Elton's lantern, which made a small yellow circle on the snow. It was getting very cold.

Harry sat down, facing the rabbit, who dropped the stick and slid slowly to the ground. "This is the strangest thing that has ever happened to me," the rabbit said. "If someone had told me yesterday that I would be sitting in the middle of the forest, all alone, talking to a fox who could talk back to me . . . !

Maybe I *am* dreaming." The rabbit shook his head. "Gods, I hope so."

"If anyone had told me two days ago that I'd be *talking* to a rabbit instead of *eat* . . ." The rabbit looked up, shocked. "Never mind," Harry said. "Do you have a name?"

"Quentin," the rabbit said. "My name is Quentin."

"What are you doing here? Who are you waiting for? Who are the rebels?"

"You heard me? Well, I'm not going to tell you."

"Fine," Harry said. He stood up and reached for the lantern.

Quentin looked alarmed. "No, wait! You're the first creature I've seen or spoken to since . . . yesterday."

"Well?"

"The rebels . . . Zack and Frank . . . are my friends. They left me behind by mistake and are coming back for me." Quentin peered into the darkening woods, as if he could hear their footsteps. "There are thousands of them," he said, but his voice quavered. "They'll be here any minute."

It was an obvious lie, but Harry was impressed with the effort. "You speak with an accent," he said.

"*You* speak with an accent."

Harry tried another tack. "Do you know two rabbits named Dan and Wally?"

"*What?*"

Harry repeated his question.

"Yes, I've . . . heard of them," Quentin replied cautiously. "Why do you ask? Do *you* know them?"

"Do you live at the rabbit warren inside the old fortress?" Harry went on. "Are all the others like you?"

"What do you mean?"

"Intelligent? Self-aware?"

The rabbit nodded. "I suppose it's the same for you?"

"Yes."

They sat in silence. Harry's stomach rumbled. "Do you have any food?" he asked. The wind was picking up and the snow began to swirl around the clearing. Harry repeated the question more loudly, striving to be heard over the wind.

"No," Quentin called back after a moment.

He's lying again, Harry thought. *I saw some interesting-looking packages in those open sacks lying about. Why would he have blankets and a book but no food?* "I'll be leaving, then," he said. "There's an Inn not far from here where I know I can get a decent meal." He picked up the lantern and turned away.

"Wait!" Quentin called. "Don't leave. I was wrong. There is some food. I'll . . . share."

Harry walked slowly across the clearing until he stood in front of Quentin, who leaped to his feet but backed up as Harry came closer.

Harry put the lantern down. He rummaged through the

217

open pack nearest to Quentin and pulled out a small, heavily wrapped package. "What's this?" He smelled it; it was sweet and scented with cinnamon. His mouth watered. "Mmmm. Smells like apples."

Quentin snatched it out of his paws. "Not that!"

Harry turned to Quentin, suddenly furious. He reached out to grab it back. "Why not!" he snarled.

"Harry." It was a familiar voice behind him. "Found you."

Elton.

A short time later, Harry, along with Quentin and Elton, was seated inside a small canvas tent that the badger had produced from his apparently bottomless sample case. The wind and snow howled outside, but the interior of the tent was relatively cozy. Two lanterns — the one Harry had "borrowed" and Elton's spare — glowed in the center. Harry and Elton sat next to each other on one side; Quentin, surrounded by several packs and some blankets, sat opposite them. He rummaged in the packs and removed three wrapped packages. "Here," he said, handing them out. "This is the end of the food, except for the apple turnovers."

"Why are you saving them?" Harry asked, angry again.

"That's none of your business," Quentin said. "I'm willing to share the sandwiches. Isn't that enough?"

"Enough," Elton said, reaching for one. "Thanks."

It had taken Quentin a long time to adjust to the presence of the badger, Harry reflected as he chewed on the sandwich, and Elton's cryptic explanation had not been overly helpful.

"Badgers talk. Problem?" Elton responded to Quentin's question while setting up the tent in the howling snowstorm. Elton had found some stones near the frozen stream bed to anchor the corners of the heavy fabric he'd pulled from his case. At Elton's direction, Harry and Quentin had searched the underbrush for a dead log; in the end, they used Elton's sample case to weigh down a corner. When Harry offered further help, the badger shook his head.

Harry learned that Elton had awakened in the middle of the night, noticed that his lantern was missing, and assumed that Harry had taken it by mistake. When the storm blew in, Elton guessed that Harry had returned to the Inn to wait it out and find Gerard. On his way to the Inn, he'd heard their voices.

At one point, Quentin walked outside with the lantern and stood staring into the dark woods, breathing hard. Harry turned to Elton. "Did you know about the rabbits?" he asked in a low voice.

"Yes."

"Why didn't you say something?"

Elton looked at him over his spectacles. "Didn't ask."

Now inside the tent, Quentin sat, his arms folded for

warmth, a blanket wrapped around his shoulders tightly. "I guess you're going to tell me that all creatures are like you — wolves, badgers, foxes — what else?"

"*Some* wolves. Ermine. Weasels. Raccoons," Elton replied.

"Oh, of course. I should have known. What about rats and mice?"

"Rats, yes. Mice, no." He glanced at Harry, then looked away. "Voles, no. Possum, no. Birds, no. Chickens, no." He turned to Quentin. "Alone?"

Quentin shook his head. "My friends are . . . with the rebels. They're a group. I don't know how many — who are living . . . I don't know where, but my friend had been contacted by them because . . . I can't say why." He paused. "Gods! That sounded ridiculous, even to me!"

Harry nodded in agreement. "And these friends who deserted you are going to return? Doesn't seem likely, especially in this weather."

Quentin looked stunned. Apparently it had never occurred to him that he would not be rescued. "Of course they'll return! Unless they're dead, in which case I might as well . . ."

"Why wait?" Elton said.

"What do you mean? What else can I do? I don't know where the rebels are!"

"I do."

Harry turned to Elton. "You do? How?"

"Customers. Going tomorrow." He put on the nightcap and slippers and began to unroll a sleeping bag from inside his pack.

Harry glanced at Quentin. The rabbit's face was a picture of surprise and relief. "Tomorrow? Then we can go together?"

Elton was asleep. In a moment the tent was filled with the sound of his rhythmic buzzing.

Harry was not in the least bit tired, although he had not slept since leaving the cabin. He was hungry. The rabbit had shared his food, reluctantly, but the aroma of the apple turnovers lingered in the air and in his memory. He wanted one.

Elton's pack lay beside him, open. Harry looked inside, then turned to Quentin. "Do you know how to play badger checkers?"

Quentin shook his head.

"Good. I'll teach you." They'd play for an apple turnover.

Harry set up the board.

15
Harry:
It's Only a Game

The checkerboard sat on a smoothed-out blanket, the odd-looking pieces carefully positioned on the gray and rose squares. In a far corner of the tent, Elton buzzed softly, his face turned away from the lantern light, his nightcap askew, a paw over his eyes.

Harry had noticed that Quentin seemed to become more calm as the evening progressed. He'd watched Elton set up the tent, asking questions and nodding at Elton's cryptic replies. He'd dragged his stuff into the shelter when it was finished and neatly piled the packs into a corner, tucking the one containing the apple turnovers on the bottom. The rabbit's wary, fearful expression was fading and he'd studied Harry with interest as he set up the board.

He explained the rules to Quentin. *I'll let him win the first game,* Harry thought, *to give him confidence.*

Quentin nodded. "It doesn't make much sense," he said, "but I'll try it."

"If I win two out of three," Harry said, "I get one of those apple turnovers."

"No. Not the turnover."

"There are two. I only want one."

"Oh, all right. I can certainly beat a fox at checkers!" he murmured to himself. "But if you lose, you get nothing."

"Agreed."

Quentin won the first game. He collected the last of Harry's pieces and smiled briefly. "That was strange," he said. "It's not at all like regular checkers, but it's close enough. May I set up the board?"

"Go ahead," said Harry. He could practically taste the cinnamon and sugar.

The second game started normally, but then Harry played the way he'd learned from Elton — distracting Quentin's attention, pretending not to notice an important move and then, on his turn, brutally taking Quentin's pieces, and when challenged, inventing a new rule that worked to his advantage. After a few angry protests, Quentin grew silent. When Harry won the third game, the rabbit stood up quickly.

"So this is a game without rules," he said. "I should have known."

"What do you mean?"

"It's cheating."

"That's what I thought at first," Harry said calmly, "but I was wrong. This is *badger* checkers — it's different. You can ask Elton." He reached over to the pack. "I'll take that turnover now."

"Here." Quentin got there first and handed it to him.

Harry tore open the wrapper and wolfed it down in two bites as Quentin watched.

"What kind of game is it where the rules are made up as you go along?" the rabbit persisted a moment later. "Where's the fun in winning a game like that?"

"I like to win. *Winning* is fun. Why does it matter how I do it?"

Quentin shook his head. "I've always hated cheaters," he said under his breath, but Harry heard him.

"It's not cheating," Harry said again, impatiently. "Besides, I hate to lose. What's the point of a game, anyway? Why follow someone else's rules? Who has the right to say what the rules should be for the rest of us?"

Quentin turned to him. "You have to follow rules. Otherwise everyone does what they want, and when that happens . . ." He stopped. "Never mind."

"Is that what rabbits do?" Harry asked. "Is that what *you* do? Always follow the rules?"

"Yes. . . . Well, almost always." He seemed to think for a moment. "I guess it depends."

"Just like badger checkers! Look — you lost. It's not the end of the world. It's only a game."

"That's like saying 'It's only a snake.' It's easy to win a game like this," Quentin said, angry again. He gestured to the board. "You just do what you want. It's harder to win when you play by the rules. You should try it sometime." But he seemed less convinced and turned away.

Oh, relax, Harry thought. What a stiff, humorless creature this rabbit could be, scolding like a skunk in an onion patch. He opened the flap of the tent and walked out into the snowy dark.

The air was cold but fresh after the warmer confines of the tent. Quentin had certainly gained confidence in a short time, Harry thought. Only a few hours ago he'd been cowering against a fallen tree, terrified, clutching a stick and pathetically threatening to defend himself. Now he was talking about hating cheaters and the importance of following rules. This new breed of rabbit was clearly more adaptable and intelligent than Harry would have expected.

A few moments later Quentin stepped out of the tent and stood beside him. "Those turnovers were meant for my friend's child."

So? thought Harry. *There's one left. Unless I can find a way to get my paws on that one too.*

"He recently disappeared, along with his mother and siblings. We were hoping to find them alive."

225

"Disappeared?" Harry said, suddenly alert. "What do you mean?"

Quentin told him. "Some of us think it's predators," he said, looking at Harry, then glancing away. "Others think it's our own government, although that kind of immorality is hard to imagine," he said. "It's probably pretty common in your world," he added.

"It's pretty common everywhere," Harry said. He paused. "So you *do* know Wally and Dan," he said, guessing.

Quentin was clearly startled. "Yes. But how could you possibly . . . ?"

"We'd better go inside," Harry said.

An hour later, Harry stopped talking. Quentin sat silently, his head in his paws; when he looked up his eyes were red. "This is the most horrible thing I have ever heard," he said hoarsely.

Harry nodded.

"And you say it's your brother who is behind it all?"

"Yes — and those two rabbits."

"Are you and your brother two of a kind?"

"What do you mean?"

"I mean, are you like him?"

"Do I seem to be capable of that kind of behavior?"

"No. But I've never talked to a fox before. For all I know,

every one of you could be like Isaac." He took a deep breath. "This trade must end. It is barbaric."

In the corner of the tent, Elton's snores stopped suddenly with a snort and a cough. The badger opened his eyes.

"Morning?" he said groggily.

"No," Harry said. "It's still nighttime. Quentin and I have been talking."

"About what?"

"I'll tell you."

While Harry talked, Elton stood up, put on his spectacles, tucked away his nightcap and slippers, and pulled on his worn brown boots and the tweed jacket. When Harry mentioned Gerard, Elton stopped and turned to him.

"Gerard?" he said.

"Yes."

Elton's face was expressionless. "Ah." He continued packing his things. He folded the checkerboard. "You played?"

Quentin nodded. "Yes. I didn't like it. It feels like cheating."

"Not cheating," Elton said firmly. "Different rules." He repacked the board and the pieces and continued until everything but the tent was neatly stowed.

Harry glanced at Quentin with a look that said, "See? I was right," but the rabbit was staring at the ground.

"I didn't think the world could be so awful," Quentin said, his voice flat and defeated. "I'm not that innocent. I know life can be hard, that you can't always depend on the gods. Good luck for some who don't deserve it, bad luck for those that do, rumors of slavery beyond the mountains. I know all that." He ran a brown paw over his face. "But this changes everything I have ever believed about what the world is like. Our own government murdering its citizens for gold! All the things I believed in and thought everyone else did too — gone." He looked at Harry, his eyes haunted. "Gods! We're all related or connected in some way — don't they see that? Doesn't that *matter*?" He buried his head in his paws again.

I understand how he feels, Harry thought, surprised. "I remember when I was very young, I thought the world was a wonderful place," he said. "Then . . . it changed."

"What do you mean?"

Harry found himself searching for words. "I saw liars and hypocrites . . . succeed. No one seemed to notice. Creatures who were selfish and greedy became rich and powerful."

Quentin looked up. "What did you do about it?"

"Do? I didn't do anything! Why would I? It's not my job to fix things!" Harry said. "The only way to survive in a world like that is to find a way to make it work to your advantage."

"And how does that make you any better than the liars and hypocrites?"

I should never have talked about this, Harry thought. "I'm getting tired of being scolded by a rabbit," he said angrily. "I don't see *you* looking for Wally and Dan to stop *them.* I see you running and hiding and whining about being lost and abandoned by your friends!"

"At least I'm not taking advantage of the situation for my personal gain."

Harry was stung. He leaped up. "What I do is none of your business!" he shouted.

"Harry," Elton said in his deep voice. "Quentin. Not argue." He paused. "Decency. Kindness. Gone. Maybe forever." The badger cleared his throat. "Sorry," he said, and patted Quentin on the shoulder. "So sorry." He took off his spectacles and rubbed his eyes.

Harry's anger melted. He had a fleeting memory of that morning in the woods a long time ago, before Isaac got sick and everything changed. *Gone. Maybe forever.* A deep sadness rose up inside him. *So sorry.* He turned away.

Outside the forest was quiet. They had been up all night; now the snow had stopped and the morning light seeped into the tent. Harry could feel the air warming. He went outside and gathered kindling and wood. Elton came out and helped build the fire; Quentin joined them. The three sat silently near the flames, rubbing paws for warmth, as the sky turned pale yellow, then rosy pink, then bright, deep blue.

16
Harry:
A Dam of Straw

As he sat before the fire, Harry thought about the folded bills deep in his pocket. *I have found a way to make this situation work to my advantage. Is that wrong? No. Money is neutral. It doesn't matter where it comes from — it's what you do with it that counts, and I am going to spend it most judiciously on myself. I have a right to think of my own survival! All the high ideals in the world won't help you if you're dead.*

He was surprised when Quentin stood up suddenly. "I can't sit here anymore," the rabbit said. "You know, I'm not very brave. I didn't want to leave Stonehaven with my friends, or jump off the fortress wall — believe me! — but I did it, and now . . . well, I've been picturing this weasel Martin delivering a . . . a sack . . . to the guards at Isaac's gate, and the next morning Isaac's rich friends secretly taking home to their kitchens. . . . If I keep thinking about it I'll go crazy, and I can't stop thinking about it. I have to do something."

"What?" asked Elton, turning to him.

"I'm going to find that cave, and when Dan and Wally

appear I'm going to . . . I'm going to stop them. Don't ask me how."

"I'll go with you," Harry said.

Quentin looked surprised and a little alarmed. "Why would you do that?"

"It's on my way to the Inn," Harry said, needing to clarify. "I'm just going to help you find the cave — that's all. What you do there is up to you. Although I have to say, I don't like this game or the way it's being played."

"I didn't think it would bother you."

"Well, it does."

"Oh." Quentin stared into the fire. "I'm sorry about what I said before." He looked over at Harry. "I've been wrong about a lot of things."

So have I, it seems, Harry thought, although he would never say so. "Apology accepted."

Quentin sat down again and rubbed his eyes. "I haven't slept and I'm exhausted," he said. "I just need a nap." He started for the tent. "Wake me when you're ready to leave." He opened the flap and disappeared inside.

I can sleep later, Harry thought. *Right now I have to make a plan. How will we manage this? Suppose Elton goes to the rebels and meets Quentin's friends. He could tell them we've gone to find the cave and let them decide if they want to join Quentin.*

Otherwise, they can all meet here, tomorrow, and return to the rebels together. That might work.

Harry stood up and stretched. The sky was bright blue without a hint of clouds, and the snowy ground and trees glittered in the sunlight. He walked over to a small spot of brightness and stood there, rubbing his paws, imagining he felt a little warmth.

Elton walked quietly into the tent and emerged holding a small leather pouch, tied at the top. He sat down again, put the pouch on the ground in front of him, and opened it up, pouring the contents before him onto the packed snow.

Harry recognized it now — the moochy-poochy stones. "Not again, Elton."

Elton was staring at the stones and shells. After a while, he picked up a flat, blue stone and showed it to Harry. "Quentin," he said. He carefully placed the collection back into the leather pouch and tightened the cord. "Ask question," he said.

"You mean about the weather?"

"No."

"What, then?"

Elton didn't answer.

Harry closed his eyes. *What question should I ask this time? Will I succeed in defeating my brother? Will Isaac get what's coming to him?* He suddenly thought about Quentin and his pathetic determination to confront Wally and Dan. *Will the rabbit survive?* "All right," Harry said. He took the pouch, untied it, shook it energetically, and dumped the contents onto the packed snow.

Harry's dark, oval stone had landed next to the blood red crystal again, nearly touching it. Elton's translucent quartz was farther away. Quentin's blue stone had landed on top of the red crystal. Elton picked it up and showed it to Harry — a large crack ran down the middle. Harry touched it with his paw and it broke into two pieces.

"Maybe that was the wrong stone," Harry said, unnerved. It was only a stone, for the gods' sake. Still. "Shouldn't Quentin be the one to pick?" he said. "And what about mine? What does it mean?"

Elton gathered up the stones and shells and replaced them. "Same thing. Path you follow. Dead end. Danger."

"And Quentin?"

Elton looked up at him. "You know."

Yes, I think I do, Harry thought.

Harry and Elton returned to the tent where they found Quentin curled up in a corner, his head resting against an empty satchel, sound asleep. Elton quietly retrieved his nightcap and slippers and in a few moments was buzzing softly. Harry sat silently for a while, thinking about the blue stone and the conversation with Quentin. His head drooped.

At dusk he opened his eyes, fully awake. He glanced outside, noticed the fading light, and began to gather his things. In a few moments Quentin awakened, sat up suddenly, and cried, "Is it late? Am I late again?"

"Late for what?" Harry asked. "We need to get started if we're going to find that cave before dark."

Quentin rubbed his face. "Sorry," he said. "I was dreaming."

Elton opened his eyes. "Night?"

"Not yet," Harry replied. "But soon. We need to go."

While Elton quickly stowed his cap and slippers, and Quentin stood and brushed himself off, Harry talked about his plan. "You can meet Elton back here tomorrow," he finished, hoping the false confidence in his voice would not be apparent.

Elton, busy organizing his things, glanced at him, then looked away.

"Sounds good!" Quentin said, with what sounded to Harry like equally false enthusiasm. He busied himself with his satchel, stuffing his blanket inside and searching the interior for something.

"Here," Elton said. He handed Quentin a tightly wrapped bundle, bulging and tied with cord. "Need this."

"Thanks," Quentin said, taking it. "You're very kind." His eyes welled up.

Hopeless, Harry thought. *A rabbit who weeps at the drop of an acorn. How in the world will he be able to defeat Wally and Dan? It will be a massacre.* He brushed the thought aside.

"About your plan," Quentin said to Harry after a moment. "I'm concerned about Gerard. Won't he and Martin be at the cave too?"

"That seems to be the way it works."

"I don't know. I'm ready to deal with Wally and Dan, although I have no idea how. Two against one is bad enough. Four, when two of them are weasels . . ."

"I see your point." Harry thought for a moment. "Well, I was planning to find Gerard at the Inn — Martin said that's where they meet — so I'll try to keep them from going to the cave for as long as I can. Is that better?"

"I guess so," Quentin replied. "And after that?"

"I'll be on my way home to settle things with my brother."

Harry and Quentin walked outside as Elton started to dismantle the tent. *I won't be seeing the badger again either,* Harry thought. *Once I've taken care of Isaac and Gerard, and collected the inevitable rewards, both tangible and otherwise, there will be no need for me to travel these paths. I can move into Isaac's mansion and . . .*

Elton stopped and came over to shake paws all around. "Harry," Elton said. "Good-bye. Good company."

"Good-bye to you," Harry replied, feeling a fleeting regret. *I will miss him.*

"I'll see you here tomorrow," Quentin said to Elton. "Thanks for everything."

Harry grabbed his walking stick, half buried in the snow, and picked up his things. Quentin took the bundle that Elton had given them and the other pack that lay on the ground, shouldering them with difficulty. Harry noticed for the first time that he was favoring his left arm.

"What happened?" he asked, gesturing.

"A flesh wound." Quentin told Harry about being pursued and cornered at the perimwall. He touched his arm gingerly. "I think it's healed but . . ."

"Bows and arrows?" This was an unpleasant surprise. Foxes only used them recreationally. Harry had never held a bow and had only occasionally attended the archery meets that were held on holidays in the summer. They were boring. What could be entertaining about shooting at a fixed target? Where was the challenge? What possible skill could be involved? Try catching a terrified possum or a family of quail, well camouflaged and dashing like mad through the underbrush! He'd walked away from the meets filled with contempt. A ridiculous waste of time.

Would Wally and Dan be armed at the cave? Martin had never mentioned it, and Harry knew Gerard carried no weapon. Martin's own rusty knife would pose no threat. But suppose

Wally and Dan *were* armed. *By the time I get there,* Harry thought, *the worst will be over.* The rebels will arrive too late to help. Wally and Dan will have escaped and Quentin will be dead. Even the moochy-poochy stones said so. The trade will continue. So much for trying to restore kindness and decency to the world.

After I confront Gerard, however, he will probably confess to everything, giving me all the information I need to bring Isaac to court.

... "Now you know it all," Gerard said. He lit a cigarette and inhaled slowly. "You know the depth of my depravity and shame. How could I have done something so terrible, so despicable!" He covered his eyes with his paws and sobbed.

"Yes, you are despicable," Harry replied. "Utterly and completely without a single redeeming quality."

"I should never have deceived you, Harry," Gerard replied, lifting his head. "I deserve to be punished, don't you agree?"

"Oh, yes. I do agree!" Harry said. "But if you come with me to the High Judge in Foxboro and tell about Isaac's part in this illegal trade, I will ask the Court to be lenient."

"Oh, Harry! How can I ever thank you!" Gerard cried. He fell to his knees. "I will tell everything I know

and with my assistance you will bring down Isaac once
and for all. It's the least I can do to repay your kindness,
of which I am so undeserving." . . .

Harry glanced over at Quentin, who walked slowly beside
him, occasionally shifting the weight of his burdens from one
shoulder to the other, wincing each time. His face was set and
determined.

Foolish rabbit, Harry thought. *You can't stop this. No one
can. It's like trying to hold back a flooded river with a dam of
straw. Greed and self-interest drive these creatures. The torrent
will wash you away.*

He returned to the delightful image of Gerard on his
knees.

17

Quentin:
The Enemy Was Among Us

It was dark when they found the cave. It seemed innocent enough, Quentin thought, and somehow that made it even worse. He noticed the rough circle of stone that had been cut out of the floor, and pointed it out to Harry, who held the collapsible lantern Elton had provided.

"I see it," Harry said. "This must lead to the tunnel under the fortifications."

"I guess so."

Harry leaned down, and using Isaac's walking stick, pried the lid up and pushed it partly open.

Quentin came closer and they both peered into the darkness as the cold, damp air of the tunnel, smelling of wet stone and mud, gusted gently into their faces.

Harry pushed the stone back and they walked into the woods.

They set up camp in a sheltered stony outcropping they found not far from the cave. Elton had managed to stuff a small tent, a blanket, a canteen, and the collapsible lantern into the parcel he'd handed them.

Harry unpacked the tent but Quentin stopped him. "Let me," he said. "I watched Elton." It was satisfying to do it himself. *If only my buddies at school could see me now,* he thought, as he pounded the stakes into the icy ground and smoothed out the floor inside. *No one would believe it.*

The snow-covered forest smelled clean and wet; the trees and shrubs, laden with snow, seemed to be silently waiting in the dark; the air was still. The sharp sound of stone against wood as he pounded the stakes for the tent into the icy ground echoed through the trees and bounced back, a stutter, each muffled blow sounding like two. What would Zack and Frank say once he was able to tell them about these last two days? *I won't have to exaggerate,* he thought. *The facts alone will say it all.*

"I'm going to the Inn now to find Gerard," Harry said as soon as Quentin was finished.

Quentin was startled. So soon? He'd been sitting in front of the tent, taking a breather, trying not to think about what lay ahead. Now, the thought of being alone again in the dark, so near the cave and all that meant, made his stomach turn over.

"You can keep the lantern," Harry said. "I know the way." He turned to Quentin. "Good luck."

"You're thinking I'll need it."

"Yes," Harry said, "I'm afraid so." He disappeared into the forest.

*　　*　　*

Alone again, Quentin thought, *and very hungry. I should be going to the cave . . . but not just yet.*

At one point, as they were collecting their things and Harry was distracted, Quentin had taken the last remaining turnover in Frank's backpack and shoved it deep into his jacket pocket, next to his book. Now he remembered. *Frank would understand,* he thought. Saliva filled his mouth as he breathed in its fragrance — it smelled heavenly — and he swallowed hard. Just a bite. He unwrapped it and the pastry crumbled. Quentin licked his paw and tasted the sweetness and the bit of slightly burned apple that stuck to the pastry; he took a huge bite and in a moment had swallowed the entire thing. He examined the ground for crumbs, which he picked up with a dampened paw, along with some dirt, sucking on each morsel. His tongue searched his mouth for the last remaining bits of pastry and cinnamon. The sugar buzzed in his head and he felt his face growing warm. *That was the best, most wonderful food I have ever eaten in my life. I wish there were fifteen of them.*

Gods! *What have I done? I have no self-control at all! Now there's* nothing *left to eat. What will I do tomorrow? And suppose they find Charlie — how will I explain this to Frank?*

A nearby crackling of the underbrush startled him. He peered outside, holding the lantern, but could see nothing. Not a sound. Quentin went back inside and lay down with his head against Elton's emptied satchel.

241

Who could be out there? The military police? He recalled Dan, handing him his induction papers on the snowy street outside the café, the high-pitched voice and the smug, self-satisfied look as he turned away, followed by his uniformed bodyguards; then Zack, in his apartment, showing him the guard duty assignment that had been left on his doorstep. An oddly fateful coincidence. Suddenly Quentin sat up. "Fakes!" he said aloud. "They were fakes."

Had he saved it? He felt deep into his pockets, pulled out a crumpled piece of paper, and held it close to the lantern. Now he saw that the official seal had been copied in an uncertain script, and that the paper itself lacked the government letterhead. He was right: his draft notice, and certainly Zack's call to guard duty, had been forged.

Quentin stuffed the paper back in his pocket and sat down. *Wait a minute.* That's *why the military police have not come for me — they probably don't even know I was drafted.*

I wasn't drafted.

I see it now. If they can fake these notices without being caught, then wouldn't that mean they're acting independently? That the government isn't behind the abductions at all? Dan and Wally are acting alone, then, murdering their own kind for profit. In fact, the enemy was *among us.*

Zack would probably say the Leader knew all along and just looked the other way, letting his advisors take advantage of our deeply ingrained love of order and need for security and using it to make themselves more powerful. "The Leader is easily influenced," Zack often argued, "and he likes to let others do his thinking for him. We are headed for a military takeover, Q." He'd shake his head ominously. "I can feel it in my bones."

Zack! I miss him. I miss my own kind. This was why species lived together, in their own territory, and were suspicious of outsiders and those who were different! For the first time in his life he understood the comfort of living in a place where the world was a mirror. The longing to see another rabbit was so deep he felt an ache in his gut.

Trying to get comfortable on the cold ground, Quentin turned on his side, away from the opening to the tent. Just a little longer. He closed his eyes, but now the images of caves and heavy sacks and wheelbarrows came back with terrifying clarity.

Why Frank's family and not me?

He sat up. *I* was *meant to stop this. I can't wait any longer.*

He was rummaging through the packs and satchels in search of a possible weapon when he heard footsteps. "Harry?" he said, suddenly hopeful.

"Q! Oh, gods! Frank, it's Quentin! Who's Harry?" said a familiar voice.

Quentin whirled around. "Zack?"

"Thank the gods! We found you!"

Quentin embraced his friends and looked at them hungrily. Zack's sad eyes were bright and his smile covered his face, but underneath he looked haggard and exhausted. Frank's eyes were red and he seemed tense and grimly excited.

"Q! It is so good to *see* you. Are you all right?"

"I am now! What about you? Are *you* all right? What happened?"

Zack and Frank walked into the tent and sat down. "It's a long story," Frank said. He took off his mittens and rubbed his paws. "The rebels found us, but they thought we were Wally and Dan. Tabor, their leader, was away. He was one of the rabbits who had contacted me. It took us a while to . . . establish our credentials. It was scary. They're a lot more militant than I expected," he said, "even though they apparently didn't start out that way."

"What do you mean?"

"They wanted to live more freely," Zack said. "You know, there have always been a few rabbits living among us who were unhappy with our orderly life. I never believed . . . Gods, it's good to see you!"

"Tell me about Tabor," Quentin said, reveling in the sight of his friends. It was all he could do to restrain himself from embracing them once more.

"Big, strong, and determined to get revenge," Frank said.

He told Quentin that the rabbit had been "peaceful as a possum" until he learned that his entire family — elderly parents, siblings, their children — had been victims. Frank paused. "I can understand how he felt."

"Q, you'd hardly believe Tabor was a rabbit," Zack continued. "He's tough and he's angry. He says he'll do whatever's necessary to destroy Wally and Dan. I've never known anyone so coldly determined. Makes me seem like an armchair zealot by comparison."

Frank sat down and rummaged around in a large knapsack he'd tossed on the ground. "Before we go on," he said, "I need to eat. Are you hungry?" He pulled out some wrapped packages and held out his paw.

Quentin swallowed hard. "Yes, I'm very hungry, thanks." He unwrapped the package and wolfed down the cold turnip-and-potato sandwich in seconds. It was terrible and wonderful at the same time. "Do you have any more?" he asked, licking the crumbs from his paws.

Frank looked at him. "Quentin! You must be starved — and the rebel food is awful. I'm sorry, I should have thought of this sooner. Here." He gave him another and handed one to Zack.

"It's fine." Quentin was able to eat the second sandwich more slowly, savoring the dry potatoes, the slightly bitter turnip, and the stale bread. *I will never take food for granted again,* he thought. *I will never turn away from a rabbit who is hungry, or keep food for myself when I have the chance to share. I promise.*

He had swallowed the last crumb of the second sandwich when he remembered. "Those apple turnovers you were saving . . . for Charlie . . . are gone," he said to Frank, unable to look him in the eye. "I'm sorry. I was hungry." This was not the time to explain about losing at badger checkers.

"I'd forgotten all about them," Frank said. Then, seeing Quentin's face, he said, "It's all right, Quentin. Don't give it another thought. Charlie will — would — understand." But he stood up, covered his face with his paws, and walked outside.

I'll be thinking about it for the rest of my life, Quentin said to himself.

He and Zack sat in the tent silently. In a few moments, Frank returned, his face calm. "Sorry," he said. "I keep doing that." He cleared his throat. "Tell us what's happened to you while we were gone. I was very worried about you, Quentin. We both were."

"It was hard," Quentin acknowledged, remembering how frightened he was when he saw his friends taken off into the forest. He told Frank about spending the night alone and waiting to be found by the MPs. "They aren't coming, by the way," he said. "My draft notice, and probably your guard duty summons," he said, gesturing to Zack "— both were fakes. I'm positive Wally and Dan are acting alone."

"Acting alone?" Zack said. Quentin could see him sorting through the implications. "You mean, the government . . . !" Zack stopped. "I can't absorb all this. My mind is numb. Besides, there's something else," he said slowly.

Frank and Zack exchanged looks.

"The morning after we were taken they picked up a weasel named Martin. He knew we weren't Wally and Dan — in fact, he saved our lives by vouching for us. I know what you're thinking," Frank said quickly. "The weasels can talk and think, but they don't smell like predators. It's all hard to believe."

"Yes," Quentin said. "Wait until I tell you about foxes and badgers."

Zack was startled. "You know a fox and a badger?"

Quentin nodded. "And I know about that weasel." Then, slowly, he told them about Harry, Elton, and the nearby cave.

Frank was silent. Then he said, "For a while, before I heard that weasel's story, I thought there might be a chance I'd find my Mary and my children. Now . . . I'm not going to think about what happened to them. I just know this has to be stopped. No other father or mate must ever go through this."

"I agree," Quentin said.

"What do you think?" Zack said, standing up and pacing

back and forth in the small space. "Frank and I have been talking. There's not much we can do on our own."

"I disagree," Quentin said firmly. "I think we should go over to the cave and wait for Wally and Dan and whoever else is involved in this. I'm not staying on the outside anymore. I've been thinking. . . . Maybe the gods want me to act." He looked away. "I hope that doesn't sound too self-important."

"Not at all," Zack said quickly. "I'm filled with admiration. And I must say, this is a new Quentin. Not the same old friend who was afraid to jump off the wall two nights ago!"

Frank stood up. "The gods Mary and I believed in would not have allowed this to happen," he said. "In my opinion, there are no gods, period. We invented them to make us feel safe. What a joke!" he said bitterly.

"Let's talk about the gods another time, my friend," Quentin said. He started rummaging through the sacks that lay on ground. "I was just looking for a weapon," he said to Zack. "Let's see what we can find."

A few minutes later Quentin picked up the lantern and they joined Frank who had walked outside and stood staring into the forest.

"Any luck?" Frank asked.

"No. Maybe we can pick up something on the way."

"Is it far?" Zack said.

"Not very. I was there just a while ago with Harry."

"Q?"

Quentin turned to Zack.

"Are we doing the right thing?" Zack asked. "Should we wait for the rebels? They'll be here soon, won't they? Isn't there safety in numbers?"

"Yes, we are, and no, we should not wait," Frank responded emphatically. "I want the satisfaction of doing this myself. Besides, every minute we waste standing here puts another rabbit family at risk." He started down the path.

Quentin and Zack followed. "I'm worried," Zack said. "We have no weapons. Wally is strong and Dan is smart. They'll be armed."

Quentin nodded.

"I know it's the right thing to do," Zack said, "but I wish I didn't have to do it."

"I know. But we have no choice."

"You sound like me," Zack said.

"You sound like *me*."

They caught up to Frank and trudged toward the cave. The air was still and the only sound was the soft crunch of their footsteps on the trail, which grew darker as it twisted into the woods. In a few moments, the moon was hidden behind the trees, the sky was black, and only the small glow of the lantern lighted their way.

18

Quentin:
Like Looking Death in the Face

It was midnight when they heard the circular stone scrape against the rocky floor of the cave. Quentin, Zack, and Frank had taken shelter nearby against a large fallen fir tree, whose girth was large enough to provide a shield against the cold breeze that had sprung up as the night wore on.

Quentin sat against the tree, the bark, rough and frozen with snow and particles of ice, jabbing him through his jacket. Zack sat close to him for warmth. They had doused the lantern; Frank had fallen asleep. The grating of stone on stone woke him.

"They're here," Zack whispered.

Quentin nodded. He grasped the rock he'd picked up on the way to the cave. *It had worked for Zack against Wally at the perimwall,* he'd thought. *Maybe it will work again.* Frank had found a fallen tree branch and had ripped off the thinner twigs to make a cudgel. Zack carried a club made from a heavier branch he now rolled nervously back and forth between his paws.

Earlier, as they had walked to the cave, Quentin had said to Frank, "At least they won't be expecting us. Maybe that will work in our favor."

Quentin had held up the lantern to Frank's face as they'd stopped for a moment. Frank's warm, open expression was now clouded, his eyes deeply sad. At the same time, his large frame appeared more tense, as if he were trying hard to contain his anger; his voice had an edge to it. The benign, jovial warmth Quentin had always found so appealing had vanished.

"I've been thinking," Frank had said. "If we can separate them we might have a chance, especially if they have weapons. Does that make sense?"

"Yes," Quentin said. *Why not?* he had thought. *I don't think I'm going to live to tell my friends about this. Wally and Dan are too vicious, too . . . evil. Those cold blue eyes that never smiled. . . . It was like looking death in the face. Then why aren't I afraid? Maybe it's because I'm so sure of the outcome.*

"Quentin — you should know," Frank was saying. "We have to be prepared to hurt them — maybe seriously. Can I count on you? What about you, Zack?"

Zack nodded slowly.

"Yes," Quentin said. "I just hope . . . we don't have to become like them in order to defeat them."

"That will never, ever happen."

Now, hearing sounds from the cave, the three rabbits stood slowly; Quentin brushed the snow off his jacket and hefted the stone in his paw. They crouched outside, peering into the darkness, as the stone slid and scraped slowly across the floor.

Quentin could barely see the light of a flickering lantern within the tunnel.

I wonder what happened to the weasel Gerard, he thought. *Harry must have found him and distracted him. But for how long?*

"Can't you hurry?" Dan's high-pitched voice asked. "Why is it taking you so long? We're late as it is. They may be gone."

"They'll be there, if they know what's good for them. And if you weren't such a delicate little flower," Wally's voice growled, "you could be doing this heavy work yourself. Then we'd see how quickly you would move through this damned tunnel."

The stone had moved to its farthest point and a paw clutching the handle of a lantern appeared at the edge of the opening. *This is it,* Quentin thought. His heart was beating fast. *Whatever happens now, at least I'll know I tried.* He looked at Zack, who was focused on the opening to the tunnel and the darkness below. Frank was crouched alongside him, staring intently. Zack looked up and Quentin's eyes met his. *Courage!* Zack nodded and tightened his grip on the club.

Dan had emerged from the tunnel with the lantern and was looking back, pulling on something. "You'd think it would have gotten easier for you after all this time," he said. "Here." He offered a paw. "The steps are slippery."

"I don't need your help!" Wally shouted. "I never have and I never will."

Dan gave a tug anyway, but there was a sudden bump and a crash, the sound of something heavy falling, a thud. "Now what! Wally? What happened?"

Dan was turning to go back down the stairs when Frank ran into the cave. Zack followed. Frank grabbed Dan from behind by the collar of his uniform and clapped a paw over his mouth.

"Not a word," he whispered furiously to Dan, whose eyes widened in surprise and fear when he twisted around and saw Frank's face. Frank jammed Dan's arm behind his back and held him tightly against his own body. "Warn him and I'll break it."

Zack moved toward them, his club raised over Dan's head. Dan stopped struggling.

As Quentin watched, he heard Wally's voice from the tunnel. "Damn those steps! Well, are you going to help me, you sniveling weakling?" When there was no response, he said, "Fine. I'll do it myself. But don't expect to get paid for this one, when I'm doing all the work."

Dan wrenched himself free from Frank's paw across his face and shrieked, "Wally! Go back! It's —"

"Do it!" Frank ordered, and Zack hesitated, then brought his heavy club down hard on Dan's head. The rabbit went limp as the blood poured from the blow, and Frank dropped him to the ground. "Good." He dragged Dan's body to the far side of the cave, where it crumpled into a heap.

"What? What did you say?" Wally's voice called from the tunnel. Then, in the ensuing silence, they heard Wally's heavy footsteps clumping back through the tunnel, the sound diminishing until there was nothing.

Quentin ran into the cave. "I'm going after him."

"I'll go with you," Zack said. He looked at Frank.

"Go ahead. We were going to separate them anyway. I'll be here with this one," he said, gesturing. "Be careful. We know what he's capable of."

Quentin held the lantern high for Zack as they tumbled down the slippery stairs into the tunnel, which was very dark and barely wide enough for them to walk side by side. The smell of mold and cold stone surrounded them like a shroud as they ran, their footsteps echoing wetly around them. Quentin heard running water. As he held up the lantern he could see the walls of the tunnel dripping with melting ice. Above him the moss-covered stones were cracked and chipped and leaking. *How old is this tunnel? How long before it collapses? Don't think about it.*

After a moment he stopped to catch his breath. Zack stopped behind him, breathing hard. In the silence, as their own breathing slowed, they heard a moaning and cursing ahead of them.

Wally.

Quentin lowered the lantern and they walked toward the

sound. Suddenly his foot hit something; he nearly fell and put a paw out to stop Zack from running into him. The dim lantern light revealed a large, lumpy burlap sack that had been dropped on the path before them.

Quentin gasped.

"What is it?" Zack whispered. "Oh. Oh, gods."

"Zack," Quentin said quietly, pointing to the sack. "We can't leave this here. Take it to the cave and wait for me. I'm going to find Wally. If I'm not back soon, go home with Frank and tell them . . ."

"Forget it, Q. I'm not leaving you."

"Please, Zack," Quentin whispered. "If something happens to me you can be there to help Frank. Otherwise we could all die."

"All right. But if you're not back in a reasonable amount of time, I'm coming for you." He grabbed the sack and lifted it. "Gods. It's not even that heavy." He put it down, then wiped his eyes, turning away. "I don't know if I can."

Quentin grabbed Zack by the shoulders and looked him in the eye. "You have to do this."

Zack nodded and picked up the sack again. "I'll need the lantern," he said.

"Take it. I'll find Wally. I can smell him."

Quentin watched Zack's dark shape and the lantern light fade until the blackness of the tunnel enveloped him again.

He walked cautiously ahead in the dark, keeping his paw on the tunnel wall for balance. *It's a good thing small, dark places don't bother me,* he thought. *Compared to the perimwall, this is a carrot soufflé.* He went slowly, placing one foot tentatively ahead to be sure the ground was solid and there were no more sacks (but there wouldn't be), then stepping forward. In a few moments he saw a faint light ahead. The groaning grew louder.

The tunnel curved slightly and when Quentin rounded the bend he saw a lantern on the floor and beside it Wally, his left leg folded beneath him, his face contorted. Wally looked up. "You!" he growled. "Vole-hole!"

"Wally," Quentin said, "it's over. This disgusting trade, the murders, the gold — it's over."

Wally looked up at him with hate-filled eyes.

"What's over? What are you talking about? I don't know anything about a trade. Besides, it was all Dan's idea, that sniveling little flower." He struggled to get up, but fell back. "Ow. Ow! My ankle! I think it's broken," he said with a whimper. "It hurts like hell."

Quentin had not expected this. Earlier in the evening they had talked about fighting, about self-defense, about using their weapons. Frank had reminded them to protect their heads and at the same time try to use the cudgel or stone to break an arm or leg. But Wally's ankle was already broken.

Was it? Then how had he managed to get this far back into the tunnel so quickly?

Quentin stepped closer, his shadow growing large against the opposite wall as he approached the lantern, his arm raised. Wally, who had turned away from him, was leaning over, looking down at his ankle. As Quentin stood alongside him, Wally suddenly grabbed his legs and yanked. Quentin fell to the ground. Wally kicked him in the side, then, jumping to his feet, he pulled Quentin up and punched him in the face, hard.

"Fooled you, Vole-hole!" he growled triumphantly.

The pain was shocking and intense; the force of the blow staggered Quentin back and he fell again. The stone dropped from his paw. His face throbbed and he felt the blood drip down his neck. Wally reached and grabbed his jacket, but Quentin turned aside and kicked. Grunting with the impact, Wally lost his balance and fell toward him. Quentin pulled himself up as Wally reached for his legs and dragged him down again. Trying to roll away, Quentin smacked up against the wall of the tunnel. Wally heaved himself to his feet and kicked, connecting with Quentin's barely healed shoulder. The burning pain was terrible.

Wally leaned over him, breathing hard and pressing him firmly against the ground. "Did you think I didn't know what you called me?" he said. "Did you think the others didn't know? Well, they did." He tightened his grip on Quentin's throat.

"Dan wanted to make you one of the first, but I told him I had to save you for myself. And I would have done it too, on the perimwall." He punched Quentin in the face, again. "You walked right into my trap. Now who's the dumb one, Vole-hole?"

"You know why the name stuck, Small Ears?" Quentin gasped, trying to twist out of Wally's grasp. "Because it was true!" *Gods, I despise you, you pathetic monster!* He reached out with his good arm and grabbed Wally around the neck, pulling him close. Then, tightening his grip, he tried at the same time to pull himself over Wally, but the injured arm was almost useless and he could get no leverage. He squeezed harder, as hard as he could. Wally's face was close to his ear; he struggled; he punched Quentin around the face and neck and kicked his knees, but the blows were weak; his breathing became thick.

Then Quentin felt a sharp pain in his ear. Wally had bitten him and the shock of it caused Quentin to release his grasp. Wally rolled away, knocking over the lantern, and the tunnel went completely black.

"Damn!" Wally said, breathing hard. "Damn! Where are you, Vole-hole? I'm going to beat you until you beg for mercy, and then I'm going to beat you some more, and then I'm going to kill you."

You'll have to find me first, Quentin thought, as he lay on the ground, trying to control his ragged breath. He felt for the tunnel wall, dragged himself to it, and gradually stood. The blood poured from his ear, his arm was numb, his face throbbed, and he could only see out of one eye. He was feeling his way along the wall when his foot stubbed against something and he almost fell — the stone. Quentin slowly reached down for it, trying to keep his head vertical to minimize the pounding in his face that made him nauseated and nearly faint.

Gripping the rock in his good paw, he listened for Wally's breathing, but the tunnel was silent except for the sound of dripping water. Wally must be holding his breath. *As long as I can't hear him he's safe. But I have to find him before he finds me.* He took the chance. "Come and get me, Small Ears," Quentin whispered into the darkness.

Wally gave an outraged cry and lunged toward him, grabbing desperately for his throat and barely missing his shoulder. With one mighty last effort, Quentin swung the arm holding the rock toward where he thought Wally's head might be. *This is for Charlie.* His arm connected with a sickening crunch, and Wally fell to the ground. Quentin leaned against the tunnel wall, panting. He stood for a moment, the blood pouring down his face. Then he dropped like a stone.

19
Harry:
Things Are Not What They Seem

It was very late when Harry saw the faint lights of the Inn far ahead of him. His stomach growled with hunger, and he quickened his pace. The moon was very bright and floated low in the sky, illuminating the icy, winding path. It was quiet, except for the sound of his own footsteps and the thump of Isaac's walking stick.

Harry stopped suddenly and listened. Someone was coming toward him. He moved quickly into the shadows and waited.

Much to his surprise, it was his brother's distinctive form that came into view. Isaac wore a dark fur hat with a brim that shaded his eyes, and a long, heavy coat of rabbit fur that fell below his knees. A large knapsack was slung over one shoulder, and he poked the ground with the mahogany cane Harry had seen before. He trotted briskly and purposefully on the snowy trail.

He was not limping.

Harry was stunned. He waited until Isaac had passed him, watching him closely for a sign of the old disability, but there was not a trace of it. Then he leaped out onto the path, grabbed

Isaac by the shoulders, turned him around, and punched him in the face. "You lying hypocrite!" he cried as Isaac staggered back and fell to the ground. Harry reached for him again, but Isaac jumped up and grabbed Harry by the throat, drawing Harry's face close and raising his cane above his head.

"Who are you — ! Why, it's Harry, my dear brother!" He struck him on the side of the face with the cane, and Harry fell, landing hard. Isaac pulled Harry to his feet and hit him repeatedly across the shoulders and head. The blows stung and Harry punched back, but Isaac ducked and whipped the cane against his legs as the momentum pushed Harry forward. For a moment, Harry remembered that they had wrestled furiously as children, before Isaac's illness, pummeling each other and swearing until Mama called from the kitchen, "Stop it, you two!" But this was different. There was no cane then. Now Isaac's upper-body strength gave a fierce power to his blows, and Harry sensed a deliberate impersonality in the vicious beating that knocked him to the ground. His shoulders and legs throbbed, and he felt the blood streaming down the side of his face. Struggling to his feet, he lost his balance, slipped, stumbled, and fell again to the path. Isaac was standing over him, grasping him by the throat with one paw, lifting him off the ground, his cane clenched in his other fist, when Harry cried out, "Wait! I've had enough!" In the old days it had been Isaac who had begged for a truce.

Isaac loosened his grip. Harry fell backward, then slowly sat up, dabbing at the side of his face and pressing his sleeve to his cheek to stop the blood. Isaac held on to the cane and reached for his knapsack and his hat, which had fallen alongside the path.

"Why did you lie?" Harry gasped.

"Because it was fun," Isaac said, panting. He sat down opposite Harry, pulling the bundle close. "Unfortunately, this particular game is over, at least for the moment. There will be others. I hear word of a slave trade on the other side of the mountain. Could be even more lucrative." He seemed thoughtful. "I didn't expect to see you again," Isaac began slowly, "but maybe the gods are trying to be helpful. . . ."

As Isaac turned, he struck Harry's left leg repeatedly with his cane. Harry tried to grab it away from him, but Isaac's grip was impossible to dislodge; instead Harry squirmed away, his leg burning inside his boot. He reached over and yanked Isaac's legs out from under him. The two struggled on the slippery path, falling and sliding. Then they fell apart, breathing hard.

"Why leave now?" Harry asked, slowly recovering his breath. "It can't be that you're running out of dead rabbits."

"So you know? Good! I always suspected you were smarter than you looked."

Harry didn't answer. He was too outraged to speak.

"I suppose I can tell you the truth since this will certainly be our last meeting," Isaac said. "There are rebels — rabbits, if you can believe it — who have discovered my connection to this trade — those treacherous foxes I sent as scouts confessed everything — and the rebels are committed to ending it. They are out to get me — even though the stupid creatures were betrayed by their own kind. I am not afraid of them," he went on. "But they have been gathering my enemies. It is time to leave.

"Back in Foxboro, I promised a permanent supply of fresh-killed rabbit, only for those select few who could afford my prices. . . ."

"Save your breath. I know all about it."

"Really? I don't think you do. You don't know that I persuaded my customers to pay in advance," Isaac said, "or that I raised the price again and again. . . . Unfortunately, the demand increased while the supply was slow in coming."

"Those must be the promises you mentioned when you came to see me," Harry said.

"Indeed. In case you're wondering, by the way, no one suspected the rabbits were sentient — not that my clientele would have minded. Once the meat was prepared properly, no one could tell the difference. Fortunately, I had the opportunity to test this hypothesis myself before agreeing to the trade."

"Lucky you."

"In any case, " Isaac went on, "due to the growing strength of these rebels and the restlessness at home, it is becoming too risky for me to keep my end of the bargain. Needless to say, I have no intention of returning the money!" he said with a short laugh. "There will be outrage. Foxes do not like to be cheated, especially by one of their own. I'm sure you can understand that."

Harry nodded slowly. "If you knew all along about the rabbits, why did you send me out to the fortress?"

"One can never have too much information," Isaac said smoothly.

You're lying. There's another reason — but what is it?

"However," his brother said, slowly getting to his feet, "all good things must come to an end. While it lasted, this was one of the best — and most delicious — *things* ever." He leaned over, opened the knapsack, and showed the contents to Harry: dozens of neat packages of bills, all of high denomination and banded with paper and the familiar logo, along with several small burlap bags that Harry remembered seeing at FoxBank. "As you can see, I don't expect to have any trouble establishing myself in a new business venture."

He stood, closed the knapsack, picked up the cane and sack, and started down the path. After a few steps, Isaac turned. "I feel sorry for you, brother," he said. "You have nothing and you're going nowhere. You're a failure — Mama knew it, and so did Dad — and you always will be." Reaching into the knapsack, he pulled out one of the small bags. "For their sake, I can afford to be generous, at least this once. Here. This is for your trouble." He tossed the bag contemptuously in Harry's direction. It landed at the side of the trail and broke open, spilling some of its contents into the snow. Then he twirled the cane, tossed it in the air, and caught it. He broke into a trot, then a run; the path turned and he was gone.

The woods were silent once again, and the moonlight was bright on the spot where Isaac had stood. Insult upon insult! Outrage piled upon outrage! Harry could hardly contain his anger and disappointment. His hopes for seeing Isaac in front of the High Judge — vanished; his chance to bring him down, to expose him for the criminal he was — gone forever. So much for revenge, for fairness, for justice. "Damn! Damn! *Damn!*" He pounded the path with his fist. He got away with it! *Again!*

And that comment about Mama and Dad — a low blow. Typical — but bitterly satisfying to recognize that Isaac's last effort to hurt him had been ineffective. Isaac was wrong. *Mama and Dad didn't believe I was a failure. They were too busy worrying about you.*

He lay back and closed his eyes.

It seemed only a moment later that he was awakened by a sharp pain in his leg. Someone had tripped over him in the darkness and fallen heavily. Harry saw a lantern on the ground and smelled the familiar scent of sassafras tobacco.

Gerard groaned and tried to get up. "What in the gods' name . . . ?" He looked around. "Harry!" Gerard reached for the lantern and held it up to Harry's face. "What happened to you? What are you doing here?"

If I stay on this path long enough, Harry thought, *everyone I know will find me.* "I could ask you the same question," he said, remembering the purpose of his journey to the Inn. "We were supposed to meet at the fortress, remember?"

Gerard shifted his position on the ground. He was out of breath and had obviously been running — with some difficulty, apparently, considering he wore the heavy fur coat and the ridiculous hat Harry remembered. Gerard looked anxious and worried. "Of course I remember," he panted. "Didn't Elton find you at the cabins? It was an opportunity I could not afford to miss. A theater troupe, looking for an experienced director, paying well — I couldn't turn it down. My old profession, the lure of the . . ." His voice trailed off.

"I thought it was your knee."

"Oh, yes. Of course. My knee." Gerard was silent. "Harry — I need to tell you . . . things are not what they seem." He heaved himself to his feet. He was carrying the heavy carpetbag Harry had opened on his bed, the bag in which he'd found the note from Isaac, *"Remember: I trust you."*

The note now seemed laughably unimportant.

Gerard held the lantern up to Harry's face. "What happened?" he asked again. "Did you fall? I told you it was dangerous to travel these trails alone."

"No," Harry said. "I . . . bumped into Isaac. Or maybe I should say he bumped into me." He watched Gerard carefully in the lantern light, but Gerard only blinked. The expression of concern on his face did not change.

"Oh? Very surprising, don't you agree?" He looked around anxiously, then turned back to Harry. "Did he say where he was going, or whether he was coming back?"

"You never mentioned you knew my brother," Harry said, ignoring the question. "In fact, you told me you knew only theater people in Foxboro."

"So I did, so I did." There was an uncomfortable silence.

"Did Isaac tell you to spy on me?" *Now that I finally have the opportunity to ask the question,* Harry thought, *I hardly care about the answer.* "Is that why you insisted on going with me to the old fortress?"

"Spy on you? Why would you think that?" Gerard said, genuinely surprised. "Really, Harry! Our meeting was nothing more than a delightful accident. It's been lonely out here in the woods, staying at the Inn, eating meals with that . . . fool and his incessant singing. . . . I needed a break from the . . . routine. When I met you, I had been considering the possibility of a permanent departure for climes unknown. An escape, you might say. A trip to the cabins seemed like a good start in that direction —" He stopped abruptly. "But I was quickly reminded that I needed to attend to other . . . responsibilities." He paused

267

again. "I confess I suspected you might be related to Isaac. There's a strong family resemblance, don't you agree?"

"I never thought so until recently."

"Did you hear something?" Gerard lifted the lantern and held it high, squinting into the dim light.

"No. Are you being pursued? Or are you expecting someone? A rabbit or two, perhaps?" Harry couldn't resist.

Gerard turned to him slowly and pulled the lantern close. "How did you find out?"

"I met Martin," Harry said. "Singing. He mistook me for my brother."

"Martin! Where is he? He's disappeared and without him I can't possibly . . ." Gerard sighed. "Oh, I don't care. It's over, at least for me, and I'm glad you know. I did not enjoy the pretense."

"Spare me the sentiment," Harry said scornfully. "What you've been doing is disgusting and illegal. You deserve to be punished."

"It's not sentiment," Gerard insisted. "I like you. You're different from Isaac. He has a heart of stone." He sighed again. "You have no idea how much I regret being involved in this business. And as far as punishment is concerned, I carry mine with me every day. It's called a conscience." He looked down, unable to meet Harry's gaze.

"Still the actor," Harry said. "You'll get no sympathy from me. Besides, there are always choices. *Don't you agree?*"

Gerard turned to him angrily. "Maybe you're more like your brother than I thought."

"Why did you do it?"

"I ask myself that question sometimes," Gerard said. He fell silent, then after a moment, said, "Haven't you ever done something you regretted, but then found it difficult to get untangled?"

Harry thought about it. "No."

Gerard smiled briefly. "No? How unusual! What a strange life you must have led! No mistakes, no regrets, no apologies. No sleepless nights, tossing and turning, wishing for a different outcome! I can hardly imagine it."

"If you didn't like what you were doing, why not stop?" It seemed so simple.

The weasel was silent. "I liked the money," he said finally. "Perhaps you can understand that."

Yes, Harry thought, *I can.*

Gerard stared at him, then lifted his bundles. "Well, I am going up North to get as far from here as possible," he said. "I never want to see another rabbit as long as I live, and if I can find a community without foxes, so much the better. Goodbye, Harry." He turned away and ran heavily down the path,

269

the earflaps on his hat bouncing against his head. After a moment he too disappeared.

At least Gerard won't be going to the cave tonight, Harry thought. *That will leave Quentin to deal with Wally and Dan. And I know how that will turn out.*

Harry's shoulders were stiff and aching, and when he took a deep breath there was a sharp pain in his upper back. His leg was swollen where Isaac had struck him repeatedly with his cane, and Harry took off his boot with considerable difficulty. He applied some snow to the spot, which helped for a moment, until the cold water ran down into his sock. *If I don't put the boot back on now,* he thought, *I'll never be able to do it.*

He pulled himself to his feet and took a step, but his weight on the bruised leg inside his boot caused him to gasp with pain; he wobbled and fell. Damn Isaac! Groping in the snow for the walking stick, he heaved himself up and leaned on it, picked up his belongings, and shifted his weight so that his pack was on one shoulder. He was weak with hunger; breathing was painful and his leg could support no weight. He turned toward the Inn, hesitated, then looked back.

There was not a sound in the forest. The burlap bag lay bulging on the path, its contents outlined clearly, the few escaped coins glinting on the snow. *I don't need you,* Harry thought. *I'm through with Isaac and everything connected to him.* He turned and made his way slowly down the path.

20
Harry: Trapped!

Harry spent the rest of the night and the next day at the Inn. Becky had fussed over him when he'd knocked at the door, very late, and Harry decided to let her. He hurt all over and was so exhausted and gloomy he slept soundly. When he awoke the next morning, he made his way painfully to the dining room and ate quickly, without speaking to anyone. Becky and Allison were nowhere to be seen, but clearly they had left instructions that Harry be taken care of, and several youngish rats, looking respectful and concerned, hovered about him. When one of them rushed to find a cushion for his leg, Harry laughed. The irony was hard to bear.

The following afternoon, he stood at the window of his room, looking out at the forest. The dark, jagged profile of the firs was backlit; the path disappeared into the woods. He closed his eyes and thought about what lay ahead.

Isaac would settle on the other side of the Black Mountains and come up with a way to profit from a trade in slaves, an endeavor as repugnant — and illegal — as the trade in sentient rabbits. He would ingratiate himself into the governing structure and use his money to buy power. Maybe he'd fake his disability again. The public would admire him because of his wealth; some would feel sorry for him because of his limp, but all would learn to fear him once they experienced his cold heart. There would always be a Martin around who could be persuaded to help. Or a Gerard — smart enough to know better but able to silence his conscience so that he could collect the gold. Worst of all, Harry would never have the chance to reveal his brother's true nature.

Too bad Dad and Mama are dead. At least I could go to them and tell them the truth.

... "So you see," Harry said to Mama, "Isaac was never as sick as you thought. There is nothing wrong with his leg. He's been pretending all these years just for the fun of it."

"I can hardly believe it," Dad said. "Why would he do such a thing?"

Mama sighed. "I never knew Isaac was so desperate for attention," she said. "I tried to give him as much as he needed. Now I see that it wasn't enough."

"But, Mama!" Harry said. "What about me?"

"I always knew you were stronger," Mama said. "You didn't need me as much as he did." ...

"That's not true!" Harry said aloud.

...Mama just shook her head. "I am so disappointed in Isaac," she said. "Won't you forgive him?"...

This was not the fantasy Harry had hoped for. "Never!" he said aloud again. "I can never forgive him," *and neither should you,* he added, but Mama and Dad had already faded away.

He sat back down on the bed. His rib cage and stomach still ached from Isaac's blows. After many applications of ice, the pain and swelling in his leg had diminished, but he still had to retrieve Dad's knife and cut a large slit down the side in order to slip on his boot. Even then, he could barely tug it over his leg and the pain was terrible.

Somehow having his boots on made him feel better. He limped tentatively around the bed, holding on to the side. Now the room seemed small and confining. With Becky and Allison away, there was no one to talk to, and the guests at meals became very quiet when Harry appeared. The books stacked on the table in the lobby were ancient and focused mainly on raccoon history and social issues that held no interest for Harry.

I need to get out.

I'll go back to Elton's tent and see if I can find out what happened to Quentin, he thought, although if the rabbit had survived, he would have met Elton by now and they would have made their way to the rebels. *Perhaps they're safely back at*

Stonehaven. Still, Harry felt he needed to be outdoors. He'd take a quick look at the tent — if it was still there — and start home tomorrow, when his leg would be stronger. The exercise would do him good.

He put on his jacket and walked tentatively across the room, but he was unsteady on his feet and could hardly stand after a few steps. *I'll need that damn walking stick.* He took it and went downstairs, and stepped out into the cold, sunny afternoon.

The sky was bright with sunlight. All around him, the snowy trees glittered; the path, turning to ice, crunched under his feet. A wet, translucent fog hung in the air and created a painful glare as the sun penetrated the dense shrubbery and trees heavy with snow. Harry shielded his eyes with his free paw and leaned on the walking stick with the other. It was slow going. The path gleamed like a mirror.

He reached the spot where he'd last seen Isaac and Gerard. In front of him now was the burlap bag, still lying on the ground, like a small, light brown rabbit asleep — or dead — on the path, spilling its entrails of gold. He reached down and put two gold coins in his pocket. Souvenirs.

"That's him!" a voice cried faintly. "It ain't nobody else! It's him, all right! It's Mr. Isaac!"

Harry looked up. In the distance coming toward him, he could see someone running — Martin, by the sound of it — followed by what looked like an enormous number of large rabbits with drawn bows and arrows.

But I'm not! he thought . . . and then he understood. *I'm a decoy!* This *is why Isaac sent me to the fortress, and why he lent me his walking stick! He didn't want information — he wanted me dead so that he could escape more easily. And the fight — my injuries, the vicious beating to my legs, my limp — now makes it impossible for me to prove who I am. No wonder Isaac thought the gods were helping him!*

What to do. I could wait till the rebels get here and explain — but would they listen? Would they believe me? Why should they? I could find a place to hide — but where? The cave is nearby, but that will make me look even worse. . . . I need someone who can confirm who I am. Allison and Becky could identify me, but can they prove I'm not Isaac?

The voices and shouts were coming closer.

He stood, his heart pounding, frozen on the path as the cries of the rebels came closer.

For the first time in his life, Harry was trapped.

On impulse, he turned toward the cave. Maybe he could hide in the tunnel. He began to run, limping and hopping as fast as he could on the uneven, slippery trail. When he looked back, he saw one large rabbit with dark brown fur, wearing a black tunic and boots running ahead of the others. "Stop!" the rabbit cried. "Isaac! Stop and surrender!"

Harry could not run faster.

The rabbits were close behind now, thundering on the path. Panting, Harry slowed to a limping trot, then a walk. The pain in his leg had become too great; his sore ribs hurt with every breath. He could go no further.

He fell to the ground.

In a moment, he was surrounded. The large rabbit grabbed Harry by the jacket collar, lifted him off his feet, and snarled, "Prepare to die, Isaac Fox!" Three even larger rabbits crowded in alongside Harry, and Martin hovered around the edges. Two rabbits with clubs raised them menacingly.

"I'm not Isaac," Harry said, trying to sound confident and calm, but he was breathing hard and his voice trembled a little. "You've made a mistake. Isaac is my brother. My name is Harry." He struggled free from the rabbit's grasp and leaned on the cane. He looked at Martin. "You remember me, don't you? We met the other night when you were pushing that wheelbarrow toward town. You mistook me for Isaac then too."

Martin shook his head. "I don't never remember no stinking meeting," he said. "And besides, I ain't never believed you neither." He turned away. "We ain't never met, Mr. Tabor."

"Then how can you be sure I'm Isaac?"

"Easy!" Martin said, turning back to him triumphantly. "That's easy! Ain't I knowed it then? You got a walkin' stick!" He grabbed it from Harry's paw. "Look!" he said, showing it to the others. "No normal fox wouldn't never need this! Ain't Mr. Isaac known for bein' a poor, helpless cripple? He can't never walk none without no stinkin' cane. I seen you limpin'! And ain't this stick got the initials Eye Eff? That don't stand for no Harry. For Harry it would need a . . . a . . ." He stopped in confusion, then looked suspiciously at Harry's pocket. "What's in there?"

Tabor reached in and pulled out the gold coins. "What's this?"

"I saw it on the path," Harry said. "It's not mine. I just picked it up." He could never explain the souvenir part.

"It's gold," Martin said excitedly. "It ain't no different from what I been paid with. This is the same."

"You're a fox who walks with a limp and is using a cane with Isaac's initials, and you have gold coins in your pocket. That's good enough for me," Tabor said and gripped Harry's arm.

Harry saw this was his last chance. Balancing his weight on his one good leg, he cried, "I'm not Isaac!" He punched Tabor in the stomach as hard as he could, knocking him down. Tabor doubled over, and several rabbits crouched down to help him.

As Martin stood, staring, Harry picked up the walking stick and hit him across the face with it. He jabbed his elbow into the gut of the nearest club-holding rabbit behind him, who fell to the ground. Then Harry ran down the path toward the cave, limping and hopping. Martin's howls of pain followed him. In a few moments, he could hear the rabbits again, shouting, their footsteps getting closer and closer. One or two arrows *thunked* into the path behind him.

Breathing hard, and with the pain in his leg again becoming unbearable, Harry saw the entrance ahead. The late afternoon sun slanted onto the front floor of the cave, leaving the rest in deep shadow.

Falling inside, he gasped for breath and was blinded by the sudden darkness before him. He crawled further into the cave and looked around. The sunlight fell on the circular stone, which had sunk partially into the ground to reveal a gaping dark hole filled with rocks and debris. The floor of the cave in front of him was smeared with dried blood. Harry could barely see that the tunnel had collapsed. His last chance for escape was gone.

Feeling utter despair, he sank to his knees, breathing hard, his head in his paws. Behind him, the rabbits' footsteps pounded on the path, getting closer. "Kill him! Kill Isaac Fox!" Tabor's voice cried, and the rabbits' shouts echoed into the sun-filled forest.

He waited for the blows that would end his life.

21

Quentin:
An Unexpected Life

The first thing Quentin saw was Zack's anxious face and sad eyes, hovering above him. Then he became aware of the pain in his arm, which throbbed with every beat of his heart, and the burning in his ear. He hurt all over and his vision, through his one opened eye, was blurred.

"Q — can you hear me?"

Quentin tried to speak, but no sound came. All he could do was blink an assent. Then he managed, "Where am I? What happened?" in a hoarse whisper.

"The tunnel collapsed last night. We got you out just in time. Wally's under it, somewhere. You've been unconscious for hours." Zack took a breath. "How are you feeling? You look horrible."

"Thanks," Quentin said. Zack had to lean close to hear him. "I feel horrible."

"Q, I'm afraid to ask this — did you kill him? Wally?"

Quentin tried to remember those last moments in the dark — the struggle, the rock. "I hit him as hard as I could," he murmured. "I don't know. I wanted to. Yes, I think so." He tried to sit up but fell back. The ground under him was cold but dry and he seemed to be covered by a light blanket. Beyond Zack's face he could see the rough canvas of Elton's tent, the one he had pitched a thousand years ago.

"Listen, Q. I'm worried about your ear," Zack said. "It needs to be more securely bandaged and there could be infection. Your eye looks terrible and your arm is bleeding again. Frank went to the Inn to get help."

Quentin closed his eyes.

"Well. What have we here?" a deep voice said, and Quentin opened his eyes again to see a very large raccoon standing at the entrance to the tent. She carried an enormous black carpetbag and was bundled up against the cold. Frank stood beside her. Behind him, peering into the tent, was a smaller raccoon carrying an armful of blankets and a large woven basket.

"These are my friends, Quentin and Zack," Frank was saying. He turned to Zack. "Allison and Becky own the Inn."

Zack nodded and held out his paw, but Allison was already kneeling down alongside Quentin and shaking her head. Becky unfolded the blankets and gently patted them around Quentin. Then she bent over the basket and began to remove fragrant packages and containers. The aroma of food filled the little tent.

"Frank told us a little about what happened," Allison said, sounding impressed. "You look awful."

"It *was* awful," Zack said.

"I can imagine the details. Male creatures fighting for power, that's what it's always about. I'll never understand it."

Becky looked up. "Let's not talk politics now," she said. "This poor rabbit needs us." She pointed to the basket. "Please help yourselves."

Frank pulled out a few wrapped sandwiches and packages of dried fruit and handed some to Zack. The two sat down and began to eat.

"That smells good," Quentin said weakly.

"Not for you," Allison said. Becky reached into the bag and drew out a bottle as Allison lifted Quentin's head. "Drink this," she said sternly. "And no complaints." Quentin swallowed a thick, bitter liquid. He coughed and lay back, staring at the top of the tent, his eyes unfocused. In a few moments, the pain began to leave him.

"This is the second serious injury we've seen today," Allison said, as she unwrapped the makeshift bandage Zack had applied to Quentin's ear. Becky winced at the sight and dabbed at it with a solution she removed from a small vial. It stung like mad, but Quentin just groaned. "It's beginning to sound like war."

"You could call it that," Frank replied between bites of his sandwich, "but we're hoping it's over now."

Allison looked at him and snorted. "War? Over? Ha! I'll believe *that* when stones float."

Quentin felt her wrapping his ear with clean bandages.

"We haven't met any rabbits," Becky said as she offered more food, "but we never believed the stories about timidity and cowardice." She turned to Frank. "Are all of you fighters?"

"Quentin is one of our bravest," Zack replied, and through his increasingly foggy mind Quentin could hear the sincerity in his friend's voice. "We all look up to him."

"I never thought of myself that way," Quentin managed. "Just the opposite."

Allison had leaned close to hear him. Then she said, "Nonsense. These are the injuries of a warrior." She finished bandaging his arm, pulled another blanket out of her carpet-bag and tucked it around him. She lifted his head. "Drink more of this."

Quentin entered a world that was profoundly calm and silent. He was alone on an island surrounded by a blue sea. A warm sun covered him, and there was nothing to be seen on a horizon that stretched beyond the forest, beyond the Black Mountains, beyond the edge of the earth, and into a distant nothingness that was peaceful and healing.

When he finally opened his eyes, he felt he had traveled a great distance. He lifted himself on his good elbow and looked around, slowly getting his bearings. He touched his bandaged ear gingerly. The sound was muffled — a hearing loss? Could be. But his bruised eye was opening, and although he still hurt, the pain was muffled too — and bearable.

There were hushed voices outside the tent. Then the flap opened and Zack peered in. "Q! You're awake! Frank — he's awake!"

The two rabbits were at his side in seconds. "How do you feel?" Frank asked.

"Much better," Quentin said. His stomach growled. "And very hungry."

"That's the best news I've heard in a long time," Frank said, leaving the tent and reappearing with some wrapped sandwiches. "Allison said you could eat these."

After Quentin ate and drank some fresh water from a large canteen, he pulled himself up with help from Zack, and leaned against the bundles that rested against the tent wall. He felt his strength returning. "How long have I been . . . out?"

"Hours."

Quentin shook his head. "Amazing. And I had the most wonderful dream. I feel much better," he said. "My eye is opening — see?" He demonstrated. "But I have a feeling my ear is going to be permanently crumpled and I'm not hearing too well, although that could just be temporary. My perfect ears!" he said with a wry smile. "Well, that will teach me to be vain."

"You were never vain," Zack said. "A little pleased with yourself, perhaps . . ."

"Ouch. Thanks. And now that I'm a 'warrior rabbit' I'm going to demand a little more respect."

"So you heard that! I wondered."

"I would never have thought raccoons could be so skilled in the healing arts," Frank said, getting up and walking to the opening of the tent. "Allison, for one, gives a very different impression."

"Yes."

"But if there's one thing I've learned from all this, it's that you can't go by appearances," Quentin said. "Now — please tell me what happened, Frank. I remember only bits and pieces."

Frank turned back to him. "First, Zack came out of the tunnel with . . . the sack. . . . That was very hard." He looked at Zack.

"Yes. The heaviest burden I have ever carried," Zack said. He ran a paw over his eyes. He had carefully placed the sack in the far corner of the cave, he told Quentin. "Then I went back to help you."

"In the meantime, I was standing over Dan with that large club in my paws," Frank said.

Zack continued, "When I went back into the tunnel, I could hear it dripping and crumbling. With the lantern I could see how truly dangerous it was to be there. I have no fear of dark, enclosed spaces," he said to Quentin, who nodded slowly in agreement, "but I have never imagined that being buried alive would be a good death. I admit I was very, very frightened."

"With good reason," Quentin said. "You were very brave to come after me, Zack. I'm in your debt forever, my friend." He reached out a paw, then winced. "*Ow*. It looks like warm gestures of thanks will have to wait."

"That's all right, Q. You would have done the same for me — or Frank."

"True," Quentin replied, falling back against the bundles. "But I'm still enormously grateful."

Zack had made his way into the tunnel and had found Quentin lying unconscious against the wall, with Wally nearby. The lantern light revealed dark stains of blood over the walls and floor. "I grabbed you under the arms — I had to leave the lantern behind — and I dragged you through the tunnel. I was feeling my way, backward. All around I could hear rumbling, like thunder, in the dark, and dust and pebbles falling around me. I expected the tunnel to come down on me at any moment," Zack said. "You were a dead weight. It seemed endless."

Frank had helped Zack pull Quentin up the stairs as the sounds of falling rock and sand came closer.

"The two of you had been out of the tunnel for only a few

minutes when there was a huge thundering crash from beneath us," Frank said. "Some dust and rock and fine sand blew out of the tunnel into the cave. The stairs collapsed. The ground shook. It was terrifying."

When Dan came to, Zack continued, he claimed the whole thing was Wally's idea and that he'd been forced to go along. "It seemed pretty clear from what he said that they had acted alone — without the Leader's knowledge, that is — except for the few hired mercenaries and goons who shot at us on the perimwall and did the other . . . dirty work."

"When he saw that we were unconvinced," Frank said, "he seemed to grow more and more desperate. He cried and then he begged me to let him go. I told him that Wally was dead and that the tunnel had collapsed."

"What did he say then?"

"He offered to cut us in."

"Cut you in? What do you mean?"

Frank turned to Quentin. "He said something like, 'There is another tunnel, I'm certain of it. I'll give both of you one-third of the income I get from trading the product in exchange for letting me go.'"

"That's unbelievable," Quentin said. "He really thought you would *consider* an offer like that?"

Frank nodded. "When I didn't answer right away, he said,

'All right. Two-thirds.' That's when I completely lost control, Quentin. I just lost control."

"What did you do?"

Frank looked away. "I took the club and beat him to death. And I don't regret it one bit."

There was silence in the tent for a long time. "Frank," Quentin said. "You lost your family to this creature. What you did is completely understandable." He closed his eyes for a moment and could see the darkness of the tunnel and the struggle with Wally. "I think I know how you feel."

"Really?"

Quentin nodded. "Wally and Dan broke the law that keeps us civilized. We did the right thing."

"And *I* broke the law that kept *me* civilized," Frank said, sitting down slowly. "My own law. What about that?"

"I would have done the same thing," Zack said, but he sounded uncomfortable.

Frank noticed his tone of voice and looked up. "You don't really mean that."

"To be honest, I'm not sure what I mean," Zack said slowly. "It's just that I've seen too much blood and death in the last few days. Ever since we jumped off the wall . . . first the rebels, then the cave, the sack, Wally and Dan . . . It's been too much for me, too much." He fell silent.

"What happened with Wally in the tunnel?" Frank asked.

Quentin told them. "I thought about Charlie just before I hit Wally with a rock," he said, and he could feel his heart beating fast as he spoke. "I bashed him on the head as hard as I could. I have to admit, it felt good at the time."

"How does it feel now?"

Quentin hesitated, then he said, "They had to be stopped. We stopped them." After a moment, he asked, "What did you do with Dan's body?"

"It was hard to know what to do about it," Zack said slowly. First, they had emptied the contents of the sack and had buried the two female rabbits they'd found inside in deep snow and covered with a thick layer of branches. "The ground was frozen solid. It was the best we could do. We'll come back in spring and give them a proper funeral."

"It was almost morning by then. We brought you back here," Frank continued, "and Zack stayed with you while I . . . I stripped off Dan's clothes and dumped his body in the woods. Eventually the feral wolves will find him, and the maggots."

"What about the rebels?"

"There was no sign of them," Zack said, "although I imagine they're probably at the cave by now."

"We needed to leave that place," Frank said, nodding.

"I take it you never saw Harry, or Elton? Or Gerard, the weasel?"

Zack shook his head. "No. Listen, Quentin — are you feeling well enough to walk? I want to go home, *now*. I need to see my old familiar house and my things. I need to see other rabbits and hear their voices. And as soon as I open the door to my place the first thing I'm going to do is get under the covers and stay there for about a week. I'm serious."

"I can understand that," Quentin said. "Then what?"

"I'm not sure. Obviously, this whole thing will have to be reported to the Leader, don't you think? Some policies will have to change."

"Actually," Frank said, "I've been imagining what it would be like to go home. I think it would kill me to walk into my house and see . . . the children's toys and clothes, and my Mary's things, all the signs of our life together but with the family gone . . . I can't do it."

"What else *can* you do?" Quentin said, surprised.

"I've been thinking I'd join the rebels," Frank said. "Don't laugh, you two. Now that the . . . trade has been stopped, the rebels may be able to return to the cooperative life they once led. Tabor struck me as an intelligent, thoughtful creature when he wasn't ferociously angry. I think I could get used to it — peaceful, nonviolent, loosely organized. . . . And they certainly need some help with their cooking!" he added with a laugh. "In any case, I think I'd like to try. Maybe you and Zack can visit me from time to time."

Quentin closed his eyes. In his mind he could see Wildwood Forest, the perimwall with its towers. *On the other side is my home, Stonehaven. I could go back and finish school, maybe make a permanent connection and raise a family. Every day would be pretty much the same. No risks — no jumping off walls or pitching tents. No foxes, no weasels, no badger checkers . . .*

"Can we talk about this later?" he said. "I think I need to sleep."

"Of course," Frank said, getting up. "We'll be outside if you need us. It's actually stopped snowing. Coming, Zack?"

Zack had stopped and was looking at Quentin. "In a minute," he said.

Frank nodded and walked outside.

Zack sat down again. "Something's wrong, Q. What is it?"

"You know me too well," Quentin said. He shifted position and sat up so that he could see Zack clearly. "I was thinking about going home. I don't know if I can."

"Q! What do you mean?" Zack looked stunned. "Why not?"

Quentin struggled to explain it. "I'm not the same rabbit who jumped off the perimwall. I've talked to a fox and a badger! I've done things . . . I never thought I could do. It's just hard to imagine living my old life. When I think about it now it seems so boring, so . . . predictable!"

Zack gave a short laugh. "After all we've been through," he said, "that's exactly what appeals to me! A world with no surprises." He stood and walked to the opening of the tent. "I *long* for peace and quiet! Don't you?" When Quentin didn't answer, he turned to him. "Maybe you just need some time. Maybe you'll change your mind once you feel stronger." He sat down again. "You're my closest friend, Q," he said. "Who will I complain to about the government? Who will listen to my radical political views — if I still have any," he added, almost to himself. "Who will I meet for lunch at the café?"

Good questions, Quentin thought. "I'll have to think about it," he said as Zack turned away and walked out of the tent.

I must make a decision, Quentin thought, closing his eyes. *I could go home and at least give it a try. I owe that much to Zack. Or I could join Frank and the rebels, which would be different, at least. But that's not what I want, either! I want to be in a place where things happen that I'm not prepared for, or didn't expect, and instead of being frightened, I'm excited. And then see that I am* ready for the unexpected, even though I didn't think I was. *Where will I find that?*

Toward the late afternoon, Quentin was able to stand. Allison had provided a large wooden staff for him to lean on, and in a short while he could walk, slowly, holding on to Frank's arm with his other paw. They gathered up what gear they could carry, along with two lanterns given to them by Becky, and set out for the front gate to Stonehaven. Zack, cold and silent, walked on ahead.

By dusk, the air was milder; snow had melted all around them. The path, covered with a coat of slush, was slippery and Quentin's boots were beginning to soak through by the time the sky darkened and the moon appeared, a silvery disk behind the clouds.

Frank lit the lantern.

"I told Zack I'm not sure I can go home," Quentin said to him.

Frank stopped in his tracks, a look of amazement on his face. "That explains his silence today," he said. "I wondered what had happened. But not going home!" he said. "I didn't think for a moment you'd be joining me! I must say I'm enormously pleased. It will be good, Quentin. Like old times at school, only better because we're older and have more sense. And it will be less lonely for me to have the companionship of someone from Stonehaven."

"No," Quentin said. "That's not the life I want either," he said. "I'm sorry. I just don't know what I want to do."

"I see. I think."

Ahead of them, Zack had stopped and was staring into a clearing. Quentin and Frank came up beside him.

There stood Elton's tent, illuminated by the moon, the packs and bundles inside, where Quentin had left them; he peeked in and saw *Rabbit Heroes for All Times* opened to the first page.

Beyond the tent was the rough lean-to that he had built that first night and the path into the woods where Zack and Frank had been taken by the rebels; there was the log he had leaned against, holding the stick, terrified, when he had first seen Harry. The bright moonlight, filtered through the trees, made the clearing seem a peaceful place.

"Let's stop here for a while," Quentin said. "I need to rest." He stepped inside the tent and sat down with difficulty near the bundles. Frank and Zack followed, and Zack picked up the book.

"I remember laughing when you said you'd brought this," he said. "Now I'm thinking they'll have to add both your names."

It was the first time Zack had spoken to him since the morning. "*All* our names," Quentin said.

Zack shook his head. "I try to imagine telling our friends what happened," he said, "and I can just see their faces. No one will believe you jumped off the perimwall, Q, or that you talked to a fox and a badger, or that there's an Inn run by raccoons. They certainly won't believe that Dan and Wally were behind the disappearances and were acting alone, or what happened to the rabbits who vanished, or that you and Frank killed . . . No one will believe me. They'll think I've gone crazy. They'll send me away. I'm serious."

"You're right," Frank said. "Not about the crazy part. But we're the only ones who will ever really understand what happened in these woods and at the cave. As far as the other things — maybe you can persuade the Leader to visit the Inn. When Allison and Becky heard about what happened — they were shocked, especially since Gerard and Martin had stayed with them so often. They would certainly vouch for you."

"You could show him the cave and the collapsed tunnel," Quentin said.

"I never want to see that place again," Zack said. "Besides, that's not really the point, is it?"

"No," Quentin said quietly. "It's not."

Zack walked outside the tent and stood staring into the woods, his arms folded across his chest.

Quentin followed, and put his paw on his friend's arm. "Zack — please try to understand," he said. "I can't see myself joining the rebels."

Zack turned to look at him.

"I suppose I could try it. But something about all that endless pacifism and cooperation — it seems so boring! I *don't* mean that I'd like to fight every so often just to liven things up," he added hastily.

"Glad to hear *that*."

"I'm not explaining this very well." Quentin sighed. "I think it's the idea that everything has to be just one way or the other all the time, forever. I want surprises."

"I guess when you're a warrior rabbit," Zack said with a crooked smile, "the world looks different."

Quentin felt a flood of relief. "I guess it does."

"Look," Zack said, trying again. "*You've* changed. You jumped off the wall. Maybe our community can change too — in small ways at first. If you're a part of it, you can help make it happen. We could do it together. What do you think?"

"Small ways?"

"Yes . . . like, well, we could encourage the others to try different colors. Rabbits don't have to wear blue all the time, for example." Zack started to laugh at the expression on Quentin's face. "Oh. Not exactly what you had in mind, I gather."

Quentin exploded with laughter. "No," he said. "Small changes won't be enough," he said. "But perhaps I could find a way to push things along."

"What do you mean?"

"I've been thinking of giving up agriculture and studying rabbit law instead. Maybe I'll run for office someday. I'll bet *that* would be an unexpected life!"

Zack's face brightened. "I like it — Quentin for Leader. You'd be a good one."

"Do you think so?"

"Absolutely."

"And maybe the first thing I'd do would be to try to get everyone to jump off the wall in the snow, just once," Quentin said with a little smile.

"Literally?"

"Literally."

"You know," Zack said slowly, "that's a really interesting idea."

Frank emerged from the tent, carrying his things. "Have you two figured it out? I need to get going. Quentin, are you sure you won't be joining me?"

"No, Frank. I don't think so."

"Then I'll say good-bye." Frank dropped his bundles into the snow. "Thank you for helping me get through this," he said to Zack. "I'll be thinking of you safe and warm under the covers."

Zack nodded.

"But don't stay there forever," Frank continued. "Don't let Dan and Wally change you permanently. Take the time you need and then come back to yourself."

"I will," Zack said. "You do the same."

"I'll try." Then Frank turned to Quentin. "One of the hardest things in the world is saying good-bye to a friend."

"It *is* hard to say good-bye," Quentin replied.

"Brothers," Frank said, looking into their faces, "we will meet again." Frank embraced Zack and Quentin briefly, then picked up his bundles and a lantern and turned into the woods.

"Well, Q?" Zack said, his sad eyes hopeful.

Quentin clapped his friend on the back. "All right," he said. "Let's start with red."

22
Harry:
Brave Fox

"Harry," a familiar voice growled.

Harry lifted his head and saw Elton step out of the shadows of the cave; at the same time, he heard Tabor and the other rabbits charge inside behind him. He felt himself roughly lifted off his feet and pulled toward Tabor, who held a knife to his throat. The edge of the blade was sharp and it drew blood — Harry could feel it. Tabor's eyes were filled with hate and rage. Behind him, the other rabbits crouched in a circle, their spears and clubs pointed at Harry.

"Isaac!" Tabor said hoarsely. "Now you will die for all the crimes you have committed. This immoral trade ends here and now!"

"No," Elton said in his deep voice. "Not Isaac."

"Elton? What are *you* doing here?"

The badger came closer and placed a paw on Harry's shoulder. "Friend," he said, and Tabor, looking shocked, lowered the knife.

Harry was about to speak, when Martin pushed his way

through the rabbit guards. "What's going on?" he asked. His face was swollen and he held a pawful of melting snow against his bloodshot eye. He looked from Tabor's face to Elton's and said furiously, "You ain't going to believe no stinking badger! Badgers don't know nothing about no foxes. This *is* Isaac. I know him. I *seen* him. It ain't no one else. Look at his walking stick!" he said again, holding it up.

"It's not mine," Harry said, wiping the blood from his neck with a shaky paw. "My brother gave it to me."

Martin looked around at the armed guards. "Foxes ain't known for never telling the truth," he said wisely.

"Not Isaac," Elton said again.

"Are you sure?"

"Sure."

"I *told* you," Harry said. "I'm Harry, Isaac's brother. You've been chasing the wrong fox. I saw Isaac two nights ago. He's far away from here by now. You'll never catch him." He was still breathing hard, and it was not only from running.

"If you're a friend of Elton's, that's good enough for me," Tabor said to Harry. "We've traded with him for a long time. He doesn't lie." He turned to Martin. "You, weasel, are a different matter."

"I ain't taking no blame for none of this!" Martin cried.

He dropped the walking stick, pushed his way through the rabbit guards, and ran.

He'll probably pick up that gold on the trail, Harry thought with fleeting regret, then sighed. *He can have it.*

"Let him go," Tabor said as the guards started after him. "There's no point in punishing an underling when the real evildoers go free." He looked around the cave and noticed the blood and the collapsed stairs, the stone cover to the tunnel slightly ajar and cracked into pieces.

"What about the others, Wally and Dan? What happened to Frank and Zack, and their friend?" Tabor asked Elton.

"Don't know."

"If Isaac is really gone," Tabor said, "then this trade is finished, thank the gods. We'll seal up this cave, and then we'll go home." He turned to Harry. "I'm sorry for the mistake."

"So am I," Harry said.

A while later, Harry was walking slowly on the melting path with Elton at his side, his leg throbbing with every step. He told Elton about his meeting with Isaac, and about Gerard. "I thought you were going to the rebel camp," Harry said. He wasn't ready to talk about the events at the cave just yet.

"Rebels gone," Elton replied.

"How did you get here so quickly?"

"Shortcut."

"Did you see Quentin or the others?"

"No."

"Why did you come to the cave? You were supposed to meet Quentin at the tent."

"Worried."

"About Quentin?"

Elton shook his head. "No. You." He looked up at Harry. "Threw stones."

Harry was about to ask what the stones revealed and thought the better of it. Finally, he said, "Elton, if you hadn't been in the cave . . ." He stopped and cleared his throat. "Thank you. I owe you my life."

Elton coughed and turned away. "Owe nothing," he said, looking intently at the ground.

They walked on in silence. "Look." Elton had stopped and was pointing into the woods at the mangled, bloody body of a rabbit, the side of its head bashed in, splayed on its stomach across a snow-covered log. The thin afternoon sun filtered through the trees and cast a pale light on the rabbit, its limbs askew. Clearly it had been thrown away, like garbage. It wore no clothes.

Harry went closer. "It's not Quentin. I see a bit of that bald spot — mange, most likely." He recalled Quentin's description.

"It must be Dan. Good. Shall we leave him?" he asked Elton. "Considering the cold, the body will probably be intact for quite a while."

Elton nodded. "Wolf food," he said. "Deserves it."

"What do you think happened to the other one?"

"Don't know."

They continued on the trail until the path forked, and then they stopped.

"Inn first," Elton said, dropping his things on the ground. "You?"

"I'm not sure," Harry said. "I had thought about going home, but now . . ."

Elton was waiting. "Plans?"

"I'm going after my brother," Harry said firmly. He saw a flash of disappointment cross the badger's face. "Well? What would you do?"

"Forget."

"Forget that my brother wanted me killed? And that he almost succeeded? How could I do that?"

Elton thought about it. "Hard," he acknowledged, then added, "for you."

Harry and Elton returned to the Inn, where Harry picked up his belongings, paid his bill, and left a large tip in his room for the considerate young rats. This time Allison greeted him and expressed concern about his leg. "The rabbit said the war was over," she told him, peering down at him from behind the front desk, "and I didn't believe him. I was right."

"Rabbit?" Elton asked.

"Three, actually," Becky said, coming into the room. "One was quite seriously injured. Quentin, I think it was — am I right, sweetie? But thanks to Allison, he was in better shape when we left."

"Do you know those rabbits?" Allison asked, turning to Harry.

"Yes," he said. "I know Quentin." *So he'd survived!* Harry thought, surprised at the relief and pleasure he felt. *Good for him!*

"Really?" Becky said. "Well, he and his friends may already be on their way to the fortress." She handed Elton some wrapped parcels of food and he nodded his thanks.

"You might be able to catch up," Allison said. Then she glanced down at Harry's leg. "Maybe not."

Becky held out a paw. "Thank you for staying at Inn the Forest," she said to Elton and Harry. "Come again."

Allison's grip on Harry's paw was firm. She gestured to his leg. "Take care of that," she said gruffly, and she closed the door behind them.

Harry and Elton walked down the path toward Elton's tent. The late afternoon sunshine was fading and the sky was clouding over; the cold air and the chill breeze suggested more snow.

"So the moochy-poochy stones were right about me but wrong about Quentin," Harry said.

"Not moochy-poochy," Elton said patiently. "Tell future."

"But the blue stone broke in half! Remember?"

"Quentin divided. Not broken." He looked at Harry. "Different."

"If you say so," Harry said, feeling once again how hopeless it was to argue with a badger.

"Say so," Elton said, and kept on walking.

Elton stopped. "Wait." He walked into the woods and disappeared.

Again? Harry thought. *Haven't I been here before?*

The badger reappeared, carrying a large branch of cedar. In a few moments he'd carved a staff for Harry and handed it to him.

"Thank you." Harry took one last look at Isaac's walking stick and threw it with all his strength into the woods.

"If Quentin is alive," Harry said as they continued walking, "I guess that means Wally is dead too."

"Quentin, " Elton said with admiration in his voice. "Saw

evil. Fought it." He walked in silence for a moment. "Brave rabbit," he said.

"Yes," Harry agreed. "But that's because he survived. If he had died he wouldn't be brave — he'd be foolish."

Elton shook his head. "Brave. Either way."

In a short time, they were standing in front of the tent, not far from the clearing where Harry had first seen Quentin and heard him talking to himself. The shock of that moment would be with him for a long time.

It was snowing again. The ground in front of them had been trampled recently with many footsteps, and there were signs that heavy bundles had been dragged from place to place, but the snow was beginning to cover the deep furrows and footprints, filling them in. *Soon it will seem as if none of this ever happened,* Harry thought.

Elton peered inside. "Look." The tent was empty except for a small book that lay on the ground.

Harry picked up the book and opened it. A piece of paper fluttered to the ground. Harry showed Elton the large, scrawled *Q* that decorated the flyleaf.

"Quentin's," Elton said. "Read."

Harry read aloud: *"Harry — Wally and Dan are dead. Thanks for keeping Gerard away from the cave. I killed Wally, and even though I was defending myself, I broke a rule I've always*

305

believed in. I'm not sorry I killed him, though. I'm just sorry I had to.

"*I know you thought my decision to go after Wally and Dan was foolish, but I felt there were much bigger things at stake than my own life. I never really knew what that meant until I saw a burlap sack lying on the floor of the tunnel. Good luck in bringing your brother to justice! He deserves nothing less. — Quentin.*"

Harry handed the note to Elton, who read it silently. He handed it back to Harry, and looked at him quizzically. "Well?"

Harry sat down to rest his leg. "I told you. I have no alternative. Either I travel North and find my brother, or I go home like a sniveling coward and try to have a life in Foxboro. Either I make him pay for what he tried to do to me, or I pretend everything is fine and let him believe that he outfoxed me and that I'm a fool who deserves what he got. Doesn't seem like much of a choice to me."

"Vengeance. Bad choice."

"What do you mean?"

Elton didn't answer. He turned away, his face expressionless, and settled down across from Harry. Then he methodically unwrapped one of the packages from Becky. "Decide tomorrow."

"I *have* decided," Harry said again. He unwrapped his own package, and began to eat.

Elton didn't say another word. He gathered twigs and branches for a fire, distributed blankets from within his heavy wrapped bundle, and sat silently watching the flames as they crackled and later died. When the stars appeared, he put on his nightcap and slippers and rolled himself into a rough, brown blanket. In a little while, he was snoring softly.

The next morning, after they had made a fire and shared the remaining sandwiches from the Inn, Elton sat quietly for a moment, looking at Harry.

"Your brother," he said finally. "Why?"

"Why what? Why do I despise him?"

Elton nodded.

Harry stood up, exasperated. "Elton, for the gods' sake! Do I have to make a list? He deceived me and my parents about his handicap — there was never anything wrong with his leg. He used it as an excuse to get attention from them and sympathy from the world. He acquired power and abused it. He sent me out as a decoy — Me! His own brother! — in the hope that I would be mistaken for him and killed in his place. And he almost succeeded!" Harry could feel his anger rising. "*And* he agreed to a trade in sentient creatures — breaking the one law that ties all of us — and enriched himself even more. He has no morals, no ethics, no scruples! He is evil! Someone has to stop him!"

Elton looked down at the ground. "Isaac. Powerful." He glanced up at Harry from the corner of his eye. "Dangerous."

"I'll take the risk. I have to," Harry said, beginning to see where this was going. He was silent for a long moment. "It's more than vengeance, isn't it. It's what Quentin said. It's bigger."

"Yes."

It was true. When he thought about Isaac's deception he could feel the outrage pounding in his veins. The trade went beyond that. It was the difference between a puddle and an ocean. *I have never been an especially good fox,* he thought. *I have had my moments of lying and cheating. But I would never have participated in this, not for all the gold in Foxboro, not for all the gold in the world.*

I am not like my brother.

"Well, whatever it is," Harry said aloud, "I'm going to find Isaac and stop him. Even if it means I have to . . ." He wasn't ready to finish the sentence.

Elton stood up and walked over to Harry, holding out his paw. "Harry," he said. "Brave fox."

Harry could feel his face get hot, but he held out his paw and they shook. "Not so fast, Elton," he said. "I haven't done anything yet, and it's a long way to the mountains. In fact, I should be leaving."

Elton went back to his pack and pulled out the checker-board. "Play," he said, turning back to Harry. He held out the feathered pine cone.

"Now?" Harry said. "Why?"

Elton did not move.

"You know I've won the last two games," Harry said, "including one I played with you, remember?"

The badger nodded. "Good coughing." Then he said, "You win. Go alone. I win. I decide."

"What does 'I decide' mean?"

"I. Go. With. You. We. Sell. Things. Play. Checkers. Throw. Stones." He struggled to get the words out. "Stop. Isaac. Together." He wiped the perspiration from his forehead with a handkerchief he pulled from his pocket.

Harry was amazed. "You *can* do complete sentences!"

"Hate it," Elton replied, looking disgusted. "Waste breath." He gestured to the board. "Play?"

Harry's first impulse was to laugh out loud. Traveling with the badger — throwing moochy-poochy stones, and all the rest — was not exactly what he'd planned for his future. He tried to imagine what it would be like. He remembered vole stew at the cabin, and Elton's stubborn insistence on sharing; he thought about the badger's nightcap and slippers, and his buzzing snore — but the most vivid picture was that of Elton emerging from the shadows of the cave and stopping Tabor's knife with a paw on Harry's shoulder and one word.

Elton sat motionless in front of the checkerboard, holding the playing piece. He stared intently at Harry through his spectacles.

"All right." Harry took the pine cone and placed it on a gray square. "I'll play. But either way, I am going to win."

ACKNOWLEDGEMENTS

Heartfelt thanks for friendship, inspiration, and support to:

Nancy Garden, Marylou Mahar, Meg Des Camp, Nancy Gallt, Joan Behn, Ann Whitford Paul, Susan Fletcher, Susan Goldman Rubin, Marla Frazee, Elsa Warnick, Ann Ruttan, Judi Davis, T. Degens, Bob and Roanne Hickok, Harriet Wasserman, Helen Greer, Marilyn Ginsburg, Cecile, Jessica, and Tom Knab, Mike Knab and Kim Zundel, Kristi Knab, Jude Knab and Dolores Moorehead, Maurice Aboaf, Jacques Aboaf, Myra Glasser and Richard Keogh, Helen Richardson and Don Hayner, Sharon and Buck Buckmaster, Eva Rickles, Chris Knab, and Sue Cook, Judy Randol, Carole Binswanger, the WIT ladies, my Kesilman cousins, and the Critter critiquers. Thanks to Mom, who taught me to read and who told me that if I wanted to find the truth I should "look in a book"; to Arthur Levine, for his perceptive and sympathetic editorial guidance; to the many talented authors I worked with over the years who, by their example, taught me to write; and of course, always, to Klaus.

THIS BOOK was designed by Alison Klapthor. The art for the jacket and the interior was created using ink and brush. The text was set in Monotype Imprint 12 point Regular, a typeface designed by John Henry Mason in 1913 based on Caslon Old Face. The display faces used were Linotype Authentic Sans Bold and Liquorstore Regular by Chank Fonts of Minneapolis. The book was printed and bound at R.R. Donnelley in the United States of America. The book's manufacturing was supervised by Jaime Capifali.